THEY SHUT ME UP

THEY SHUT ME UP

CASSANDRA MYERS

WINDING ROAD STORIES

NEW YORK   LOS ANGELES

Copyright 2023 by Winding Road Stories

Jacket design by Rejenne Pavon
Jacket Copyright 2023 by Winding Road Stories
Interior book design by A Raven Design
ISBN#: 978-1-960724-18-2 (pbk)
ISBN#: 978-1-960724-19-9 (ebook)

Published by Winding Road Stories
www.windingroadstories.com

To my family, who aside from being Irish, are nothing like the Callaghans.

"Most unavoidably, and therefore first, on the list of risks of being deposed is the simple, inescapable fact of mortality."

—*The Dictator's Handbook*, Bruce Bueno de Mesquita

PROLOGUE

January 14

Today, I burn it all to the ground.

Today, I burn *him, John Callaghan,* to the ground.

He'll get up this morning, swing his legs over the side of the bed, and go shave. On his way to the bathroom, he'll grumble that it's too early to be thinking, too early to be alive. He'll rub his face and watch his reflection in the bathroom mirror. He'll note his graying temples with his usual combination of dismay and bluster—he's getting old, but he's earned those gray hairs, goddammit!

He'll go out to the kitchen. Deirdre will be there, or maybe she won't. It doesn't make much difference to him, or to me.

I'll be lighting the kindling.

ONE

BRENDAN

SIX MONTHS EARLIER

I don't read all that much, but there is one book I like. It's an old one, written in the 80s by Chet Harmon. You've probably never heard of him. I hadn't either. But the book's fucking insane—it's the story of this real guy, Eddie "the Yeti" Hoffman. He was a button man for one of the big families in the 70s. I don't remember which—some Italians. They called him the Yeti because he was a monster. He liked strangling people and vanishing without a trace. Sometimes, he'd use tools. When he did, he preferred the ice ax. Because of the yeti thing, I guess, or maybe that came later.

Why the fuck should any of that matter? Because it's a good book—*Dark Was the Night*. And I was reading it that morning, the first time I heard about Casey.

"You hear about this guy?" Jimmy asked me. Jimmy's one of my oldest friends (in the US, which means we go back three years). None of my Irish friends are allowed to "associate" with me now, because Uncle John said it's too dangerous. Jimmy's a fucking idiot, but he has his moments. We were in The Bar, our favorite place. It was probably 9 a.m. No jobs that day. At least not yet. So far, we'd been listening to

3

Colin drone on and on about how much he wanted to fuck this girl Kylie who worked at the coffee shop three doors down. I like tits, but ten minutes of description is nine too many.

"What guy?" I said. I cared more about the book—I'd just gotten to the good part, where Eddie starts offing people. "*He began with the ones nobody would miss, the drug-addicted, the homeless, the crack whores of the grittiest, darkest streets. He'd see a girl stumbling down an alley, half-dressed in the middle of winter. She'd spot him and think greedily of a customer. He'd spot her and think of how it would feel to have his hands encircled around her skinny, heaving throat. This psychopathy served him well as his hitman career blossomed, and his killing went from mere pleasure to a heady mixture of business and pleasure.*"

Jimmy huffed in impatience. "The guy they're bringing in today. Jesus, do they tell you anything?"

I looked up from my book. Colin had finally stopped talking, and he was sniggering. As if he knew what the fuck was going on. "They bring in lots of guys," I said slowly. "To whom are you referring?"

Jimmy rolled his eyes. He doesn't like it when I get all "European" on him—he thinks everyone across the sea thinks they're fancier and smarter than he is. I told him pretty much everyone is, regardless of birthplace. And I was born in Ireland, the land of his forefathers.

"I'm talking," Jimmy said, "about the guy who's been causing trouble for our boys in Richmond." Colin, who'd been swiveling on the barstool, stopped suddenly.

"Trouble? You mean—" Colin glanced at the door, and then at Archie the bartender, who was rubbing a glass, staring at him. There was no one else there at 9 a.m., of course.

"The guy who's been messing up our...." Again, Colin hesitated. Archie knows some of what's going on, and he's paid well not to know most of it, but Uncle John doesn't appreciate us throwing around words we don't need to.

"...business arrangements?" he asked.

"Specifically, the *deliveries*," Jimmy said. He raised an eyebrow to demonstrate the significance. "He's been muscling in on *our customers*. And we *got him*."

"When did you hear?" I asked.

He shrugged. "Last night. They said they'd be bringing him in soon."

"Here?" Colin asked.

I rolled my eyes. "Yes. Here. *In broad daylight*."

"Where then?"

I shrugged. But I had a feeling we'd know by the end of the day.

———

"That night was a cool, clear night. The stars shone brightly in the heavens. It promised to be a night like all other nights for Luke Harbach, family man and father of three. But the devil has a way of catching up to a sinner like Luke, and that night, the devil took the form of Eddie Hoffman."

I read mostly all day. And that night, like I'd guessed, we had a job again. The phone rang at the bar—Archie answered, told us about a "pickup truck" they were selling that we had to go look at. There we were, 10 o'clock at night, cruising through downtown in the ugliest, most beat-up looking tan Volvo you'd ever seen. Colin had always complained about this car until Uncle John overheard once, fixed him with one raised eyebrow and told him, "Gaudiness isn't the goal." After that, Colin never dared to question it again.

It wasn't a long drive down to the old piers on Embarcadero, but we got stuck in traffic. Fucking night construction. With all the fog, it took even longer. Finally, Driver Tim let us out a few blocks away from the pier. We walked in, past the big skyscrapers and shitty little homeless guy sleeping bags. There was a long black driveway down to the main warehouse, which used to hold crabs or some shit back in the old days. I could hear the sea slapping the wood pilings like they owed it money. Jimmy tried to explain the history of these warehouses to me once, when I first got to the US and was finally ready to come out of hiding. As if I give a shit. Now the warehouses (and the little office up above, and a few more little rooms) belong to the Callaghans, and that's all I or anyone else needs to know.

We knocked on a side door. Someone let us in.

It was a big open space, with concrete walls and floor and an industrial door at one end. Pitch black everywhere but the center of the room, where one panel of lights shone on four men, huddled in a horseshoe, staring at a man duct-taped to a chair. As we drew closer, I blinked in surprise.

I was surprised for two reasons. One: We're just a cleanup crew. They're usually dead by the time we get here. This guy wasn't. Two: The guy looked like he was hardly worth a sneeze. A weaselly skinny guy, like an IT idiot, about half the size of a guy I'd stabbed in Ireland, and not nearly as mean looking. He had those fucking stupid wire-rimmed glasses that teachers wear in the movies, although his were slightly crooked, and one lens was splintered. He had floppy, curly hair, and when he turned his head slightly, I could see a swollen cheek and taxi cab ears. He looked about my age, twenty or so.

"*That's* the guy?" Colin whispered. We closed the door, and the men in the circle looked up. They were all wearing ski masks, so I wasn't sure who they were, but I thought I recognized Peter—he was the shortest one, and he was standing right in front of the chair, facing the glasses guy.

Peter is my youngest uncle, Uncle John's brother, sort of his second-in-command. One of his gloves was darker than the other, like he'd spilled wine on it.

"You're fucking early," he said. Yeah, it was Peter all right. I recognized the rasp. "We're not finished."

"They picked us up," I said. "What the fuck were we supposed to do?"

Peter glared. He doesn't like lip from anyone, but I'm his nephew. I get one snap a year.

"It doesn't matter," a voice said. Everyone turned back to the circle, but it was a while before anyone realized who'd spoken: the guy in the chair.

"You're not in the position to be bargaining," Peter growled.

The guy smiled, then winced at the pain. "I think that's precisely the position I'm in, actually," he said. "And it's rather an uncomfortable one."

No one responded. Peter gestured us forward, and we moved so we were standing a few feet away from the circle.

"Ah, intimidation," the guy said. "A nice tactic. But if you'd wanted to kill me, I'd be dead already. And you wouldn't have come, sir," he said, nodding to Peter. "And—"

"Do you know why you're here?" Peter pushed in.

"I'm causing problems for you in Seacliff and inner and outer Richmond," the guy said. "I'm selling drugs in areas you own, but without paying you your cut. What's more, I don't appear to be affiliated with a specific gang yet, and that makes you uncomfortable. Maybe I am affiliated, and you don't know about it. Maybe this is just the beginning of something bigger..."

"Shut the fuck up!" one of the men in the circle yelled. He slapped the guy across the face, and the guy's glasses flew off and clattered to the floor. He sighed.

"You want to talk to me, don't you?" he said, still

addressing Peter. "You had your goons—" he lifted his nose at us, "come in here 'early' so I'd think you were about to kill me, and I'd blurt out everything you want to know. But in case I don't fall for that, you'll settle for a nice interrogation and ransom—that way you can figure out who I'm working for *and* make a nice chunk of change."

"Who *are* you working for?" Peter asked.

"I'm self-employed. But my guys will pay my ransom. You just need to pick a number."

Peter considered this. A few of the guys in the ski masks shifted. The dull buzz of fluorescent lighting filled the silence. So we'd been called in "early" on purpose, and then yelled at for doing what we were told. What a crock of shit. My nose itched. I hoped someone would punch the guy again. He was smirking, even with his shiny, swollen cheek. I wanted to make it shinier, or better yet, darker, the darkest purple you could imagine. I remembered the feeling of my fist connecting with bone, and I wanted it again.

"Okay," Peter said finally. "We may still kill you, but we'll take your gang's money first. A hundred grand. By the day after tomorrow. We'll send a note out—" he gestured to one of the other masked men, "tomorrow."

"Two hundred," the guy in the chair said.

"What?"

"Two hundred grand. I'm worth at least that much. Please don't shortchange me."

Peter made a noise, somewhere between a grunt and a laugh. "You've got balls, kid, I'll give you that."

"And it's only fair to ask them for another day, since it's twice the amount."

This time Peter really did laugh. I clenched my fists at the sound. "Fuck you. Day after tomorrow." He shook his head. "But I tell you what: We'll have them take you somewhere real nice to wait for the money." Obvious sarcasm, but the guy in the chair seemed pleased.

"That's only fair," he agreed. "Now, could you—"

But I didn't hear anything else. Without taking his eyes off the guy, Peter gestured to one of the masked men, who pulled us back toward the side door. "You're done," he said. "Go home. The car will be waiting where it dropped you off." Jimmy and Colin turned to leave.

"Wait a minute," I said. "What do you mean, *we're done*? You drag us out here—through traffic—and then we get kicked out after three fucking minutes?"

"Let's go," Colin said. "Come on."

"*No,*" I said. "This is *ridiculous, you*—"

"Hey." Jimmy grabbed my arm. "Don't be a fucking idiot. Sorry," he added to the man. "Irish temper, you know."

"We're all fucking Irish," the man grumbled, but he let us go, back out into the night.

TWO
HARRIS

"I respectfully decline to answer your question on the grounds that it may incriminate me."

That's all most of these guys have to say. You wouldn't think it required index cards, but more often than not, I have to drill them before it comes to trial. Low-level gangsters aren't usually gifted with sharp memories.

Today, though, things were going well. I had Ryan McDonald on the stand, our gambling guy, and he was a pro. It was the other lawyer's turn to sweat, and sweat he did, profusely. His cheap blue suit was dark under the arms. I chose to see the circles as a personal victory: a symbol of his determination leaking out, melting into nothing.

"I respectfully decline to answer on the grounds that it may incriminate me," Ryan McDonald said. He was a little man, like a sparrow, with brown eyes darting every which way. I'd had to calm him down before testimony—juries take that kind of nervous movement as proof of guilt. (Although in this case, I couldn't really blame them.)

"Mr. McDonald," the other lawyer—Halloran—said. He'd just rubbed his head in frustration, causing several gray hairs to stick up right over his bald spot. I had a flash of pity—his suit was too big, he badly needed a haircut, and he sighed like a coal miner at the end of a long shift. "Will you answer *any* of my questions regarding how this money made its way into your possession?"

"I respectfully decline to answer on the grounds that it may incriminate me."

Halloran's mouth twisted. "Your Honor," he said, looking up at the bench. "This trial can't go on like this."

"Legally, it can," Judge Mayhew said. She pursed her lips. She hated interruptions almost as much as she hated sloppy appearances—hadn't he done his research? "Please, Mr. Halloran, continue."

"This money," Halloran said, pointing at a picture, evidence exhibit J3, "was found in a black duffel bag outside one of your bosses' casinos, near the dumpsters. It's one hundred thousand dollars in cash. One. Hundred. Thousand. Dollars."

He should've brought the duffel bag with him. Juries love a good prop, and a prop that looks like it came from a crime procedural is even better. Most people have never seen that much cash. You can practically see the cartoon dollar signs lighting up their eyes.

"Objection, Your Honor," I said, standing up. "Does Mr. Halloran have a question?"

"Sustained. Mr. Halloran, please ask your question."

"Yes, Your Honor." He turned back to Ryan.

"Have you seen this money before, Mr. McDonald?"

Ryan sat still and looked right back at him, just as coached. "I respectfully decline to answer your question on the grounds that it may incriminate me."

"Do you know where it came from?"

"I respectfully decline to answer your question on the grounds that it may incriminate me."

"It was found at the casino where we're told you work as the unofficial manager. Is that correct?"

"I respectfully decline to answer your question on the grounds that it may incriminate me."

Halloran sighed, a little too loudly. A black woman in the jury box covered her face with her hand to hide a laugh. I grinned inwardly. We had them now. I took a moment to appreciate the scene: McDonald in the witness box, cool as anything, and Halloran deflating before our eyes.

"Are you or are you not a member of John Callaghan's crime syndicate?"

"I respectfully decline to answer your question on the grounds that it may incriminate me."

It had been three days of pleading the Fifth, and before that, a lengthy fight over discovery. Poor Halloran was exhausted. The court reporter had whispered to her friend that he hadn't had a real night's sleep in weeks. That explained his rumpled look; even though he tried to paint over his exhaustion, he looked ill. That was our fault—mine, specifically, in fact. When he'd asked for the casino's books, we'd showered him with paper, literally hundreds of boxes of evidence that we knew his budget-gutted staff would never be able to sift through.

We hadn't helped him during the trial, either. Halloran had chased McDonald down every possible road, trying to trip him up with double negatives or piss him off with something insulting. But my men—or rather, John's men— were well-trained. McDonald barely spoke, just his name and the phrase from the index cards, over and over.

"Will you say anything of substance to the court, or will you just continue to hide behind the Fifth Amendment?" Halloran said, rubbing his eyes.

McDonald smiled. He couldn't help it. Usually, I hate when defendants go off book, but this time it worked. "I respectfully decline to answer your question on the grounds that it may incriminate me."

Halloran actually let out a little groan of frustration. I allowed myself a small smile. McDonald was Halloran's last witness. Barring closing statements, I was willing to bet the jury would finish deliberating within a couple of hours. It was getting late—they'd want to get home to their kids and dinners. This had been a long trial, and I'd done my damnedest to make sure it was a boring one, too. Most of them had stopped listening two days ago. A woman in the third row was knitting; the balding Indian guy behind her was doodling. Pleading the Fifth doesn't exactly make for high-octane viewing.

I was right—just two hours later, when Halloran had gotten too tired even for sighing, and settled for shaking his head a few times, the jury was out for deliberations. I told McDonald to go stretch his legs. A few reporters shuffled out, yawning, as did the judge and most of the spectators. I went over to Halloran, who was nodding gravely and whispering to the redheaded AUSA standing next to him. He stopped when he saw me. I expected him to glare. Instead, he shook his head and laughed.

"I lost this one," he said. He had a strange, wheezing laugh, like a fish sucking in air. "I fucking lost it." I looked at him, surprised. I'd never heard him swear before, and I'd done more than enough to provoke it.

"You're good," he said. "*Very* good. I get it. Use my momentum against me. I'm the sad old man with a vendetta, going off his rocker in front of everyone, insisting on *numbers* and *facts* and *evidence* in a case about a bag of cash. No one was killed, no one was really even hurt. Why am I making such a fuss? Who gives a shit about illegal gambling? And there you are, on the other side, the cool, handsome black attorney with a dark, dangerous client."

All of this was too true to argue with, so I didn't. I almost asked why he hadn't changed his strategy if he'd figured out mine so neatly, but that seemed like rubbing salt in the wound.

"You seem like a good guy, too," he added, gathering up his papers. "I wonder what you'd be like if you worked for the light." He eyed me to let this sink in.

"My goodness," I said. "That's quite a morality play you're working on."

"You're gonna tell me the Callaghans are good people? That that money was just casino winnings that someone happened to leave behind?"

"I wouldn't insult your intelligence."

"So you respect me?"

"I do."

"And yet you insist on coming to court and shitting on everything I like about this country?"

He really did have a flair for the dramatic. A shame. I could've shown him how to move it in useful directions. Instead, I just laughed, and so did he.

"They'll be back soon enough," he said. "I'd better go assemble my gracious loser face." The courtroom door creaked behind him when he left.

They found in our favor, of course. A long deliberation means jurors are wavering about conviction, and this was a nice long one. I'd known it would go our way.

But where are my manners? Let me introduce myself properly. I'm John Ellston Harris, son of Marlene and Douglas Harris of Oakland, California. I'm forty-one, fit, tall, often described as "handsome," although I'd be more likely to say "well-dressed and toeing the line." I'm a lawyer, obviously. I have my own firm, with a few partners—Harris, Kaur, and Burgoyne—but I'm hardly ever there since I mostly just focus on my main client: John Francis Callaghan.

As you probably know, John Callaghan is a gangster. He runs pretty much everything in his sections of San Francisco (and a fair amount of other people's sections, too). Guns, drugs, prostitutes, unions, illegal gambling, protection: all the rackets the government is too unenlightened to regulate and tax. I know about most of it, but I'm not foolish or arrogant enough to think I know about all of it. Only John does, I think. And maybe not even him. The weird thing about these big institutions (and you're fooling yourself if you don't think a crime family is an institution, like the Catholic Church or the Boy Scouts of America) is that they end up knowing more than any one individual. John Callaghan may be in charge, but if you ask me, it's the Callaghan Syndicate that really holds sway.

People who know what I do don't ask questions, but I can see the questions in their eyes. *Why? Why do you do such a bad thing?* But even an unintelligent person knows the answer to that: money and power—the two pillars of our civilization.

I don't rationalize my decisions. I know they're wrong. This is soul-staining stuff. Some gangsters live in the shadows of their justifications, whole cities they build to redeem themselves. They'll tell you they're just doing what corporations are doing. But at least gangsters have the honesty to do it dishonestly.

Work that one out, if you can. It wouldn't hold up in court unless you had someone like me arguing it. It's like if a kid breaks a window, and when his parents ask him why he did it, he says, "Well Billy down the street broke seven windows, and he lied about it." It may be true, but it's not really relevant to the question at hand.

John likes this justification. A lot. He uses it whenever he can, when he holds sway in a room of our people and gets to speechify. I think he likes it less because he believes it (I don't think he really does), but because it ties him to the big corporations. His dad always wanted him to be either a CEO or a president, and that's as close as he'll ever get.

All gangsters have daddy issues. I bet you didn't know that.

The question most people want to ask me, especially when they find out I work for the Callaghans, is "Why them?" The Callaghans, if you haven't already noticed, are white—Irish. And I'm Black. Gangsterism has progressed in the past few decades, but it's still mostly broken down along race lines, and there are plenty of Black crime families and organizations for me to represent. Hell, this is San Francisco —I could go with any ethnicity I chose! The Chinese in Chinatown, the Mexicans in the Mission, even the Italians in their little slice of North Beach.

As a matter of fact, Tom "Tomcat" Marks, the head of the Bayview/Hunter's Point gangs, asked me that exact question a few weeks ago at one of the semi-annual under-the-radar San Francisco gangster meet-and-greets. This one was at a hotel buffet. Tom cornered me by the bacon-wrapped shrimp, and demanded to know why the fuck I was working for that white guy.

"Dance with the one that brung you," I said. That horrified him enough to make him leave me alone. But it's a fair point—John saw me at a debate event in high school (one of his older nephews was competing) and we struck up a friendship. He paid for my college and then my law school, and I became his lawyer. More than that, even: his *consigliere*. Counselor. Sort of a crime consultant.

So why do I work for the white guy? Habit, I guess. And money—the pay is very good. My father is a paramedic, my mom is a teacher. They raised me right, as anyone would tell you. And I would've done just fine on their salaries, as they've told me repeatedly. But the money—well, it's nice to have real money, money that can say "fuck you" or "welcome" or any other number of things. My parents never had that kind of money.

But it's more than that, too. I remember it at that first debate event, when John was sitting in the audience. He was in the bleachers, wearing a suit, of course, and a blue pocket square. He was there "supporting" his nephew Charlie, who I trounced soundly in a debate on the death penalty. (Our side was taking "pro," an irony not lost on me later when I went to work for a man who doles out death far more regularly than the United States government.) John was...well, for lack of a better word, he was *fun*. After my team had won, he shook my hand and then, in front of Charlie and Deirdre and my parents, he said, "Well, Charlie, how does it feel to get your ass handed to you by a junior?"

My parents were appalled, but I had to stifle a laugh. Charlie had been awful, preening and snotty, reciting statistics from a discredited source with the tone of Moses descending from the mountaintop. I remember thinking, now *that* is a man to emulate: a man who could see his own nephew that clearly, and cut through his ego so easily. John was so unlike my father, who was sober and measured and humorless.

And when John clapped his hand on my back and invited me to dinner that night, something began. I've never looked back; or if I have, it's only been temporary. John Callaghan is a fire—a source of light and heat. Once I got used to him, no other job would do.

I couldn't say any of this to Tomcat, though. So he rolled his eyes and called me an "Uncle Tom," something I've heard from other powerful Black gangsters trying to bait me into switching sides. But as I always say, if you're going into the crime business for racial uplift, you're bound to be disappointed. At least it's nice to be the only Black guy in San Francisco who never gets pulled over.

———

A few days after McDonald's trial, I met with John again. Today, he said we'd meet at Cocina Linda in the Mission, which was code for an Italian place in North Beach. (John is nothing if not paranoid.) I drove over early—we were meeting at eleven. He was already there, of course. "I'd rather be early than be the late John Callaghan," he likes to say.

He was drinking Americanos, his fingers tapping a quick rhythm on the red and white tablecloth. I always like the first few moments of our meetings, when I see him before he sees me. He's a well-composed image: the tailored suits, the slicked-back hair, the pocket square. That day his pocket square was black, an omen. John keeps an extra black pocket square in his suit at all times, "for contingencies," meaning unexpected deaths. I wondered who was dead. I wondered if I should feel responsible.

"Harris!" He'd spotted me. He motioned me over.

I sat down. "The trial went well, sir."

He nodded. "McDonald did well. You did better."

"Thank you, sir."

"I have another request for you, if you think you can handle it. I know you're busy, but..."

"I can handle it, sir."

"Good." He drummed on the table decisively. The waiter came over and I ordered lunch. No messy pasta when you're with the boss—John hates when his underlings look ridiculous. And Irish gangsters are already off their game in an Italian restaurant. I got antipasto. John ordered the veal scaloppini, "No mushrooms."

We chatted pleasantly for a few minutes, small talk about the weather, his kids, and my "pile of papers." John went out of his way to bore any potential eavesdroppers at the beginning of a meal, so they'd tune out by the time we got to the good stuff.

When the waiter set down our plates, John took his first bite, then leaned in, lowering his voice. "I've got Brendan Rorke and his crew on a job right now," he said. "Frank Salvare is dead."

I faked surprise. "Really?"

"Heart attack."

"Death by chocolate?"

John couldn't help it—he smiled a little.

"Don't make me laugh, Harris. It's a day of mourning."

My eyes flicked to the pocket square. "Of course, sir."

"Anyway," he said, leaning back and stretching his arms, "I need you to go see Emilia, his widow. She's going to be distraught. Assure her she'll be getting the usual package."

"The good soldier pension," I said. "Got it."

"Bring her flowers," he said, "nice ones. She got any kids?"

"All grown up now," I said. "Two daughters. The oldest is married and in England, and the youngest just moved to Seattle."

John frowned. "Shame to think of her all alone in that house. Frank was a good man."

"Of a sort."

"Harris," John said, "one day that mouth of yours is going to get you in trouble."

"Not with you, though, sir. You appreciate a good mouth."

He rolled his eyes. "Stop being cheery. Go help the widow."

"On my way, sir."

I stood up to go, but John stopped me. "Keep an eye on this one, will you?" he said. "She's going to be upset, and upset people like to talk. Let her. Give her the money, a nice chat. Keep her happy. Happy widows are quiet widows."

THREE
BRENDAN

After the warehouse, things went back to normal. We picked up some small jobs in the next few days, and I kept my ears open, but there was no word about the guy or the ransom. I figured they got their money and killed him. I wished I'd been there to see it, or, better yet, to help the process along. That smarmy weasel-faced fuck mouthing off to Uncle Peter was playing on repeat in my mind.

On Tuesday, we got a call first thing. It was a cleanup, kind of. One of Uncle John's "dear friends" had "passed on," and he'd done his passing on in a diner near North Beach. We needed to get there before the police did. The owner of the diner, who'd been spoken to, had graciously agreed not to call them.

The diner wasn't far from The Bar. When we got there, it looked empty and almost totally dark, with a shitty little "SORRY WE'RE CLOSED" sign hanging off kilter on the front door. I knew the place—Rickie's. It was one of our guys' favorites. We came in through the back and saw an old man sitting in a corner booth of red vinyl, slouched over with his head on the table like he'd had too much to drink.

"This him?" I asked the only other person inside—it was Robins, one of John's lieutenants. He was standing near the body with his lips puckered, smoking a cigarette.

"What do you think?" he muttered. One of the overhead fans was still whirring, making the paper tablemats wave up and down.

The man was big—huge, in fact, with a beer gut the size of a barrel. "You didn't think to move him out of sight before we got here?" I asked Robins.

Then I turned back to the body. I couldn't see any blood. The man was wearing a dark pinstriped suit. As I stood there thinking how fucking impossible it was going to be to carry him, I noticed that he'd missed a spot shaving, close to his jaw line: I saw several dark, prickly hairs. I put my gloves on and poked at him. I still couldn't see any blood, although the side of his face was sort of blueish. "What the fuck happened?"

"Heart attack," Robins said.

"Why do we have to move him?"

Robins scowled. "He needs to be found at his house in Russian Hill. Fuck off and go do it."

"I don't need to take that kind of shit from you," I growled, but Colin and Jimmy had their gloves on and were already grabbing the body. I knew I'd end up hauling the thing either way, so I might as well start now. It took us a good five minutes to drag him into the kitchen, where we set him on a dumbwaiter. It made me think of Eddie Hoffman—there's a great scene in the book where the Yeti kills six guys in a diner shootout. But I don't remember him sticking around to haul a dead guy's fat ass off the premises.

The guy looked worse now that we saw him close up. His eyes were open and glassy, and his face was white with a weird bluish tinge. His body was stiffening already, and his comb over was starting to flop out of place. When I moved him, some of his hair flopped into my mouth. I spit it out in disgust.

By the time we had him folded into the dumbwaiter, we were all sweating. I wiped my forehead. "Another fucking wonderful day with the Callaghans," I said.

"I thought you'd be used to this by now," Jimmy said, slightly out of breath.

"What the fuck are you talking about?"

"After that time with Annette Luciano," Jimmy grinned, "you must be used to having a fat ass on top of you."

I swiped at him, but I couldn't help laughing a little. "Fucking asshole," I muttered.

"What's taking so long?" Robins yelled from the door. "Hurry the fuck up!"

We got him to his fancy Russian Hill house after all, where his wife was waiting for him. She knew he was coming, I guess, but knowing didn't soften the blow.

"Frank! My poor Frank!" she wailed. We took him up the stairs and put him in his giant green bed. The whole fucking house was green, like the Grinch had puked everywhere. The woman followed us to the bedroom, crying as she readjusted the stuff on his nightstand over and over. We had orders to undress and dress him. She'd laid out a pair of green pinstripe pajamas. Fucking awful work, and difficult. She made it worse, too, still crying and watching every second.

"Make him look peaceful," she said between sobs, as we ruffled the sheets to make them look slept in.

"Would you like us to read him a bedtime story?" I asked.

The look on her face almost made the whole thing worth it. It even stopped her crying. But she didn't say anything, just pointed us downstairs.

She called the cops just as we were leaving the house. I

heard her on the phone, sobbing and doing a good job of seeming surprised. "*It's—it's my husband. I think he had a heart attack. It's been a few minutes...I don't know if he's—I think he's—*"

By the time they got there, we were long gone.

FOUR
NEIL

I need a new name.

Neil Bowes just doesn't dominate the top of a film poster. It doesn't have the dash of Willis Scott, for example, or Hart Mankin. My agent keeps submitting me for pretty boy parts, but I really think I should be up for something a little more rugged. And rugged names are the ones people remember.

I tried explaining this to John when he met with me on Friday. He seemed to agree but couldn't suggest a better alias. I'll admit I was hoping he'd suggest Callaghan. I mean, it's a little uncouth, since his daughter Katie married *me,* but the Callaghan name is what I bought, and I think I should get to use it.

"Katie's well," I told him as we walked. We were in the Conservatory of Flowers, which I found to be an odd place for a clandestine meeting, but I knew John would have his reasons. At the very least, I thought, it's tough for anyone to bug a bed of tulips.

"What?" John asked. He was ogling a woman in white leggings who had the most perfect ass I'd ever seen. When John ogles, it's classy, just a few quick glances and then, if the woman ever turns around, a grin that seems to suggest danger and excitement all at once. I notice these things—it helps with my craft. And John does it with so much panache.

"Your daughter's well," I repeated. "I left her at the house this morning. I think she was gardening."

"Good." John was still looking around. Harris, John's lawyer, a big black man who wears suits almost as expensive as John's, was making his way towards us. His suit was, I noticed, a little in need of pressing, but I have to admit, Harris cuts quite a figure. Of course, this reflects well on John—and me, too, as part of the family.

We met Harris at the roses. John welcomed him and Harris turned politely to shake my hand. We all fell into step.

"Neil," John said. "I called you here because I have an exciting opportunity for you. My production company, Emer Productions, is about to embark on a new project, *The Reddened Hand.*"

"How intriguing."

John smiled. "It's a story about people like us. Well," he added, almost shyly, "between you and me, it's more or less about me. About my rise, and my...empire."

He paused, with an actor's flourish. I rubbed the gold band of my wedding ring.

"The main character is basically my doppelganger," John continued, "Aiden Trask."

"Hell of a name," I said. Excitement bubbled in my stomach.

"I'd love for you to audition."

I stopped dead, forcing them to stop with me.

"You want me to audition?"

"If you'd like to," John said smoothly, starting to walk again.

"Oh, of course I'd like to!" I said, probably a little too enthusiastically. I took a breath and then looked him right in the eye. "John, you won't regret this." He shrugged. We walked on in silence for a few moments.

I was excited, of course, but something nagged at me. I couldn't understand why John wouldn't just cast me outright. But maybe, I reasoned, he wanted the process to seem more legitimate, and so had to go through the whole charade of holding auditions. Then I had an idea.

"Harris," I said, as we rounded a corner and startled a few doves nesting in a nearby tree. "Would you come to the audition with me?"

John, who'd lit a cigarette, exhaled, and the wind drifted the smoke into my eyes. I coughed.

"That's a good idea, Harris," John said. "With you there, I'll know that things are going smoothly."

I grinned. It was, in fact, a *great* idea—Harris was, let's face it, a pretty threatening presence to a casting director, even in an expensive suit. Having him there would be like an extra guarantee. Cast the son-in-law, or else.

When I left them in the rose garden, I was secure in my triumph. Some people may not think actors are worth much, but I know how to get what I want.

———

Katie was at the kitchen table when I got home, scribbling in a notebook. She jumped when I walked in, and then blushed. "Writing erotica?" I asked airily. She frowned.

"Daddy wants me to take that accounting class, help a little with the business," she said. "But I just can't get it—why is math so hard?" She looked up helplessly.

I shrugged and put my keys down on the silver plate by the door, enjoying the familiar chime. "Anything happen while I was gone?"

"My mother called," Katie said. She picked at the lilies on

the table. "To invite us to dinner. She said Daddy was with you today."

I nodded. "Yes, John and I had a meeting. And you won't believe what he offered me!" I quickly explained everything about *The Reddened Hand*.

She got up and raced to hug me. "Sweetie, that's wonderful!" she said. "This could be your big break!"

I snorted. "This *is* my big break," I said. "I've got the part."

She stopped. "I thought you said he wanted you to audition."

"That's a formality. I'm family. And I'm an actor. What could be more perfect?"

———

Perhaps now would be the time to explain my situation with Katie. It's simple, really. I married her in the old-fashioned way—for her father and her connections and her money. She's okay-looking, don't get me wrong, when she makes an effort, but since we got married, she rarely does, and she could stand to lose a few pounds. She doesn't quite compare with her aunts and all the women John surrounds himself with.

Like I said, though, she has her merits. She has nice eyes, I suppose, and she's sweet. She really loves me a lot.

And she's a good wife. When we fuck, she's always attentive to my needs, and she keeps the house running smoothly. Of course, we're more than able to keep a maid and a cleaning service, but she coordinates everything. I don't actually know much of what she does during the day. Between auditions, workshops and meetings with John, I don't have the time to keep track. She's on some charity boards, I guess, and now that accounting class. Maybe she really is writing erotica. Her brothers would crack a rib laughing if they found out.

———

The news traveled fast. By late afternoon, I'd already gotten several hearty congratulations, and Liam, Katie's youngest brother, offered me his own prize: a trip to a strip club. I don't tend to like those places. My ideal woman is refined, elegant, someone who could pose for *Tatler*, sit a horse, wear a crimson riding jacket. But Liam knows women, and there's a particular honey blonde at Lacey's that I find irresistible.

She hadn't heard of Emer Productions, she said, (or rather, shouted over the incessant dance music in that place) but she was duly impressed by my audition. She knew who Liam and I were, and she knew what that meant. Professional women of that stripe often know more about business than their rich counterparts, like Katie. Katie hasn't worked a day in her life. She doesn't understand people. Honey blondes do. They get their blonde out of the bottle and their wits from the streets. (That's a nice turn of phrase—I should include it in my noir script, if I ever get the time to write it.)

"So, are you going to be a big star?" she purred at me. I was looking at her breasts, which were huge and so real looking I needed to touch them to make sure.

"Oh yeah!" Liam answered from his corner of the couch, where a beautiful Mexican girl was giving him a lap dance. "He'll be fucking *huge*! But he's pretty big already. Have you ever seen that commercial?"

She stopped grinding for a second and flipped her hair back. "What commercial?"

I grinned a little. "Oh, it's nothing, really. Just a stupid little thing."

"No, come on," Liam said. He stood up, making the girl on

top of him stumble forward with a little yelp. "You're not giving yourself enough credit, Neil. It was a *big* commercial."

"What was it for?" the blonde asked. Liam's girl was listening too, now that she'd picked herself up off that disgusting floor.

"A large pharmaceutical company," I said.

"He's being modest!" Liam shouted. "He was the guy in the Adraxa allergy commercials! The one in the bee costume? Dressed as a bee and talking about how allergic bees made him!"

"Irony," I muttered.

"Oh yeahhhhh," the blonde said. "I remember you!" She started laughing. "That bee costume, with the little yellow tights. Didn't leave much to the imagination, did it?"

I turned back to my champagne, which had gone flat. She was still laughing, and Liam's girl had joined in. Their eyes were drifting down my frame.

"Liam," I said, "I'm bored. Are there any better whores around?"

That stopped her laughing.

I hated the little bitch quite a lot in that moment, and her face stuck in my mind. I don't know why, exactly. Maybe she was a symbol, an amalgamation of all the girls—all the people—who'd thought I wouldn't amount to anything. But really, I should've thanked her. Her scorn was yet another motivation to me in the weeks ahead, as I began my climb to the top.

FIVE

BRENDAN

That thing with the old woman in the green house was weird, but I took it as a good sign. A new task meant new responsibilities, according to some business fuck I'd heard on TV once. And soon after that came one of the biggest events on the Callaghan family social calendar: Sunday dinner. Uncle John does them right, the whole Nob Hill house shiny and clean, a huge fancy tablecloth on the dining room table (and a separate, smaller one for the grandkids and younger nephews in the other room, although if they ever sat still and stopped shrieking, I'd drop dead of shock). It's family only at the big table—just Callaghans and their offshoots. After "dinner," which is served at noon sharp, the other "family members" come. But at eleven thirty, as I walked up the steps to the house, it was us: just real family.

Aunt Deirdre was at the door. She's John's wife. She's fucking weird and smells terrible, like too much perfume and mothballs. She's super quiet, but she also has this little creepy smile she does, where you can only see the very bottom of her teeth. I had to hug her, of course, but only for a second.

"John's in the den," Deirdre said as she led me down a

31

long hallway—the Hall of Fame. It's covered in family photos —all three boys, Katie, Uncle Peter and his family, Uncle Simon, and the grandkids and all. I'm not up there. But I guess I shouldn't be, for legal reasons.

The den is my favorite room in the house. It's quiet and filled with booze, and it smells like money. It's dark in there, too, which was nice after the glaring sun. Uncle John was in there with his three sons: Owen, Martin, and Liam.

Liam came over and slapped me on the back. "Brendan, you feckin' eejit!" he grinned. He likes to make fun of the Irish accent I no longer have. I wouldn't take that shit from anyone else, but Liam's okay. He's a pretty boy, but at least that means he can get pussy. A *lot* of pussy. So much, in fact, that when you go out with him, it spills over. That's worth putting up with a little bullshit.

"Oh, faith and begorah!" I shot back. Owen and Martin looked over, and Owen raised his glass of whiskey. I flipped Liam off and went over to them.

Owen, the oldest Callaghan son, was lecturing Martin. "Honestly, you have *no* clue what Dad's aiming for, your projections are *way* off. At the GSB we always were told..." He patted his pot belly like a satisfied cartoon character.

"Oh, did you go to fucking Stanford for your MBA?" Martin shot out. "You haven't mentioned it in fifteen minutes!"

"I didn't even *say* Stanford," Owen whined.

"It's a good school," I offered. They both stopped and stared.

"No one asked for your fucking input!" Owen snapped. His cheeks were going red already, that telltale Owen flush that meant he'd scream at anyone who didn't frighten him, from cleaning women to his current whore to his underlings.

Owen's the oldest Callaghan son. Everyone figures he's going to take over for his daddy someday. I call him the

Potato. He's tall like Uncle John, with Liam's dark brown hair, and he wears expensive suits to compensate for a wandering hairline.

Martin's more of the same: skinny where Owen is doughy. He looks a little bit like God's first, fucked up attempt at making Owen. He likes sweater vests and khakis. Last I heard, he was mostly running the dry cleaners down on Geary.

And these are the guys who think it's beneath them to look me in the eye.

Uncle John walked over to me and shook my hand. "Brendan," he said, "nice to see you."

Uncle John is way better than his sons. He's tall, well over six feet, and he has black hair with these cool silver streaks and this great voice: low, rich, and kind of slow. And he knows how to dress: beautiful suits, double-breasted with pocket squares and nice ties. Like a real old-school movie gangster. Like the Yeti.

"Sir," I said.

"Thank you for all your help," he said. "Enjoy your lunch." He turned to his sons.

"Was that really a heart attack?" I blurted.

John half-turned back to me. "Excuse me." It wasn't a question.

"I—I was just wondering if it really was a heart attack, sir," I said. "The guy, I mean, in the restaurant."

"What do you think it was?"

I looked at Liam, whose face was blank. "I don't know—" Owen and Martin were frowning.

Then John laughed and clapped me on the back. "I'm just fucking with you," he said. "Of course it was a heart attack. That was my old friend Frank Salvare. You know Rickie's, where you found him?"

I nodded.

"He used to do business there. A lot. Always did business

there, in fact. People—even people outside our business, people in uniforms—were starting to *know* he did business there. If he'd been found dead there, it would have raised the issue again: what he was doing there, who he was talking to. No need for that."

I nodded again. Finally, someone was telling me things.

"Now why don't we go see how Deirdre's doing with the roast?" John said. He looked to his sons, and we all filed out to the kitchen.

Deirdre smiled when we walked in, that little creepy smile. Katie was in there, too, the only Callaghan daughter. She may have been cute once, with those big brown cow eyes, but genetics are taking over her waistline. She was wearing an apron with stains on it and stirring a big pot of cabbage. It smelled fucking horrible.

"How's it going, Katie?" Liam asked, plopping down on a stool next to her. "Managed to fuck up the cabbage yet?" He winked at me. Katie blushed and muttered something.

We headed out into the dining room. I stopped dead.

There he was, sitting at the table. I'd last seen him in that huge warehouse, his face half bashed in and his glasses on the floor. But here he was: glasses repaired, bruises faded, with that same fucking smirk on his face.

"Oh, you've met," John said, smiling. "I'd forgotten. But that wasn't a real introduction. Casey, this is Brendan Rorke, my favorite nephew and the head of one of our crews. Brendan, this is Casey Moore. He's going to be joining our team."

I looked at John. He was still smiling, but I knew from the look in his eyes that he wouldn't be explaining. It was one of those John Callaghan things, and the rest of us just had to accept it.

Deirdre came back into the room, with Katie behind her.

"Dinner's ready," Deirdre said. "We just got the kids all settled, so now it's the grownups' turn."

Owen stood up from his chair and yelled "DINNER!" in the direction of the living room.

"That's how you call your wife?" John snapped. "Sit down, Owen."

Owen hesitated, but he sat. His wife Anna, along with Peter's wife Lena, filtered into the room. Anna's okay-looking, maybe a 7 out of 10: brown hair, decent body. She met Owen in high school, and she's been glued to him ever since. I'd fuck her, I guess, if I was desperate, but she's getting old.

Martin doesn't have a wife, or doesn't want one, I guess. He likes whores, mostly.

"Please, Brendan, sit," John said, gesturing to the spot next to Liam. I realized I was still standing there, staring at Casey. I sat.

Halfway through the roast, Casey started talking to John and Owen, actually *yelling across the fucking table* at them. Stupid shit, too, about how "wasn't the weather so unseasonably warm this year" and "were they as excited about the prospect of their new business venture as he was"—on and on. Every time he said something, all the other conversations had to stop so that Uncle John could hear him. But John didn't even seem pissed. He just smiled and nodded. I only got through dinner by thinking Uncle John must have some kind of plan for Casey, some humiliating death or some torture. *Something.*

I tried not to listen, but the only people near me were Katie and her husband, this blond prick of an actor named Neil who clearly fucking hates her as much as he loves the idea of being a Callaghan (although he isn't really). He spent the entire dinner telling me that he'd been reading some really interesting scripts and going on some really good auditions and that his career was "just about to take flight." I tuned it out. He has a wife to listen to his bullshit—why the fuck would he bother me?

After dinner, John, Peter, and Owen went into the den. Visiting hours were about to start. I waited to be invited because that's how it's done. Casey just fucking strode in after them like some phony cowboy. So then I had to follow, too.

Harris was already waiting for us. Harris is John Harris, our lawyer. There can't be two Johns, though, so we call him Harris. He's a big black guy, but not scary at all. The Yeti could kill him in a second, and if I had him surprised, I'd bet I could stab him before he even realized I was there.

Harris nodded in my direction, and John turned around.

"Brendan, why don't you go watch the game?" John said. "We'll call when we're ready for you."

I saw Casey smile. My eye twitched, but I'm not fucking stupid—you don't argue with John, especially during visiting hours. I left.

I didn't go into the living room, though. I went to the basement. There's another TV down there, even bigger than the first one, and a huge leather couch. I don't know why I went down there, really—I was sick of this room. When I first came to the States, before it was safe for me to show my face in the great outdoors, I spent *weeks* down there, playing video games and eating whatever Deirdre brought me. I found *Dark Was the Night* down there, and read it cover to cover about a million times. It was where I first decided I wanted to be a real assassin, a button man for the Callaghans.

I spent the rest of the afternoon in there, thumbing through books and old hunting magazines (John's favorite is *Fortune's Hunter*). I didn't want to go stand outside the door waiting for Casey and John, like some fucking puppy begging for table scraps. I tried to be calm, but I flipped a *Fortune's Hunter* page too hard and tore off half an article ("Beef Up In 16 Days"). Just when I'd decided to leave without saying anything, I saw Owen on the stairs. "Oh, there you are," he said. "Dad wants to see you."

When I got to John's office, there was a crowd of mostly low-level guys hovering in the hallway, their eyes all glued to John's door. "What the—" I asked, but they all shushed me. There was shouting coming from behind the door. John soundproofed his office, so you couldn't hear words, but the shouts were fucking loud. Louder than I'd ever heard on a Sunday. And then the unmistakable *thud* of a body hitting the floor. All of us jumped. The shouting stopped suddenly, like someone had flicked a light switch. More muffled sounds, fainter this time. Talking. I looked to Owen and almost laughed at his big moony face. He opened his mouth, but before he could say anything the door opened again and a man ran out, white-faced and clutching at his ribs. The men waiting in the hallway all moved automatically to let him past, and Harris emerged from the door, buttoning his suitcoat. He spotted me. "Oh, Brendan," he said airily. "John will see you now."

The other guys all gaped at me. I had to admit, I liked the feeling. I strode into the office. Harris followed me in and closed the door. John was sitting behind his desk, rubbing his knuckles, sighing at a half-empty glass of whiskey. I could see from the veins in his forehead that he'd been the one screaming. But I saw no other sign of a disturbance.

John saw me looking and rubbed his hands. "Just a little business." He sighed. "I wanted to tell you that I think you've been doing a terrific job lately. And we're going to ask more of you—soon. Don't fuck it up."

"I won't, sir," I said. Finally, a little responsibility. Maybe I would be a button man soon after all. My jaw unclenched.

John nodded, and I knew it was my cue to leave, but I couldn't go just yet.

Harris looked at John, then at me. "He wants to know about Moore," he said.

For a minute I didn't know what he was talking about. Then I realized: Moore was Casey's last name.

John rubbed his face. "I'm not going to tell you about Moore, Brendan. That isn't part of your job."

"I'm—" I tried to think of how Owen or some other Ivy League fuck might've put it. "I'm just...eager for more responsibility, sir."

John's lips pursed. "If you do your job, and you do it well," he said slowly, "you might be looking at a promotion." I waited. He sighed again.

"Brendan," he said. "If you really want to be a bigger part of this family—"

"I do, sir, I—" I stopped at the look on his face. No one interrupted John.

"As I was saying, if you want to be higher-ranking, you'll have to learn first. Call it—" he turned to share a look with Harris "—an internship, of sorts. You'll go with Harris on a few errands when he needs you. He'll show you the ropes."

I swallowed. Higher-ranking was all well and good, but fucking *Harris*? And fucking *errands*?

"I—thank you, sir. That would be great," I said. I looked at Harris, whose face was blank. I reached a hand out to him—a nice touch, I thought. He moved from his place in the corner and shook it.

"Good, then," John said. "You can go." As I left, I saw him cluck at his bruised fist. "Gonna take forever to get back to normal," he muttered.

"You should see the other guy," Harris said lazily. The door shut behind me, silencing John's sharp, cutting laugh.

SIX

HARRIS

I always tried to skip most of the Callaghan Sunday ritual. That particular Sunday, not long after McDonald's trial, I slipped in after dinner, just in time to see Casey Moore, fresh off the assembly line of flashy drug dealers who tried to mold themselves into our competition, invited into John's den.

Casey immediately started talking. "I've been thinking, Mr. Callaghan, that I should really keep doing what I'm doing. If it ain't broke, don't fix it, right?" He grinned in my direction. I grinned back tightly. He was my kind of operator —demanding a higher ransom when they kidnapped him was a nice move—but he didn't exactly make it easy to like him. "I have lots of ins with the Herreras and..."

My attention wandered. And then, somehow, I blinked and there I was in the den with John and his nephew Brendan Rorke, and Brendan was being named my—what, criminal intern? He'd been called in for a classic "you're doing a great job" speech from John, and I'd struggled not to laugh at the look on his face. He was trying to look tough but was actually beaming at the praise, so he ended up just looking constipated.

Brendan is like a toddler in a bulldog's body. He thinks his army-regulation buzz cut makes his curly red hair less noticeable. He's not smart enough to grow it out, or to realize that his natural ginger altar boy looks could be handy for a life of crime. He'd rather look like a thug. He just wants to be obvious.

Brendan is ruthless as anything, but he can't keep even the smallest bit of emotion off his face—in a flash I saw all his disappointment and all his wishes and dreams for John Callaghan, his official father substitute. Just as quickly, that was replaced with rage and a fierce glare. At least he wasn't stupid enough to glare at John—he settled for glaring at the sofa. I took the opportunity to examine him again.

He stabbed someone once, back in Ireland—that's why he came to the US. He thinks it's made him a legend, given him a reputation to build his life on, but no one really cares. He might be violent, but he's way too hot-blooded to be real leadership material. Only cold bloods can run corporations.

I wish I could tell him. Maybe then he wouldn't glare so much or get so addicted to the drama of his personality.

The afternoon's meetings passed. I found myself struggling to pay attention, even during the interesting ones. Usually I appreciate a good bullshitter, but that day I couldn't really focus. I waited for whatever low-level guy to finish, and then when John started talking, I tuned back in. John's brother Peter had turned up and was adding in his updates.

"...don't care, Peter," John said. "You shouldn't be bothering me with this."

"Wei says that Kertner's buying up a lot of new real estate near Chinatown, and making a name for himself with all the right people..."

"Kertner? Will Kertner?" John snorted. "Call me when he grows a dick." He sighed and ran his hands through his hair. "Now. Lagrimas will want to meet within the month. We'll need to have all that money waiting for him. You have that taken care of?"

Peter nodded. He's the head of most of the drug operations, and he can be a bit of a wild card, but he's learned over the years to be careful with his money. John doesn't care for chaos. I like watching him nod at John—it seems almost impossible to imagine the two of them as little boys in Ireland, fighting over trucks. No, actually, it's impossible to imagine *John* as a little boy. Peter I can see just fine: a little pouty, a little small, with a greedy eye for his oldest brother's toys. They have another brother, too, Simon, who runs a winery in Napa. He's mostly useless: "fatty wing meat," John calls him. He runs one of John's "legitimate" businesses, the dry cleaners. I secretly think that Owen and Martin both take after Simon more than John.

And Liam, the third of John's sons? Liam inherited the worst parts of John and Peter: he's handsome and reckless and impatient for praise. My grandmother would say he "thinks the world was made to watch him go by." When I see John argue with Peter or try to reason with his sons, I feel for the man (and for myself) for getting saddled with such unimpressive relatives. But again, I wasn't listening. I sat up straighter and tried to focus. John had called Casey back in for some reason, and he was hovering near John's chair.

"...Mulligan says voluntary donations are up," Peter was saying.

"We have such kind, charitable people in our unions," John said, smiling at Casey. John has a lot of smiles, but this was his perfect lazy cowboy smile, which he uses sparingly. When he flashes it on you, you feel like you're part of a gang of outlaws. I watched Casey to see if he'd melt—gangsters try to act like they don't care about other men, but power is all about seduction, and John is the ultimate seducer. Casey

41

smiled back, but not as broadly as someone like Brendan might've. I was impressed. He was one to watch, for sure.

The meeting broke up soon after that—we were gearing up for election season, but that was still some time away, and mostly things had been quiet. Eventually Casey and Peter left, and Owen leapt forward with the next set of agendas: the meet and greets. I sat down on the couch with a pen and paper, ready to start taking notes.

Finally, after a few hours of complaints and bureaucracy and putting out fires (Could you believe Harry Rogers was telling everyone he'd made the most whores when really it was Skinny's nephew Luke?), the evening was winding down, and John sent me into the kitchen to get Owen.

When I got there, Owen and Martin were standing around the counter, arguing.

"Owen, I swear to fucking *Christ* if you tell me 'consistency is key' *one more time!*" Martin shouted. He was in his favorite Sunday uniform: a sweater vest and khakis, and his face had its permanently rumpled look.

Owen swelled like a bullfrog. "I only mention it, Martin," he hissed, "because *someone* isn't doing the books for the drycleaners the way he's supposed to..."

"I'm not a fucking accountant!" Martin snapped. "I *delegate*. Rhodes does that shit. Anyway, Katie's supposed to be his fucking assistant, so bug *her!* Dad's not going to waste my brains on some dusty little office where I sit and shuffle papers all day!"

"You're not upper management material, Martin, you're really not," Owen sighed.

"Oh, fuck you, Owen, you're about as useful as a...a... fucking...dirty diaper!" Martin shouted.

I'd heard ninety different versions of this argument, and I was just about to interrupt when I heard a little, quiet laugh. Owen and Martin kept arguing. They didn't even look up, but

I turned. There in the corner was Katie Callaghan, John's daughter. She'd been helping the maid load the dishwasher, and I turned just in time to see a smile vanishing on her face. Strange. I'd never known her to have a sense of humor before, but I suppose even the dullest of people laugh at their brothers' expense. And Owen and Martin were certainly ridiculous enough. I felt a little swoop of pity for her.

"Owen," I said. "John needs to see you." I jerked my head upstairs, where I could hear muffled shouting. That poor balding fuck.

Owen nodded, made a face at Martin, and straightened his tie on the way out of the room. I headed for the door, even had my hand on the knob when—

"Harris!" John yelled down. "Did you leave yet?"

"No, sir," I shouted back. I sighed.

I rubbed my temples and went back into the den.

———

When John wasn't sucker-punching people who displeased him (which, I swear, happened very rarely), he was a surprisingly deft touch with condolences. It took me a while to clear space in my schedule, but eventually I did as he'd suggested and went to see Frank Salvare's widow. After all, we'd had Brendan lug her dead husband's body upstairs and then re-dressed him like the world's least popular paper doll —the least I could do was bring her some flowers. So there I was, at the widow's house with a bouquet of white lilies, which, as I'm sure you know, symbolize the innocence of the newly departed soul.

The porch creaked as I made my way up the steps, but the paint was fresh and there were flowers everywhere, blooming in pots and hanging over my head, lots of pinks and yellows and greens. The house was one of those old Victorians that white people always seem so attached to, the kind that must remind them of times when their empire was uncontested. It was painted bright green, which isn't so unusual in San Francisco, but this particular shade was just south of chartreuse, and it was starting to make my head hurt. I rang the doorbell. After a few seconds, I could hear her feet padding along the passageway.

She looked exactly the way I'd imagined: a small, frail-looking Italian woman in her early sixties, with a slightly hooked nose and her gray hair tied back in a messy bun. Her makeup was smudged from crying, but her jewelry sparkled, and her black dress was immaculately tailored. You could smell the money on her. A huge diamond gleamed on her bony finger, which was painted a violent red.

"Mrs. Salvare," I said, handing her the flowers. "I'm John Harris, I work for Mr. Callaghan. We're so sorry for your loss."

"Come in, come in," she said. "You can call me Emilia." She opened the door wider. The smell hit me immediately: the thick, cloying stink of too many flowers. It made my eyes water as I followed her down the hallway, which was crowded with lilies on every possible surface.

"I know, it's a little much," she said dryly. "Frank's been gone for two weeks now, and I still have an entire botanical garden." Her voice was lower than I'd have guessed, and smoky. Her smile was a little crooked. "I guess that's what happens when everyone's terrified of your dead husband."

She motioned me into a little living room with a green plush couch and a bunch of little marble figurines. They were like Hummels, but not quite: cupids, babies, little girls kneeling in prayer. I almost knocked one off a dresser but caught it just in time. It was a little bearded gnome about six inches tall with his legs raised like he was about to skip off to a meadow.

"Horrible, aren't they?" she said, taking it back. "Frank used to buy them for me; he thought I loved them. Would bring one home from every trip. Limited editions, keepsake memories, you name it. You know what they call these? The Heartsakes Collection." She shook her head. "I have a *million*. I had a million ten years ago, even. But Frank always bought one when he saw it, even shelled out like a thousand dollars for one they discontinued in the seventies."

"He was a good man," I began.

She raised one eyebrow, ever so slightly. "He was good to me," she acknowledged. "Well, most of the time." She was quiet for a long time, looking at the gnome. Then she looked back up at me. "I appreciate the visit, I really do, but my sister and her kids are coming all the way from Santa Clarita to stay with me, and I still have to deal with all the funeral arrangements and everything—"

"You should feel free to make any decisions you like," I said, "but Mr. Callaghan will be paying for the funeral."

She laughed and shook her head. "You guys. You're too much. First John has his guys come and deliver the body upstairs, like a fucking *package*, and now he wants to pay for the funeral. You know that an Italian can't have an Irishman pay for his funeral, right? That stays within the family. Frank's men are taking care of it."

I nodded.

"Why did they deliver him anyway?" she said. "That fucking prick of a little boy never told me." I assumed she meant Brendan Rorke. I hid a small smile. Then she held a hand up. "You know what? Don't tell me. Frank always said, 'It's better if you don't know.'"

"Ma'am—Emilia, you're not in any legal trouble, and if we were, we'd do our absolute best to protect—"

She held up her hand again. "I know," she said, not unkindly. "Thank you."

I didn't respond. The smell was really starting to get to me now, and I wanted to leave, but I sensed that she wasn't finished yet. She thumbed one of the lilies, already in a vase on the counter. "I had to call the police and pretend he'd just died," she said.

"Of course that must have been awful, I'm so sorry—"

She eyed me again. "It *was* fucking awful," she said. "Mostly because I haven't been on stage in about fifty years, not since I played Cinderella's ugly stepsister in the third grade."

That time I really did smile. She didn't seem to mind. She wasn't looking at me anymore; she was gazing all around the room like she couldn't remember how she'd gotten there.

"John—Mr. Callaghan—also wanted me to let you know that you'll be taken care of, a real pension, three thousand dollars a month for the rest of your life," I said. "You own the house?"

She nodded.

"Then it should be plenty."

"Yes." She sighed and lifted the curtains in the window, looking out onto the street. I couldn't tell if she was even listening. Her eyes were suddenly veiled—all the wryness had vanished.

"Thank you for coming," she said. "It was kind."

SEVEN
NEIL

I spent the next family dinner observing. Some people asked about the audition, of course, and I was glad to update them, but I also wanted to get right to work. If I was going to play Aiden Trask (and of course I was going to—it was inevitable) I needed to really soak up the atmosphere around me. I zeroed in on Brendan Rorke, John's nephew, the real Irish article. He's so salt of the earth: eats like a rabid dog and scowls at everybody. That night I paid special attention to the way he held his fork. He gripped it with his fist, like it was some kind of trident. Excellent for a dinner scene. Brendan is so...authentic. Some of the other members of the family are theatrical, using gangster terms like "button man" and "house painting" that sit awkwardly in their mouths. But for better or for worse Brendan can't help being who he is, and that's something I really want for the role in *The Reddened Hand*.

After dinner that night John and the others had their usual business meetings. I went into the backyard, and after a while, Katie joined me. She stripped off her old ratty apron and wiped dish soap off her fingers onto her jeans. The sun was just starting to set, and the backyard was getting cold, the threat of autumn in the air.

"What'd you think of Casey?" she asked. At first, I didn't know who she was asking about, but then I remembered the guest at dinner. "I don't know," I said. "I didn't think much of him at first: this boy, maybe nineteen, with ears the size of car doors and those ugly old-fashioned glasses like my stepfather's. But he's what my acting coach would describe as a first-rate character actor—an unattractive little man who ends up having a surprisingly watchable quality." Katie's mouth quirked upward in a half smile.

"He does," she agreed.

"Better to keep him inside the tent, pissing out…" I said. I wasn't really listening, though. I was thinking about Brendan again, and how he glared all the time like the sun was permanently in his eyes. Another good tic for my character.

"My brothers are in there now, arguing," she said. She made a noise, somewhere between a laugh and a cough. "I wouldn't go back in if I were you."

"I wouldn't dare," I said, smiling at her. She smiled back. Her brothers (excepting Liam, of course) are pure milquetoast.

"…seriously, Anna, I don't know how much more I can take," I heard, as the screen door opened. Owen had emerged into the backyard, holding a beer and yelling back into the kitchen at his wife. I heard her mutter something I couldn't quite catch—she's a nice girl, that Anna, if a little mousy at times—but then he saw us and made a beeline for Katie.

"Mom said she needs you," he said. "To look at some pictures for the hospital opening. Something about diagrams of a layout." He yawned.

"I'll be right there," Katie said, but she didn't leave. She put an arm on Owen's shoulder. I noticed that her wedding ring needed to be cleaned. "Are you all right?" she asked him.

He shrugged and cracked his knuckles, displaying his red and gold Stanford class ring (which was, in contrast, in sterling condition). "I'll be okay," he said. "Just Martin getting on my nerves, as usual." He rolled his eyes, and I nodded, trying to edge my way out of the conversation. "He has no real idea what it means to run a business, and he thinks he can just ask Dad to let him in..."

"Maybe Dad gives him too much leeway," Katie said. "Dad should listen to you more often."

That certainly wasn't true, but Katie's always this way with her brothers, coddling and overestimating their abilities. It's sweet, really. She's like a teddy bear that just wants everyone to be friends. I watched a bee buzz around the gardenias and felt a flash of irritation again about that damned commercial.

"...not Dad's fault," Owen was saying, rubbing his bald spot. "It's Martin—he just..."

"Dad asked him to look at the books for the drycleaners," Katie added, her hand still on his arm. "You didn't think he should've, and you were right. Maybe you should talk to Dad..."

Owen shrugged off her arm. "God, Katie, I have enough to worry about without you chiming in."

She blinked. "I just think you aren't getting your due," she said, and she floated away to do Deirdre's bidding.

Owen sipped his beer, watching her leave. "You think she's right?" he grunted at me. Classic Callaghan son insecurity. I had to hide a smile. This was all great for my audition. "You think Dad thinks *Martin* should take over?"

"I don't know," I replied. I looked out at the neighbor's yard behind us, which was overgrown with weeds. "Anything you need from the production offices, by the way? I'll be heading out there soon, for my audition."

He said he didn't need anything.

EIGHT
BRENDAN

Days after that dinner, I was still pissed about the whole "Harris' intern" thing. I'm nobody's fucking intern. But that Friday was one of Liam's parties, and that helped take my mind off it. Being the youngest Callaghan son certainly has its advantages, and Liam uses all of them. Every few months, he has a huge party at some fancy bar, one of those places full of trendy shit like glass tables and linen umbrellas and drinks he knows my crew can't afford advertised on bamboo clipboard menus. We come anyway, though. I had to admit the man had style.

That night, I invited Kristie, this girl I'd been seeing. She wasn't as hot as some of the girls Skinny was running (her face was kinda rumpled up, like one of those weird Chinese dogs), but she gave the best head I'd ever had.

We headed out together, her, me, Colin and Jimmy and two girls they'd scrounged up somewhere. A heatwave was just starting, and the night was warm. When we got to the bar, we were whisked up into the elevator at the first mention of Liam's name.

We were pretty early, but there Liam was, his arm slung

over this gorgeous black girl's shoulder, a drink sloshing in his other hand while he told some story (I heard the word "pussy" repeated several times). The guys he was with (I saw Harry and Ian and some of Liam's rich private school friends, and even Neil fucking Bowes, Katie's husband) were all laughing hysterically. "That's Liam?" Kristie whispered. She sounded impressed. I didn't like the way she was looking at him.

"Yeah, that's Liam," I said. "Now go get me a beer, cheapest they have." I waved a twenty in her direction and she disappeared, along with Colin and Jimmy's dates.

"Pretty nice, right?" Jimmy said, looking around.

I shrugged. "It's okay." I usually don't go in for trendy shit, but even I had to admit this place was pretty cool: a rooftop bar in the Mission, with glass all around and huge views of the city, all the way out to the Bay Bridge, which was playing its fucking stupid light show: black and white, black and white.

I felt a hand on my shoulder. "Brendan!" Liam said. His breath was thick with alcohol already, the black girl still on his arm. "You came! All the cleanup crew!"

"What cleanup crew?" the girl asked, scrunching up her nose like we worked in fucking sanitation.

"They work for my father," Liam explained, "and—" he laughed, "for me." He patted me on the cheek. I tried to smile. Liam had a tendency to buy everyone drinks when he got really sloshed, and I couldn't afford more than one beer otherwise.

The girl was still looking like we were something she'd glimpsed in the gutter. "Liam, honey," she said, "let's go get another drink."

"Right behind you," Liam said. He slapped her ass and sent her off ahead of him. "Pretty unbelievable, right?" he said as she walked away. "And I don't have to pay for it like you fucks."

"That's not what I heard," I said.

For a second, I thought he'd be pissed, but he just shook his head, grinning. "Next round's on me," he called over his shoulder as he followed her away.

Kristie appeared with the beer. "I missed him?" she said, looking in Liam's direction. "Damn, I was going to make Gina so jealous, she's never even seen him before."

"Why the fuck do you care about Liam so much?" Jimmy asked her. His eyes flickered to his own date, who was still waiting to be served at the bar. "What's the big fucking deal about Liam?"

Kristie just looked at him.

I drank my beer, looking around at all the girls and wishing I'd left Kristie at home. "I'm going to the bathroom," she announced, and off she went, gossiping with Jimmy and Colin's dates. Soon after that Jimmy and Colin drifted over to Liam again, but I stayed where I was. I liked the feel of the wind in my hair and the cold beer in my hand.

Then Casey walked in. He had a guy with him—one of his henchmen, I guessed. When Liam saw Casey he grinned and waved, and they slapped each other on the back. My stomach twisted.

Casey of course saw Colin and Jimmy, and then he spotted me. He waved his guy off and made his way over.

"Couldn't even find a whore to come with you, huh?" I asked. "That's a shame. That's my date over there." I pointed to Kristie. She'd made an effort tonight, and she looked pretty hot in her red dress.

Casey just smiled. "How are you tonight, Brendan?"

"I'm well, Mr. Moore, *thank you*," I said in my drippiest posh voice.

He was still fucking smiling. "Are you drunk enough yet?"

I looked down at my beer, which was almost empty. Liam's usual free round hadn't appeared yet. "For what?"

"To tell me what happened in Ireland."

"I thought you already knew everything."

"I've heard rumors," Casey said. "But not from the horse's mouth."

I snorted and turned away. I expected Casey to leave, but he stood there, looking out at the city.

"If this were a movie," he said, his eyes still on the view, "I'd be telling a parable now that reflected my feelings towards you, or some kind of warning."

I sighed. "Do you ever get tired of hearing yourself talk?"

Liam ran back over, his hand slung around Neil Bowes' skinny neck. Behind them, a waiter followed with a tray of drinks. "Casey!" Liam said, handing him one. "And Brendan Rorke! Two of my favorite people! What a night, right? The fucking city is *ours*!" He let go of Neil, who was grinning at him, and hooked an arm around me and Casey, gesturing outward. I quickly took a drink off the tray. Fog was starting to roll in now, bringing cooler air with it. We couldn't see much.

"Gentlemen," Neil said, clinking his glass (whiskey, which looked expensive) with ours. I tried not to roll my eyes. Neil's blond hair was all slicked back like he wanted to be John and he looked at Liam like he wanted to fuck him.

"My dad doesn't talk a lot about the future," Liam said, "except for going on and on about legacy. But you've met my brothers—*Owen* and *Martin*." He laughed, then coughed a little. His slicked-back hair was starting to fall in his eyes, which were having difficulty focusing. "You know them. They're not worth shit. They're not *real gangsters*, like us."

I saw Casey smile. "I don't know if I'm much of a gangster," he said, "but Liam Callaghan certainly is."

Liam blinked, then roared with laughter. "Moore, you

crack me up!" He turned to me again. "Brendan—Sam—" he laughed. "I don't even remember your real name half the time." I glanced at Casey. Liam did, too, and then tried to lower his voice, but a drunk's whisper is louder than a fake fucking stage whisper. "I know what you did in Ireland, even if no one else does, and I appreciate what you can do. When I'm the boss, you'll be my button man."

He was really close to me now, with his fucking awful breath in my ear. But this was all music to me. A grin spread across my face. I knocked back half my whiskey.

"Too bad you're a fucking ugly ginger!" Liam laughed, pulling away.

"Too bad you're a fucking prettyboy cunt!" I shot back, and Liam grinned as big as I was grinning. Then he stopped suddenly and wobbled a little. For a minute, it looked like he was gonna hurl, but then: "I gotta take a shit," he said, and he disappeared.

I stayed where I was, watching the fog slowly covering everything below us, until all I could see was a closed Mexican grocery and the restaurant across the street, which was pulsing with music and the dull flashes of a strobe light. Neil was still lingering, but for once in his life he was quiet.

And of course, Casey was still there, too. I wanted him to leave. I could feel him breathing there, rotting the air, and I wanted to enjoy the fucking moment. If Liam meant what he said, I'd be a button man in a matter of years. John was getting older, and rumor was he'd started talking to his boys about retirement... I downed the rest of my drink in one go, letting the fire spread through me.

"You have to tell me the Ireland story now," Casey said. "You've got whiskey in yer belly and a smile on yer face," he added in a terrible Irish accent designed to piss me off. I wanted to punch him, but my background was an open secret anyway, and the story was better than a fist.

"Oh, yes!" Neil said. "I'd love to hear it, too."

"Fine," I said. "I'll tell you. But—" I saluted a passing bartender and turned back to Casey, "—you have to buy me another fucking fifteen-dollar whiskey first." Casey agreed. When he pulled out his wallet, I laughed. A ten and three ones. "What a haul," I said.

I looked around for Kristie, but I couldn't see where she'd gone. Whatever. I'd find her later, or I'd find someone else.

I took that whiskey all in one gulp again. It burned going down, and Casey raised his eyebrows. "Not bad," he said. "You Irish can really hold your liquor."

"That's nothing," I said. I felt that sick, sweet looseness in my veins. Just like the night it had all happened. "When I was in Ireland..." I paused. "Three years ago, when I was seventeen—" I paused again so he'd realize how young this was, "I was in a pub." Neil was leaning in now—whatever. He could stay, too.

"The drinking age in Ireland is eighteen," I added. I blinked. My head was starting to buzz. "Wait, let me go back. I was in Ireland. Because I lived there. I was born there."

I'd never actually told anyone the full story except Uncle John, and he tended to be impatient when anyone else was talking. I looked up at the sky, at one star blinking down through the cloud. I took a long breath, thinking of what Liam had said and the fire inside me. At that moment, it felt like the whole fucking world was in my reach.

Then I looked at Casey. He barely looked interested. I saw his eyes flicker over to Liam, who was now singing loudly, probably some shit his dad told him all Irish people sing— "Danny Boy," if I had to guess.

"Brendan Rorke isn't my real name," I said, a little too loudly. Casey looked back to me, quiet and waiting. "I got that name because I—but I'm getting ahead of myself." I took a breath, ignoring Liam. I got the fire back.

"That night, I had a bit too much to drink." I grinned. "I was with my friend Tony, this kid who'd lived down the street from me since fucking forever. We go way back. Used to ride bikes together and throw rocks at seagulls. We were pretty good, too. I nearly took the leg off one once...

"Anyway. He and I were talking to some girls, and this guy came up out of nowhere and told us they were *his* girls, him and his mate's. He was this big fucking ugly guy, with a gut and a beard. I didn't know how he thought he could get *any* girls, looking that shit." I could hear it now, my Irish accent starting to creep in a little, and I stopped to swallow it. "He told us they were *his* girls, and I said he could go fuck himself and I'd do whatever I wanted with any girl I chose. And that's when he pulled a gun on me."

Casey was listening now. His eyes were on me, and Neil's were already wide. I felt the thrill of memory.

"People scattered. The pub fucking emptied. The fuck just stood there, though, didn't even pull the fucking trigger. Too much of a pussy. I bet he thought just *taking out* the gun would end it, but he was wrong." My heart started beating faster. This was it, my story, as good as anything in *Dark Was the Night*. "My blood was up. I felt it roaring in my ears. Without even thinking, I reached into my coat and pulled out my knife. It was between his ribs, sunk into the innards of that fat stomach before he even knew it was out. For good measure, I stabbed him two more times, right in the gut. He looked at me, blood bubbling up from his mouth, and then he took this big rumbling step back and fell on his ass. There was a huge fucking crash. Tony grabbed his gun and pointed it at the guy's mate. He took off, fast as you can imagine." I grinned just remembering it. The look on that guy's face. "He shat himself, too. I remember the smell."

Casey didn't say anything. He was scratching his chin, his

eyes shadowed by the darkness. Neil opened his mouth to ask a question, but Casey held a hand up to silence him.

"That was meant to be the end of it," I said. "Only it wasn't. The cops were on their way, we could hear the sirens, and the bartender told us to leave (he was an old friend of ours). So we ran. Wasn't until a few hours later that we heard that I'd somehow nicked the fat fuck's *hepatic artery*. He bled out in the ambulance."

I'd told this part of the story before—I remembered Colin's eyes as big as saucers and even Jimmy had muttered "fuck me." I heard Neil swallow. But Casey was still silent.

"I had to leave, obviously," I said, looking out at the city. "Being wanted for murder is no joke. So, we called Uncle John, as we often do in 'difficult times,' and he suggested that it was the perfect time for a long holiday in America and a quick name change."

I looked up to see how Casey was taking all this. He was watching the other side of the bar.

Liam was making out with his date. The others had disappeared somewhere, probably to the bathroom. I was missing all the good drugs, but it was worth it just to feel that story again. And Casey had needed to hear it. He finally turned his eyes back to mine.

"Your first kill," he said.

I liked the sound of that. "Yeah," I said. "Yeah. My first kill."

Casey raised a glass. And maybe it was the whiskey, or the story, but I didn't hesitate—I clinked it with mine.

He disappeared after that, but Neil lingered. I was about to tell him to fuck off when he motioned the bartender again and got me another drink: a scotch this time. My head was starting to spin, so I sipped this one. "Impressive," he said. "Very impressive."

I nodded. Then a thought occurred to me, and my

stomach lurched. "Uh, don't tell John I told you," I said. "Right?"

"Oh, of course not!" Neil said quickly. "We're family, after all."

Fucking *family?* Just because he fucked the boss' daughter? I wanted to snort, but the scotch was good shit, so I let it slide.

"As you know," he continued, "I'm up for a part in John's movie—well, the movie John's financing. *The Reddened Hand?*" He didn't stop for a reply. "Anyway, it's sort of a character based on John, a gangster type, you know." I was barely listening. Liam was standing next to Kristie now. Was he whispering something in her ear? What the fuck?

"...if you could help me out." Neil tapped me on the shoulder. "Brendan? What do you think?"

"What?" I asked dully, taking another sip. Each sip was probably four bucks.

"I think you'd be really good for research," Neil said. "Into that type of man, you know, the ultimate gangster."

I turned back to him. "The ultimate gangster?"

"Yeah, yeah!" Neil said. He put his glass down on the table. "You're the perfect type: tough, gritty, violent past, seedy underbelly from the old country...that glint of danger in your eyes."

I blinked. That didn't sound so bad.

"Come on," Neil said, "don't be modest—you know you're like that, don't you?"

"Don't lick my ass," I muttered, but I probably cracked a smile. Neil laughed.

"That's great, see?" he said. "That's exactly the kind of dialogue I need!"

"For what?"

"For my audition!" he said. "Maybe I can shadow you sometimes—you know, for research for the part. Learn your mannerisms, the way you do the things you do." He took a step back and stood tall—well, short, because he's only like five-foot-six, but I had to admit, he sort of got how to stand. All of a sudden, he looked tougher. "You're like John's right-hand man!" he said. "You're perfect!"

I considered this. Liam had moved away from Kristie and was back talking to the other guys, who were all gesturing so quickly I was sure they'd been taking multiple trips to the bathroom. "What's in it for me?" I asked.

"You could finally see yourself on screen," Neil said. I looked back at him. I couldn't tell from his face whether he was fucking with me or not. But he seemed decent enough. I was starting to wonder if he wasn't as much of a pussy as I'd thought he was. I mean, he'd married Katie, and that was fucking bizarre, but if he just wanted to be part of the family...

"All right," I said finally. "Let's do it."

"Fantastic!" He held out a hand and I shook it. Just two guys, bonding over an expensive scotch.

Not a bad night, all in all, I thought in the taxi on my way home. At least some more people knew about Ireland. And it was always a good memory to relive. I closed my eyes and savored it again, that sharp blaze of power that had flared up right as I thrust the blade into the man's stomach, turning me immediately into the man I always knew I could be.

NINE

HARRIS

So now I had another Callaghan hanger-on to babysit. Brendan Rorke, who'd clearly been boning up on some management TED talks or something, had asked for a promotion. And that meant that I was supposed to take him with me on a few of my errands, to "show him the ropes" and see if anywhere down the line he'd be useful as more than just a glorified murder janitor. Lucky me.

A few days later, we were in the car on the way to the widow Salvare's ridiculous green house. I made my way up the slightly creaking steps to that bright green door, trailed by Brendan, who fulfilled the promise of his personality by promptly stubbing his toe on one of her pots and swearing up a storm.

"Be polite," I murmured as I rang the doorbell, "and don't say anything."

"I can't do both of those things at the same time," he growled, but under his breath, at least.

The widow opened the door to us with a soft smile that stopped at her eyes. She was still wearing black, but this time it was pants and an ill-fitting shirt that ballooned around the sleeves. She hadn't done her makeup, and her hair was slightly matted. She nodded to me, but her eyes stopped when they got to Brendan, like he was a red wine stain on white carpet.

"You're welcome in my home," she said to me. "He is not."

"Oh, he's all right," I said brightly, stepping past her into the house. "He's here to learn." She didn't move. "At Mr. Callaghan's insistence," I added. Reluctantly, she opened the door wide enough for him, too. As he crossed the threshold he managed, "You have a lovely home, ma'am."

"Didn't notice that last time you were here, did you?" she said, but she gestured both of us into the living room.

I tried not to laugh at the sight of Brendan, in ripped jeans and a stained army jacket, perching on her white couch, which was still covered in plastic. I guessed this wasn't the first time a gangster had sat there, but that didn't make her eyebrow raise any less emphatic. To distract her, I asked for a tour. She insisted Brendan couldn't come. He was, of course, devastated by this.

The whole place was green, and just as full of chintzy white figurines as the living room, although every curtain was drawn, and the exact shades were hard to make out in the dimness. She took me upstairs, through two kids' bedrooms in varying states of preservation, a guest bedroom, and two horrible chartreuse bathrooms. When we got back to the ground floor, she led me out through a sliding glass door in the kitchen to the backyard, which was large for San Francisco. It was a gray day. The yard smelled like the rain that had just fallen, and the warm earthiness of freshly cut grass. At one end was a little plastic playground (green, of course) with a slide, monkey bars, and swings. I walked over to it, my head tilted sideways. It was off center. The slide was leaning too far to the left.

She laughed when she saw me. "It's supposed to look like

that," she said. "Crooked, you know?" When I didn't answer, she laughed again. "*Crooked*. Frank was *crooked*, so our playground is *crooked*. He had them build it crooked on purpose, as a joke."

"Ah," I said. "Wouldn't that be dangerous, with little kids?"

She shrugged. "That's Frank for you."

I tried to smile. She'd already moved on to her flowerbeds.

"The cyclamen aren't doing too well," she said, bending over to look. I noticed suddenly that she was in slippers, and they were starting to soak in the dirt of the garden. "Frank used to take care of the gardening," she said. "Weird, I know. But he said it calmed him." She stood, groaning a little. I put my hand on her arm to steady her, and she smiled, looking down at the garden like a mother gazing at her sleeping child. We stayed there for a while, not speaking. I felt a raindrop on my nose, then another. I looked up at the gray sky, feeling more and more drops gather on my face, but still Emilia didn't move. It wasn't until it thickened into a drizzle that she finally straightened and looked at me. "Let's go inside," she said, patting my arm. "I've got biscotti."

She led me into the kitchen. Brendan's name wasn't acknowledged. The biscotti was dry and served on a pink china plate with a doily. She served me first, then herself, and she sank into the chair across from me. "It's a little stale," she admitted. "Left over from the wake and the funeral and all that."

"I'm sorry I wasn't able to attend—"

She waved it off. "John came," she said. "Mr. Callaghan, I should say. He's always so dapper—the famous pocket square and everything. And the Cerullos came, of course, even old Victor, and he can barely walk anymore with his hip." She paused, remembering. I thought I could picture it—I'd been

63

to enough of them. A crowd of sleek, elegant mourners all in black gathered around an open casket (a heart attack, unlike most other crime boss deaths, made this possible) in a well-lit beige room with a chandelier. It never seemed to trouble these people (my people) when Robins waited politely at the door to check everyone for weapons. For them, it was all about "the camaraderie and the canapés," as John had put it once during a toast. And then of course the inevitable exits to black luxury cars, with cops posted surreptitiously across the street from the funeral parlor, trying to act like they weren't looking.

"It was a good turnout," Emilia said finally. "Frank would've been proud." She stopped suddenly, and the faraway look came back into her eyes. I thought of the pile of work on my desk, folders upon folders, including a property dispute that would not end, and wondered how much longer I'd have to stay. Brendan was probably out of his mind fidgety, and his type couldn't stand boredom for long. He'd start to break things.

"You can go, you know," she said, as if she'd read my mind. "I don't imagine you'd like to spend your day with an old lady who can barely serve a snack without *reminiscing*."

I smiled and sat further back in my chair. "But I haven't given you your pension yet."

She smiled, too. "I figured you were winding up to that."

I reached in my suit pocket and drew out an envelope— the thick yellowish-brown kind that gangsters always use for cash in the movies. John insists on that specific kind. He even had me call a producer once and find out which brand of envelope it was, so we'd be accurate.

You can tell a lot about a person by how they react to an envelope of cash. A lot of lower-level guys grab at it like a wild animal presented with food. The bosses, like John, don't touch envelopes, even when one is held out in front of them.

They shrug and turn away like a disdainful cat, letting their underlings handle the evidence. Emilia Salvare took the envelope elegantly, weighing it in her palm.

"There's five thousand in there," I said.

She nodded and put it down gently, as if it were fragile. "I won't pretend it's not welcome. Turns out, Frank had a fair amount of debts with the Cerullos, and I know this house isn't exactly a shack, but it's old, and it needs more repairs than you'd think, and..." She stopped and sighed. "There I go, boring you again. Frank always used to say even if my head was chopped off, it'd still keep talking." She laughed as if this, along with the crooked playground, was an endearing anecdote. "Eat your biscotti," she said, eyeing me. I obeyed immediately. It lodged in my throat, sharp as a tooth.

"I feel like I can trust you," she said. She was looking out, at the rain splashing on the windowpanes. Then she turned back to me. "I also feel like that's what you want me to feel."

I smiled. "Yes, that's the general idea."

"But I shouldn't trust you."

It wasn't clear if it was a question. "That depends on what I'm here for," I said. "There are times when you—when *one*—shouldn't trust me. But you can trust me now, and you should."

"Because you'll just be delivering my pension."

"That's right."

She crossed her legs. Her slippers were filthy with garden dirt. "But they won't send John Callaghan's lawyer every time they need to deliver an envelope. This is just the first time, for show, so I know I'm being noticed by the bosses."

"You'll be well taken care of."

"Of course." She smiled. "Frank wouldn't have it any other way."

I nodded and took a sip of coffee for something to do. It

was cold now, and the room was dark from the rain and the closed blinds. But for some reason, now I wanted to linger.

"If you want to tell me about Frank," I said, "you can. I'd imagine you have lots of stories, and some may not be appropriate for even your family's ears."

"You're right about that," she said. "Some of them may not even be appropriate for *your* ears." I looked down, embarrassed, and she laughed. It was a cackle, almost like a witch's, deep and throaty.

"I'm just teasing," she said. "I didn't think I'd be able to embarrass you, a big lawyer for John Callaghan, but old women saying dirty things never fails to make a young man blush."

"I didn't blush," I protested, but I stopped and grinned when I realized how silly I sounded.

She cackled again. "Since you'll only be here the once..." I started to deny this, but she held up a hand to stop me. "I figure I get to tell a story, and you have to listen."

I nodded.

"I'm going to tell you how I met Frank." She took a sip of coffee, from a pink china cup that matched the plates, her pinky held elegantly in the air. She noticed me notice it and laughed. "I'm not fancy, you know," she said. "Not by birth, anyway. I met Frank forty years ago, when I was a barmaid at his place. You wouldn't know it; it was before your time, but it was this cute little red-and-white-checkered tablecloth kind of place here in North Beach, over on Columbus. A nice family restaurant during the day, with a big, long hardwood bar that gleamed. My boss insisted we clean it every morning. It was called Silvio's, because Silvio was Frank's cousin who had nothing to do with *our business*." She raised an eyebrow.

"Frank owned it, basically. A silent partner, I think you call it." She gestured in my direction. "But he didn't stop by much—he was pretty busy then. In those days he was a button man for Cerullo, although I didn't find that out until much later. I grew up in that neighborhood, you know. We all knew Cerullo was The Man, and it was clear that Frank was The Man's man, always wandering around with his long coat and his hands jammed in his pockets. He used to give my little sister lollipops whenever he saw her. Maybe he even gave me some. He was fifteen years older than me, so it's possible, but either I don't remember it, or I blocked it out, given our history later." She paused to smile again, and I got a flash of what she must have been like as a young girl: all sly grins and bright eyes. "Anyway. Frank came into the bar one night right before closing. I almost kicked him out, I was that tired. I think I even yelled at him to leave, only he walked in and before I could yell again, I saw his face. And he saw mine. He told me it was the prettiest face he'd ever seen."

I wondered how many times Frank Salvare had said that in his life, and to how many women. Emilia twisted her mouth, as if she wondered, too.

"So that was it. Frank said that, and I laughed. He told me he was in love. I told myself I was in love. And he started paying for *everything*. He visited my house once when he came to pick me up for a date. It was a shithole, this little dingy, gross walkup. My dad was too drunk to care, and my mother had enough trouble cleaning up after us to bother with dusting. I thought for sure that when Frank saw it he was going to dump me for being some poor piece of shit who tries to act like she's somebody, but—" She smiled a secret smile. "But he just took me aside and told me—he *told* me— that my family would start getting money." She laughed. "We'd only been dating like two months. He was actually still married to Loretta, his first wife, although, again, I didn't know that at the time."

She stopped again, for long enough that I didn't know if I should start getting up. Finally, I put my coffee cup down, and she blinked, looking up like she'd just been woken from a dream. "Was that a long enough story for you?" she laughed. "God, off I go again. And I didn't even ask if you wanted more coffee or biscotti or anything."

"I'm fine, thank you," I said. I stood up and buttoned my suit coat. The rain had stopped, finally, but the house was still cold, and I could hear the loud ticking of the living room clock—a big, gilded monstrosity with a picture of an angel on its face. I shivered. I had the strange feeling that if I stayed any longer, I'd get trapped here forever, like a mosquito in amber. "Thank you for the coffee and the food, but I'd better get going."

"Of course." She ushered me back into the hallway. Her dirty slippers left marks on the carpet. "Thank you for coming. And please be sure and tell John—Mr. Callaghan—thank you from me. For everything."

I made a move back to the living room to collect Brendan. She sighed as if she'd just remembered him and led me through again. "Better make sure he's not pocketing anything," she said. We walked in just in time to catch Brendan handling one of the figurines, a cross-eyed golfer. "See anything you like?" Emilia asked.

He jumped. The figurine fell to the floor and immediately smashed into three neat pieces. To his credit, he knelt to pick it up, but Emilia knelt in front of him and snatched the remnants out of his hands, eyes blazing.

"I'll get it," she hissed. "First my husband, now this."

"Sorry," Brendan muttered. "But I didn't break your fucking husband."

I sighed. The widow snapped back up to standing like a puppet whose strings had just been pulled. "You watch your fucking mouth."

He went pale, and I almost laughed. Maybe a nun

sometime in far-off Ireland had used the same tone, and it struck a chord. "Sorry, ma'am," he muttered.

But she wasn't finished. She made him look at her again. "What are you most sorry for?"

He blinked. "Uh..."

"The figurine, that last comment, or the way you treated my husband's body?"

He bristled. "Hey, I was *asked* to—" he started. I moved forward and stepped on his foot.

"We should be going," I said. "Sorry about that." I gestured to the pieces of the broken golfer, still in her hand. "Just add it to our tab." She smiled, just for a second, and I hustled him out of the room.

The minute the door closed behind me, I took a long, deep breath, clearing the house's cloying smell from my nostrils. The rain-damp city air was better. Even Brendan's sulky company in the car was better. When we got in the car, I put my hands on the wheel but didn't start the engine. I'd promised John I'd teach the boy *something*.

"Don't do that again," I said.

"What?"

I eyed him. "Any of it."

"Am I going back?" he asked. "Is that how I earn my promotion, not breaking shit in an old Italian ghost's house?"

"Do you think that's the way you should talk to me?" I asked. I kept my voice soft, but my hands tightened on the wheel, and he sensed the change in the air. He managed one more quick muttered sorry.

I let the silence sit for a while, then sighed. "Brendan," I said, "mobst—men in our line of work aren't just—" I stopped. "There's such a thing as...institutional ritual. You need to—whether you think you do or not, you need to learn how to behave."

He snorted.

"Look," I said. "You know better than to scream at John, right? And you call him sir?"

He nodded. I could tell we were both thinking of the terrible thump of that body hitting the floor of John's office.

"So you know and follow some of the rules already," I said. "We all do. It's how you get by."

"Yeah," he agreed, "but there are street rules, and then there's just bullshit."

"The bullshit matters more than you'd think," I said. I started the car.

―――――

"Sir, I'm starting to hear rumors about this labor consulting firm...."

"Oh, hush with that already, will you?" John said. He was waving and beaming out at the crowd with a shovel in his hand. It was that same week, a Thursday, and yet another stop on the John Callaghan Is a Well-Meaning Philanthropist Tour. This time it was a hospital wing he'd donated to St. Christopher's, a Catholic teaching hospital in the Tenderloin. The John Callaghan Proves He's Not A Criminal Wing, I believe it was called, or maybe that was just the working title.

I don't like these events. I play no part in them except standing next to John, holding a clipboard and wearing a hardhat, smiling out at the crowd of bored reporters, a few even more bored hangers-on, and several grateful and either genuinely or willfully oblivious hospital employees. It was a sunny day, at least, but the sun was directly in my eyes, and my cheeks were starting to hurt from smiling. John always insists I go to these things, and he never lets me get anything done while I'm there.

"But sir—"

"Harris," John said, "does this really seem like the

moment to talk about this?" He waved again and then put both hands on the shovel and thrust it into the ground. For one horrible, impossibly long second, the ground didn't give. I almost laughed. John smiled his rage-smile and sank one foot on top of the shovel.

Another second passed, then two, then three. John sank his entire weight onto the shovel. It finally gave. John's smile relaxed. He turned back to the crowd's scattered applause.

"Ladies and gentlemen," he said, sweeping his arm out wide, "I give you the John Callaghan Wing for Pediatric Oncology!" The applause was much louder this time. The Black woman standing off to the side beamed—Mary Perkins, the hospital administrator. She shook hands with John and gazed out at the crowd. "Thank you all so much for coming," she said, "and thank you to Mr. John Callaghan for his incredibly generous donation of two million dollars to get this wing going. With his help, we will make this the best child cancer treatment center the world has ever seen!"

Take it down a notch, Mary, I felt like saying, but John looked pleased. He'd worn a white and red pocket square for the occasion (to match the Red Cross, I guessed), and his eyes were bright as he took in yet another round of applause.

Mary spoke more after that, as did a few other people. Let me sum it up for you: John Callaghan is great for giving us money. No, this is not a bribe. Thank you to all rich men who deign to give us money that they could just as easily have spent on hookers and cocaine. We'll take your questions now.

There was a cocktail reception after that, in the hotel a few blocks from the hospital. It was meant to be a fundraiser, but really it was an excuse for John to meet with all the rich legitimate(ish) businessmen from this area. While he schmoozed, I tried to find as much shrimp cocktail as I could get my hands on. My property dispute case was finally coming to an end, but I'd skipped lunch to work on it, and I needed food. More importantly, if I was eating, I wouldn't have to talk to anyone, and the full hospital board was here, including Katie Callaghan, who could bore anyone into the ground.

But I was too late—she'd already spotted me and headed right over, waving. "Harris!" she said. "So good to see you."

I smiled. "Hi, Katie."

"I didn't know you'd be coming," she said. "Quite a spread, isn't it? Diet starts tomorrow!" She patted her stomach, and I tried to smile.

"How are things?" I asked. "How's Neil?"

She blushed. She actually blushed. They'd been married five years now, and she still acted like a groupie around him. I wondered, not for the first time, if they still fucked. It wasn't that she wasn't attractive—she was. She had beautiful eyes, and thick dark hair, she was just heavier than average. But she was so...*beige*. And Neil was...well, it was like a peacock marrying a gopher. "Oh, he's good!" she said. "Busy with all this movie stuff, of course, you know Neil, he loves to prepare...He's just researching up a storm, I can't believe how many questions he's asking John and Brendan and Liam..." Like many lonely people, she spoke as fast as possible in order to get out as many words as she could before someone interrupted her. She'd keep going like this if I didn't stop her.

"...board member meetings can be so dull, you know, yawn a minute, but Daddy says they're important and I do like to be involved in the business, you know, help out when I can. Deirdre says it helps to get out of the house."

"Deirdre?" I asked. She didn't seem like the type to call her mom by her first name. I didn't even call her that.

Katie blushed again. "Mom, I mean." She put her fingers on mine. "I never know what to call them with you. Mr. and Mrs. Callaghan?" She laughed.

"By the way," she said, dropping her voice and putting a

hand on my arm, "I heard something earlier about that guy who was at dinner not too long ago? Cary, or whatever?"

"Casey?" I asked. John was walking over, eyebrows raised at the two of us, and I shrugged my shoulder a fraction of an inch.

"Yeah, Casey," she said. "Does he work with Daddy?" She giggled. "I shouldn't laugh, but those *ears!* He seemed a little..." she wrinkled her nose. "...obnoxious."

Rich coming from her. "He's new," I said. John was almost on us, and I wanted to plan my escape route before all three of us had to make small talk. I couldn't imagine talk that small. "He hasn't gone through his Callaghan orientation yet."

"Ah," Katie said, nodding as though she understood.

I felt a pressure on my arm and turned to see John smiling at us.

"Go back to the other board members, darling," he said. "Leave poor Harris alone."

"Oh, she wasn't—" I started to say, but Katie had nodded obediently and drifted away.

"She's never that chatty with me," John said. "I think she has a crush." I agreed, but it didn't seem polite to say. So I just let John steer me over to the next group. I knew the routine. Sure enough, standing in front of me was a big Black man wearing a checkered suit with a purple tie. Ernie Spellman, I remembered, a tech millionaire. He was smiling, a little uncomfortably, at John and me.

"So. How'd you end up working for John?" he asked, after a few minutes' meaningless small talk.

Ask what you really want to ask, I thought, but I just smiled. "His was the best offer. And I have many other clients, too, from all walks of life."

Ernie frowned.

"I get it, Ernie," John said, laughing. "You're wondering

why Harris works for an Irishman like me. But as it turns out, we're not so different. He's black Irish!"

John grinned and paused expectantly for laughter, which Ernie politely gave. This is John's number-one favorite joke, and his main reason for bringing me to these functions. I'm John's diversity beard.

"Excuse me, won't you?" John said. "I've just seen Mayor Wong's assistant Martha, and I promised I'd say hello. Ernie, please come to our house for dinner sometime. My wife Deirdre is a wonderful cook. And I've heard so much about what you're doing with your company—'revolutionizing the world,' didn't *Forbes* say? We certainly could use some of that in our Callaghan businesses." He shook Ernie's hand, giving him the special John Callaghan Business Smile, which softened Ernie somewhat, and then strode away. Ernie's eyes followed him.

"He's quite a man, isn't he?" he said, watching John hug a woman in a red suit. It wasn't clear whether it was a compliment or an insult, but if he'd been on my jury, I'd have bet on him leaning toward compliment.

"He is," I agreed. A young smiling blonde waitress offered me a canapé. I took it; it was still hot.

"You like working for him?"

"He may be a little out of touch, but he's fair. John Callaghan is what I call an equal-opportunity oppressor." Ernie's eyes widened. I laughed and slapped him on the back. "I'm kidding," I said. "John's been wonderful to me. Raised me like a son." I always paused on that part. Usually that was enough to sell women on him, but sometimes men (particularly businessmen) needed more. "And then, of course," I said airily, "there's the money." If Ernie had been a dog, I think his ears would've perked up. "There's a lot of it, and plenty to go around, if you're his partner."

Ernie swelled a little. "I'm not accustomed to partners—I

built everything I have on my own, with my two hands." He held them out as proof.

"Of course," I said. "But I'm talking about a fully equal, mutually beneficial partnership. Like the Allies in World War II."

Ernie frowned, but I could tell he was intrigued. "I guess I'd better come to dinner, then."

"I would."

I turned and walked back to John. He'd just said goodbye to Martha, and he looked at me. "Well?"

"Is he looking over?" I asked.

John raised his cocktail in a toast to someone behind me. "Yes," he said, smiling.

"Then we've got him."

"Wonderful."

"Now, sir, about this labor firm guy, his name is Bhat and—"

"Oh, please, *enough* with that, Harris," John sighed. "I heard about Bhat. He's trying to shake down unions."

"He hasn't gotten to ours yet, sir, but—"

"He's asking them for money to prevent *terrible things* from happening," John continued. He took a sip of his drink —Irish whiskey, of course—and waved to someone else over my shoulder. "Standard procedure, Harris. We wait and see. If he looks like he's not just going to flame out on his own, we'll figure out something, but I'm not worried, and you shouldn't be, either."

"If you'd just let me—"

"Someone else will handle it," John said. He looked back at me, a little amused. I saw my reflection behind him in one of the silver chafing dishes. I looked tired. "Anyway, Bhat's small time, just a hustler. Don't you think it's a tad below your pay grade?"

"The biggest threats are always the unseen ones, sir."

"Then you should *really* be worried about the threats that haven't even crossed your mind yet."

I laughed in spite of myself, and opened my mouth to argue again, but he was looking elsewhere: at the blonde waitress, of course. She was smiling at him, her earlier smile to me apparently forgotten. I sighed. At least that meant I wouldn't have to spend the night "arranging company" for him. "Sir," I said again.

"Harris," he said, "I'm going over to speak to that young lady. Don't worry about Bhat. If the time comes, we'll take care of him. I need you focusing on your other responsibilities, okay?" He turned his eyes back to me. "You're the best I've got, Harris. I shouldn't have to tell you that. Have you *met* my brothers? And my sons? God, they're even worse! Did you see them, at the last dinner? Arguing about the fucking dry-cleaning business?" He rolled his eyes and put his hand on my arm. "If you're feeling unappreciated, it's probably because I've been neglecting you. Should I take you out on a date, buy you some nice orchids, treat you to a massage?"

"Only if there's candlelight, sir," I said. We were both grinning.

"Damn, sir," I said, "I can't stay mad at you."

John laughed, his eyes back on the blonde. "Have another shrimp cocktail. The hospital's paying for everything." Then he strode off. The blonde met him halfway.

TEN
NEIL

After I'd locked Brendan down as a consultant, it was time to do my authenticity research. I was eager to really dive in and sink my teeth into it. One lazy afternoon I decided to take Brendan up on his offer to see The Bar, where the "real crew" hung out. I stepped out of my car to a dingy looking dive, complete with a neon sign missing two letters (it read "T e BA") and an image of a woman opening her red mouth wide to let in a stream of beer. "Classy," I muttered to no one. But I strode in anyway, hands in my jean pockets. Here was my first chance to blend.

It was so dark inside that when I flung the door open all the men inside swore and blinked like reptiles in the nocturnal exhibit exposed to sunlight. I spotted Brendan right away, sitting with his two guys at a table inexplicably covered in salt packets. I made my way over, trying not to choke on the combined smell of stale beer and cigarettes. The floor was sticky with what I prayed was just spilled alcohol. There was a pool table, and a wooden bar with brass finishings in desperate need of a polish, and every corner was filled with degenerates, oozing liquor and glaring at me.

It was perfect.

I pulled an extra chair over to Brendan's table and sat down. His guys—Colin and something—just stared at me. "Is now a good time?" I asked, and without waiting for their permission, I filled them in on the basics of my deal with Brendan. "And of course," I said, trying and failing to wave the barman over to take a drink order, "I can learn from you guys, too." They looked at each other, probably just astonished that anyone like me, practically the boss' son, would even talk to them. I offered to buy the next round and asked for the most authentic beer they had. They picked an expensive draft—I should've guessed, I thought ruefully, but I went along with the game. Another great little trick for the movie.

They were hesitant at first, guarded and shifty. I could feel other eyes on me, too, the even lower-level guys who didn't merit a table at the center of The Bar. But I kept buying rounds and started telling them stories about my early, seedy days in LA (I may have embellished a bit, but most of the ones about pussy were true enough), and slowly, surely, they started to warm to me. They were like dogs, really—give them a few treats, and they'll start coming to eat out of your hand.

"How do you treat the guys who are, like, middle management?" I asked one fat guy.

He frowned.

"You know," I said, "like not *John*—"

"We don't call him *John*," Colin said quickly. He was the nervous one—no need for inspiration there. I'd let the ugly bit-part actors take all the nervous guy characters.

"Yes, I know *you* don't," I said with a wolfish grin. "But he's my father-in-law."

"Bet he doesn't like you fucking saying it, either," Brendan muttered.

"He hasn't stopped me saying it," I said. "And isn't that the important thing?"

They all knew it was. "So," I repeated, "how would you address, say, the red-headed man who handles...I don't know what. The one who always looks angry?"

"Tomato Mulligan?" Colin said. He looked at Jimmy, then at Brendan. "We don't really call him anything, I guess, I mean—I kind of avoid naming him, but I guess I'd call him sir..."

"I fucking wouldn't," Brendan grunted. I was taking mental notes. A short exchange, but it spoke volumes.

"Did you ever meet anyone famous?" Colin asked.

"Of course," I scoffed. "I was in a commercial with Morgan Freeman."

Even Brendan looked impressed by that one. He pulled out his phone to Google it, but I had to stop him. "It's not on YouTube," I said. "For copyright reasons."

———

They were laughing hard at one of my stories (about a girl with a lazy eye and a circus performer) when the door opened again, and another group of guys came in. They said lazy hellos to Brendan's crew and let their eyes skate over me. At first, I didn't really pay attention—they looked vaguely familiar, and I knew they were low in the pecking order. But there was someone new with them—someone who stood in the background, but with his feet somehow planted more firmly on the ground than the rest. His eyes were brighter, too. One of the others introduced him to us as Mikey Fitzgerald, a new union guy. He grunted hello.

He was shorter than some of the others but stocky and well-built, with a handsome sturdy face and a short, ragged beard. His clothes were dirty in patches and smelled like rust and oil. Seeing him next to Brendan, I couldn't help thinking that he might be an even better guy to know for the movie. He just *oozed* working class authenticity.

"I'm Neil Bowes," I said, shaking his hand.

"John's son-in-law," Brendan added.

"I work for the production company," I said. "I'm an actor."

Mikey raised his eyebrows. "An actor, huh? And the son-in-law? What're you doing in this shithole?" I liked his voice; it was raspy and deep, like a jazz singer's. And his eyes were bright blue. They held mine, a little threateningly, but not unkindly. Yes, I thought—this, *this*, was Aiden Trask! Put his intelligence and masculinity together with Brendan's temper and vocabulary, and I would really have something.

One of the other guys asked him about his new job, and another one talked about its "perks." I asked for more details, knowing I wouldn't get any, but Mikey winked at me and said, "I bet you can guess. The big man's your father-in-law, isn't he?" And I smiled. Yes, he would come in handy.

I bought another round, which entitled me to ask more questions.

I turned to Mikey when I plopped his glass in front of him. "Have you worked on the docks long?" I asked. The others laughed at the question.

"What are you, a fucking reporter?" the one who wasn't Colin snapped. I let the laughter ripple through the Bar, then looked at Mikey.

"I know, I know," I said. "I'm the shiny Hollywood guy who doesn't...what's the phrase? Know shit from Shinola? But then again—" I leaned forward, with just the right amount of dramatic pause. "You're all fucking actors, aren't you? You're playing the part of gangsters, making it real. And doing a damn good job, most of the time." Another pause. "But you know the rankings. I don't have to tell you, or maybe I do. I'm the leading man son-in-law. The leading man son-in-law who has John Callaghan's ear and can make your lives either way easier or way harder."

I saw several clenched fists, but no one moved. I had them. "And I can make your lives fun, too," I added.

"How?" the fat guy snorted.

"Anyone want to be an extra?" I asked. "Or actually get a line in a movie?"

Brendan scoffed. "We're real gangsters," he said. "We don't need that shit." But I could see a little shimmer of interest growing in the others.

I crossed my arms, leaning back and down in my chair, eyes half-closed.

"Suit yourselves," I said.

Aiden Trask, eat your heart out.

———

That night Katie came into my room after dinner. She'd been away, at some charity dinner for orphans or ALS or war widows—she was involved with every white liberal sob story you could imagine.

She plopped onto my bed. "God, I'm exhausted," she said. "Those meetings..."

"They'd exhaust anyone," I said, sitting delicately on the bed next to her.

She laughed. "Exactly. I stopped by the house tonight, too, to pick up my mom's knitting stuff. And my dad...well..." she hesitated. She doesn't like to talk about her family with me. It's another one of the things I find so tiresome about her.

"What about John?" I asked.

She plucked at the bedspread with her fingers. She wouldn't look at me. "He's...stressed," she said. She ran her fingers through her hair, which was newly cut, I was pleased to notice. She wouldn't dye it, though, even when I asked. I could see several gray streaks.

"Of course he's *stressed*," I said. "He's running a rather large empire."

She looked at me. "I know that," she snapped. Then she sighed. "Sorry, I'm just tired. He said something about Owen driving him crazy, and needing someone else to take over, and not trusting Martin..."

Jesus. Leave it to Katie to bury the lede. "He wants someone else to take over?"

"No, not like that," she said quickly. She sat up and pursed her lips. I hate when she does that. "He was just blowing off steam, I'm sure." There was another pause. "If he meant it, though..."

"What?"

"Neil, you'd be perfect. Don't you think?"

I started laughing. "No no no no no," I held my hands up in surrender. "I couldn't possibly. I'm an *actor*, I don't know anything about business."

"But I heard him talking about you, saying he really depends on you..."

I blinked, pleased. "Really." I could only half believe it, but maybe he was talking about the movie? It was important to him, after all...

She nodded and slid closer to me. "Neil, he loves you. He always has, ever since I first brought you home for dinner. Why do you think he asked you to be in the movie?"

I remembered that dinner. My first caviar, served on little crackers. John had worn a dinner jacket, and I'd thought, *Now there's a leading man*. I'd made him laugh, doing my impression of Katie. A good night.

"He's not grooming me," I said. "That's ridiculous. He has two sons and two brothers."

"None of them hold a candle to you," she declared.

I patted her hand. "That's sweet," I said, "but I'm not exactly qualified."

"Well..." She twisted her mouth. She was quiet for several seconds, but her fingers tapped on the bedspread like she was playing an invisible piano. Finally, she said, "You're right. It might be a bit of a stretch. Let's just focus on your audition and go from there."

"Yes. The audition." I brought my focus back. "They told me sometime in September. I just got the sides."

"The sides?"

I rolled my eyes. "The part of the script I'll be using for my audition. That's what they're called."

"You're too Hollywood for me," she laughed.

Far too true. I went and got the script, and we moved to the living room.

———

"*Just see that it's done.* No, no, see, I said it different last time. In my Aiden Trask voice."

"I really don't think you did, Neil."

Katie was on the couch, her legs crossed as she frowned down at the script in her lap. I was pacing. "I'm the one with the audition," I snapped. "Not you."

"Okay, okay, I'm sorry, honey," Katie said, grabbing at my sleeve when I paced past her. "Calm down. We'll get this."

I sighed. "Sorry. It's just—" I tried to think of a way to articulate what I was thinking (*I'd rather just fuck someone else and call it a night*) into something that wouldn't hurt her feelings. "I'm just under a lot of pressure right now..." I sighed. "That's kind of a lie, I guess. I just...I've been auditioning so long for so much shit and I still haven't..."

Katie stretched. "I know. But focus on this audition right now. One day at a time." She sighed and linked her arms together, cracking her back. "There's no way you're not going to get it. Unless—"

"Unless *what?*" I hissed.

She sighed. "Neil," she said, "I don't know, okay? I just—I don't want you to get your hopes up."

I rolled my eyes. "Let's just get back to the script, okay?" I said, standing up again. "Go from the beginning."

"*I—I'm sorry, sir, it won't happen again.*" Her voice was so wobbly and over the top I almost laughed, and I forgot my line.

"*It's way past—*" she prompted.

"*Way past the moment for excuses,*" I finished. "*Just see that it's done.*"

But he—Katie's character, Roscoe—doesn't leave. He wants my approval, you see, and my love, more than he wants to keep his own dignity. So, he stays.

"*What are you still doing here?*" I said, after a few beats.

"*Sir, I'm sorry I screwed up—the shipment was fine, though, wasn't it? No harm done?*" Katie was making the script shake with feigned fear. The mark of a weak actor: overly physicalizing everything.

"*No harm done is not good enough...*" I said, drawing myself up to my full height. I thought of John, the way I'd seen him stand. He kept his arms at his sides, loose but coiled, ready to strike. It was a tough combination to imitate, but I thought I had it down. "*No harm done is not good enough,*" I repeated, "*when we are speaking of empires.*"

There was a pause. I heard the thrumming of a car engine down the street.

"It's your line," I snapped at Katie.

"Oh, sorry," she said. She shivered. "You just gave me the chills."

"That's the general idea," I said. But I smiled.

———

I went to a party that Friday night in Marin, a sort of an Emer Productions meet and greet. Katie had wanted to come, but I told her I wanted to network, and she got that. It was held at Terry Mannix's house—besides John, he was the biggest producer on the project, a legitimate film guy who'd just relocated from LA. The house was gorgeous but gaudy—not at all in keeping with the usual minimalistic floor-to-ceiling glass you usually get in Marin, but that only made it clearer he was an LA guy, which was encouraging. There it was: all marble columns and topiary. The light was just starting to fade, and the golden glow of well-placed lights highlighted every detail.

The house was packed, mainly with young women wearing false eyelashes and not much clothing, but towards the back of the house I spotted Terry, a little bald man in a semicircle of men in tuxes, all old and far too unattractive for their surroundings. They had to be the money men. I hovered near the buffet table, pretending to focus on a conversation between an older couple next to me. Then I saw a flash of black and white out of the corner of my eye; Terry and the producers were on the move.

I caught them just as they were heading upstairs. I introduced myself, dropping John's name as subtly as possible. "I know who you are," Terry said. "Come join us." I nodded and followed them up the stairs, noting the gold banister and the fine, thick carpeting.

"Neil Bowes is married to the Callaghans," Terry said, smiling knowingly at the men.

One of them, a farm animal with a truly unfortunate goatee, mirrored his smile, his eyes on me. "Nice work if you can get it."

I laughed. "Yes, it is."

At the top of the stairs Terry turned left, opening a thick oak door into a huge study, complete with a fireplace and a mantle mostly taken up by a giant statue of an eagle. This was clearly another decorator's work: everything in here was wood and leather. It looked almost exactly like John's study, actually, if John felt he needed to prove something. Terry headed for one of the bookshelves, which housed a series of shining silver bottles full of amber liquid. He brought one out, grinning, and gestured us all onto the couches near the fireplace.

I sat down next to Terry. Up close he was a little owl of a man with eyebrows that seemed determined to leap out of his face. "So, Neil—you're an actor. What are you up to these days?" he asked.

"Aiden Trask, at your service," I said.

He smiled. "I didn't think that part was cast yet."

"Oh, it hasn't been," one of the other men said breezily. He was the youngest of the group, a blond man with thinning hair whose suit was too tight. "But maybe Neil here figures, what with the family name and all, he's got a bit of a leg up." He winked at me.

I crossed my legs. "Of course, I won't stand for nepotism," I said. "I'll earn the part on my own esteem."

"Of course," the man said. He grinned at Terry. I poured all of them another drink, then settled in to sell myself.

———

Later that night, I drifted outside. The pool, long and kidney-shaped, changed colors as I watched, morphing from blue to purple to green, and beyond it, past the fence, you could look down on the lights of the town and harbor so far below. The whole house screamed "new money." I had to admit, though —the pool was oddly soothing. Steam wafted off the water to mingle with the night air. I sat down and dipped my feet, watching them sway back and forth underneath the purple-blue water.

A young woman walked by me, wearing a dress so tight it looked painted on. She carried it off well, all bronzed shoulders and long, shiny golden hair. "Miss?" I said. She turned back to smile, her teeth glittering as much as her eyes.

"I recognize you. Are you an actress?"

She giggled. "No," she said. "I mean, I did some modeling, once upon a time..." She shrugged and looked off into the distance. "But it wasn't for me. They said I was too fat."

She laughed again as my eyes traveled up and down her body. "They look for size twos now. I'm a four."

"You're a ten."

More laughter. She pushed her hair behind her ears. Another trick I'd seen a million times, and it always worked. I'd thought I was tired of blondes, but...

"...now I'm more or less free," she was saying. "Out of the cuffs, I guess."

She paused. I was noting her lack of bra, but she seemed to expect a question. "What do you do now?" I asked.

She took out her purse and pulled out a joint, as if stalling for time. "You want some?" she asked, lighting it. I nodded. She took a long drag, then handed it to me.

"I'm an aesthetics expert," she said, coughing. "Jesus, that's good shit."

I took a hit. She was right—it was good. I closed my eyes and absorbed the night. When I opened them again, the pool's colors danced in and around me, and music from somewhere inside thrummed in my blood.

"An aesthetics expert," I said. "What exactly does that entail?"

She shrugged. "It's more of a consultant than anything

else," she said. "I go to people, or to firms, and I tell them how to make themselves, like, hotter, trendier, classier, whatever."

"You seem to be an expert." I took another drag. I was starting to shiver, but I loved the way the water looked now, the light fractured and remade by passing shadows.

"Well, I don't know," she said, smiling shyly. "I do ads, too. And slogans, sometimes. And windows."

"Really? Would I have seen anything you've done?"

She looked down again, so shyly I wanted to kiss her right then and there. "I did a window once, for Primal Urges. The store downtown?" I nodded, although I'd never seen or heard of it. "It was all leopard-themed," she said, "you know, the beast within, or whatever. I had hunters, loincloths, the whole bit. Very erotic—but tasteful. That was what the client required."

"Very impressive," I said thickly. Again, another silence. The weed was really starting to get to me now. My mind wandered back to Terry and his league of producers. Were they still up there, plotting in the den? *Don't think about it,* I told myself. *Think about her.*

"This pool is cool," I said dully. She looked at me as if she'd suddenly realized how stoned I was.

"What do you do?" she asked. Her nose was slightly wrinkled. As if someone who designs store windows should have any sense of upper-crustness.

"I'm an actor."

The wrinkle vanished. "Oh, really? Would I have seen you in anything?"

I smiled. "I've done a few commercials, but I'm waiting for my big break. It looks like it's coming." I shifted my weight, inclining my body towards hers, and started to tell the story.

ELEVEN

BRENDAN

After Liam's party and the little field trip to the widow's, I figured my stock was up. But then a few weeks passed, and I didn't hear anything. My whole crew was tethered to The Bar, waiting for calls to come in on the landline. (John doesn't trust cell phones, except for the burners he only hands out to the higher-ups.)

There we were, day after day. We got so bored we started making bets on when the fog would clear up each morning. By that Tuesday, I'd lost a hundred and fifty bucks, and fucking Jimmy, who always chose 10 a.m. no matter what, was up by fifty. Colin was yammering on and on about Kylie, this girl from the coffee shop who he'd fucked the night before.

"I fucked her two days before you," I said finally. That shut him up. We went to lunch.

When we came back, our usual table was occupied. I grunted and went to chase the guys off, but then I saw those fucking taxicab ears. Casey turned around. He was sitting at my table with three guys I'd never seen before.

"Afternoon, Brendan," he said brightly.

"You've got a lotta nerve," Jimmy began. I held up a hand to cut him off.

"Afternoon," I said. If Casey wanted to play this game, I would play too.

The guys with him looked to be about our age: twenty, twenty-one. Two were little white guys like him, and one looked Mexican. They were all glaring. I guess we were supposed to be terrified. I sized them up. If it came to a fight, they'd lose. The Mexican looked tough, but the other two were nothing. I'd seen Jimmy try to bite a guy's ear off (points for drama, although he didn't succeed), and even Colin could really land some punches when he was pissed off.

"We're here with a message from John," Casey said.

I bristled. But I didn't want to give him the satisfaction. "Is that so?" I asked politely.

"John requests that you be on standby for an event that will occur in the next few days," Casey said. The Mexican guy sniggered. He had a stupid little mustache that looked more like a caterpillar than facial hair. "At the home of Mrs. Lavella. He said to get all your tools ready. And a tarp. When the time comes, Tim Smith will pick you up."

"We gonna kill an old lady?" Jimmy huffed, but I shushed him.

"A cleanup job, I believe," Casey said. "A *specialized* one. Botched burglary is what I hear. John will pass along instructions when the time comes."

I nodded, but Casey didn't leave. His eyes were running around The Bar, looking at Archie and the wooden walls and all the posters of girls and beer and pool tables. "Nice place," he said, grinning.

"John's a silent partner," I spat. "If you like it, you should let him know."

Casey's eyes turned back to me, and then flicked to the table. *Dark Was the Night* was lying open next to my beer. I'd been thumbing through it. He picked it up, wiping the beer stains off the front. "*Dark Was the Night,* by Chet Harmon." He examined the cover: a picture of a man throwing a monster-shaped shadow. "A little light reading?"

I snatched it from him.

"Don't get too comfortable here," I said. "John thinks he needs you now, but when he doesn't, you'll be gone faster than..."

"Than what?" Casey said. "The people who stole your Lucky Charms?" He turned behind him, to his guys. "John also wanted me to introduce you to a few members of my crew. That's Jack and Len," he pointed to the two white guys, "and this is Javier." The half-assed mustache raised a hand in salute. "They'll be working with me, so if you see them around, know they're in with the family."

"They don't look like they're going to be much fucking help," Jimmy snorted. Casey looked at him as if he'd just spotted him.

"Good," he said to Jimmy. "Then you understand our strategy. Hiding in plain sight."

When they left, we got to work. You'd be surprised how much gangster work ends up being a fucking list of errands. First, we had to go to the warehouse John keeps above one of the auto shops, to pick up our things. Jimmy whined the whole way about Casey, and Colin was sulking about Kylie.

We picked up two duffel bags worth of tools, and five huge tarps. Then we waited in a dank little warehouse room for instructions.

"Jesus, five fucking tarps," Jimmy said. He turned to me. "What do you think—"

I cut him off just as Uncle Peter entered the room, growling like an old car engine. But I felt the hairs on the back of my neck stand up. This was gonna be good.

———

As it turned out, Casey was right. It was a botched burglary, of a sort. Uncle Peter explained it this way:

"There was a little...misunderstanding a few nights ago. A string of burglaries in a neighborhood we own. They hit five houses on one block, and it just so happens that many of *our* friends live on that block. Poor Mrs. Lavella's old TV set is gone. We're arranging for a new one, of course, but as you can imagine, it isn't quite the same. We'll need you to do a little... extra work for this one."

Then he told us to head back to The Bar and wait for the call. It would come soon.

———

We got the call at 9 p.m. a few days later. The Bar was practically dead, with only a few of the most dedicated drunks clinging to their stools. We'd been there for like twelve hours, playing cards and talking. I told Jimmy and Colin not to drink—we had to be sharp. Colin had a cold, which was annoying 'cause he kept fucking sniffling, but he promised he'd taken nondrowsy shit.

Our bags were behind the counter. I sat at the table after Colin and Jimmy had nodded off, and a little shiver ran down my spine. I could see the moon, thin as a splinter, through one of the bar windows. I knew we could handle a bigger cleanup, but five tarps' worth was fucking frightening, even to me. And I couldn't help thinking of the instructions for that "extra work" Peter had mentioned...

Finally, I put my head down, and I must've fallen asleep because the phone jangled and I jumped up, heart pounding. I grabbed Colin by the neck and yanked him up with me.

Jimmy ran for the phone and handed it to me wordlessly, his eyes big even in the dim bar lights.

"Hello?"

"Abraham Lincoln is waiting," a voice said. I didn't recognize it. "At the entrance to the state capitol."

"He can wait all damn night..." I heard Jimmy mutter grumpily. I shushed him. I was trying to remember my fucking code name, and I'd never been good at American history, which wasn't exactly prime information in Ireland. Something to do with the Depression, and vacuum cleaners? "Uh, Hoover is down in Hooverville," I said finally.

"About fucking time," the voice growled. The line went dead.

"Abraham Lincoln" was Tim Smith's code name. Why a driver got such a fucking heroic code name is beyond me, but I wasn't invited to that meeting.

The night was cold and sharp, a punch in the ribs. Driver Tim yapped at us to hurry up while we loaded our bags into the trunk in the alley behind The Bar, and then we were off. It wasn't a long drive—two blocks or so up the hill into the swankier, older houses. I understood why Uncle John was especially pissed: his house was only a few blocks away. If any neighborhood was his, this was. Burglaries here were unacceptable.

We pulled into an alleyway next to a big Victorian duplex, and Tim let us out. "Which house is it?" I whispered.

"The one at the end," he snapped. "Big fucking pink one with the sunflower in the window. Mrs. Lavella's." He yanked the door shut and clicked the automatic locks.

It didn't take long to get into the house—we did our usual: over the fence and through the back door, which was unlocked. Peter had told me that "the party was in the living room." It didn't take long to find.

"Holy *fuck!*" Jimmy said.

"Shut up," I hissed, clamping my hand on his face. "You want to get us fucking killed?" But he had a point.

There were five bodies in front of us, all men in their early twenties, if I had to guess. They were in unusual shapes, twisted at odd angles like balloon animals. One guy's head had been blown off—half of it was on the wall behind him. And he'd been the lucky one. By the looks of it, the rest had had their arms and legs broken before they died. Another guy had a bullet wound in his gut and a white shirt dyed red. Their eyes were open. I've seen enough dead bodies to know that doesn't always happen naturally. Someone had wanted their eyes open.

It made me think of *Dark Was the Night,* when the Yeti used to take people to a deserted house and kill them as slowly as possible, to "preserve the moment." *"He always wanted to watch the light in their eyes die, like the world's most twisted sunset."*

Colin had stopped at the edge of the room, his eyes screwed up like a fucking toddler about to cry. "What the fuck is wrong with you?" I hissed at him. "Get started, or we're going to be here all night."

I pointed him toward the pink carpet, where a guy lay with his neck twisted sideways. Bad way to go, easy way to clean up. Colin needed to start with something simple. I went for the other easy one: the guy with bruises covering his neck. When I turned him over, though, I smelled something awful.

"Oh, *fuck,*" I muttered, "he shat himself."

That happens a lot with strangling. Bet you didn't know that. But here's the silver lining to that particular cloud: It's easier to haul out shit-filled pants than to clean a brain smear off a fucking wall. Although we had the right chemicals either way.

The last guy's hands were all bloody—he was missing a few fingernails. From far away I couldn't figure out how he'd died: no obvious bullets, no pools of blood. And then I saw his face up close. His head was half-bashed in, so his skull turned into a little valley on one side. Even worse, though, one of his eyes was scooped out, basically hanging by a thread, a little reddish pink thread of muscle or nerve or God knows what. It looked like something my mam's cat used to play with. Colin took one look at him and nearly barfed, and I'll admit: I had to swallow a few times myself.

It took a few seconds to remember our instructions: look for the guy wearing the black beanie. The eye guy (as I came to think of him) was our guy. He had been their ringleader, the last to die. He was short and kinda fat, with a bushy, prickly beard. His other eye looked brown, although I couldn't really tell in the moonlight.

"This is him," I said. "When you're finished with the others, we'll take him separate."

———

It was a long fucking night. For one thing, there were *five* fucking bodies. Each one had to be stripped of all clothing and potential evidence, then tarped, then dragged out (one by one, very slowly and on tiptoe in case any of the closer neighbors were insomniacs). It took a while. We had to stop every few steps with each body, and we almost dropped the black beanie guy when a cat shot out of an alley and ran across Jimmy's feet. Then one guy's arm flopped out halfway down the back steps, and Colin nearly dropped *him*. I was on edge the whole time; the moon was too bright, our shadows too stark. I prayed for the clouds to move.

But we made it. And once they were all safely loaded in the van, we became like fucking housecleaners, lugging our chemical solvents all around and squeegeeing walls, cabinets, tables, couches, everything everything *everything* for splatter.

I have no idea why they hadn't thought ahead, knowing the carnage, and laid down a bunch of sheets. But they hadn't, so we had to scrub every inch of the room and then replace the carpet. All told it took us two full hours. Colin's cold kept getting worse, so he kept sniffing and honking and whining the whole time.

I didn't think we'd ever finish, but finally we did. We trudged back to the van and sank into our spots on the floor —close enough to the tarps that we could adjust if they started banging around, but of course there were no actual seats for us. Nope, we were just a bunch of bodies in the back of a van, three alive, five dead.

"Do you know where we're taking them?" I asked, wiping sweat off my face with a clean rag from the duffel. Tim grunted and started to drive. I should've known. We're never told where we're going or why, in case the cops are onto us. He drove a long time, or at least it felt like it—long enough for me to get antsy. In *Dark Was the Night*, "a long drive only means one thing: a quick death." Jimmy fell asleep. My attention drifted—I knew we were leaving the city, though, through the Presidio and over the Golden Gate into Marin County. "We going fucking sightseeing?" I muttered. Tim just kept driving.

The moon disappeared behind clouds; we were on a long stretch of two-lane highway, with city lights blurring in the distance. Tim turned off abruptly and went down another road. This one was uneven and jerky in places. I started to smell something thick and ugly.

The car went over a bump. Jimmy jerked awake. "Are we in Golden Gate Park?" he asked dully.

"We're at Sears Point," Colin said. "Near Tolay Creek, if I had to guess."

"What a fucking Boy Scout," Jimmy muttered.

They bickered while Tim went on, farther and farther

down the road. At one point the road turned to dirt, and I had to get out and cut a chain-link fence with my wire cutters. Then we drove on past the fence on rougher dirt roads, past a clump of what looked like water treatment buildings. Tim turned right, away from these and down an even smaller and bumpier dirt road that made my fucking teeth rattle. "We almost there?" I hissed, but he didn't answer. Finally, he pulled the car over and we got out. The smell was even worse now: the thick sourness of marsh water and sewage and fuck knows what else. And when the clouds shifted, the wind bit at me.

There was a weird triangular shadow in front of us, and the outline of what looked like a wall. When the clouds moved again, I saw what it was: a crane with its front end down close to the ground, in front of a wall of tightly packed dirt. Behind the wall was more water: the sea. I could taste it on my lips.

"Hurry up," Tim growled. "We don't have all night."

"Where do you want them?"

He pointed to a spot directly beneath the wall, just to the right of the crane. Jimmy and Colin went to the van to start unloading the bodies. We had strict instructions—just four of the five buried here. Other plans for the leader.

I didn't move. "Why the fuck would we bury them there?" I asked. "In clean ground with the crane right next to them like a fucking neon sign?"

I couldn't see Tim's face, but I assume he glared. "Just do it," he barked. "I'm freezing my balls off. And you clumsy fucks shouldn't take this long anyway. Fucking amateur hour."

I opened my mouth to argue, but he was right: it was fucking cold, and the smell was starting to get to me. It was weird out here, too...exposed. I could hear rustling in the little scrubby bushes and the hooting of some bird. When the clouds disappeared, the moon felt like a fucking searchlight fixed right on us.

It doesn't take long, burying bodies. Not if you know how to do it, and the ground is soft like that marshland was. Jimmy complained the whole time, whispering so Tim couldn't hear, but it was easy enough work. "Why the fuck didn't they dig the hole ahead of time?" I muttered as we dug. "If they knew we were coming and how long the cleanup would take. And they should've put plastic up at that house so it'd be easier to clean. That's what I would've done," I sniffed, "if I were in charge."

"Not a bad idea," Colin grunted.

Jimmy snorted. "You're not in charge," he said. "None of us are. We're fucking glorified monkeys." I opened my mouth to snap at him, but then I closed it. I was fucking exhausted, and my arms were aching from all the cleaning and hauling. I just went back to digging. Towards the end I even started to fall into a rhythm—the soft *crunch* of the shovel on the dirt, the scrape of it pulling away, and the *thunk* when the shovel hit the earth again.

But the rhythm wasn't soothing that night, like it usually was. Instead, it just made me madder and madder. Was this the extra work Peter had dangled in front of me? More meat to thump into the cold ground? What about my promotion?

Why the fuck—*crunch*—were we out here—*scrape*—in the middle—*thunk*—of the fucking night? Why did fucking Tim Smith—*crunch*—get to stay in the warm car—*scrape*— while the rest of us ruined our clothes—*thunk*—getting some fucking dumbasses' bones into the ground?

When we finished, Tim flashed the lights, and we made our way back to the car. "Shoes off," he said when we opened the door. "There's a plastic bag in the trunk. Any dirty clothes, too."

"What the fu—"

"John's orders. No evidence."

That's what he said, anyway. He probably just didn't want to deal with the van's fucking cleaning bill.

———

Now it's probably time for me to explain what happened to the fifth body. You see, usually when you dispose of a body you do just that: dispose of it. For four of these five guys, that's the route we'd taken. Simple and fast, even with the drive.

But this killing was a message, and the message needed to be clear. As Owen Callaghan once put it during a staff meeting that wouldn't fucking end, "when marketing, the message is everything!"

We kept the leader's body and drove back into the city to another one of Uncle John's properties: a butcher shop.

Forty-five minutes later, we'd disposed of that body, too —well, most of it. The leg was separate. Colin had it in its own little black garbage bag. We drove to the harbor through back streets and got into one of Uncle John's "tourist fishing boats." Tim drove us out into the bay. It was still freezing, and the sky was just starting to turn blue at the edges, like a fucking bruise. I guessed we had about an hour before dawn.

We went out a ways, until we were practically in the shadow of Alcatraz, and then Tim turned the engine off. The waves were high, and I swallowed again. I fucking hate floating on the ocean. It's unnatural.

"Hurry up," Tim said. He went back into the cabin. I nodded to Colin, who grabbed at the bag, shivering a little, and opened it up. There it was: the fucking hairy, fat leg of the burglar. I felt a little proud, seeing it there in the light. It was a clean cut, a professional's work. I let myself admire it.

Then Colin sneezed. He was holding the bag, and he

sneezed all over the fucking leg, snot and spray going everywhere.

"What the *fuck,* Colin?"

In his shock, he dropped it. Jimmy caught it and snatched it away from him, cradling it like a baby.

"What the fuck is wrong with you?" he yelled at Colin.

"Don't fucking yell!" I hissed. "You want to wake the fucking Coast Guard?"

"You're going to get us all fucking killed!" Jimmy said, only slightly more quietly.

Colin blanched. "You—you think? I didn't mean to, I just, it wasn't that *loud*—"

"You just fucking *sneezed,* in the middle of the fucking job. I can't even fucking—" Jimmy stopped for a second, as if words weren't enough. His hands were shaking. I looked around for Tim, but he was still in the cabin.

I rubbed my temples. I felt a headache looming, but I tried to stay calm, like Uncle John. "Colin. Don't fucking tell me you fucking sneezed on that fucking leg."

Colin looked at me. "What?" he said. "What's bad about that? It's not going to hurt him anymore, is it?" He laughed nervously.

I am surrounded by morons. "You're going to have to bleach it," I said. "Get out your tool bag."

"What? Why? We're supposed to throw it overboard once we get into the right current, that's what you said John told you—"

"Because your fucking snot has your fucking DNA in it," I snapped. "And it can be traced back to you if the police ever fucking find the leg. And according to Uncle John's plan, *they are supposed to find it.*"

Colin went even whiter than before. "Are you serious?"

Jimmy looked at me, and I nodded. "Fucking bleach it

right now," I said. "And do it quick, 'cause we're running out of time."

Colin nodded and took the leg back from Jimmy, rushing into the cabin with it.

I heard a chuckle behind me. Tim Smith, out on deck and fucking laughing at me. "You got a problem?" I asked him.

"Cut the Al Capone shit," he said. "I know more about DNA than you'll ever know. A sneeze is only really good for DNA evidence if it's in a concentrated area, like a tissue."

"How the fuck do you know that?"

He shrugged. "I used to work for the city."

As if that fucking explained it.

———

When we finally got off the boat, I wasn't talking to any of the others. My lips were cracked from the salt, my arms ached, and I was fucking done with all of them. Colin had barely apologized, Jimmy was still whining, and Tim Smith hadn't even said goodbye, just grunted us off the boat. None of them had thought to thank me for all my fucking work and leadership. Even though every single fucking one of them needed me, my knowhow and all my fucking expertise. Only they wouldn't admit it. That day, as I walked home with the dawn rising, I promised myself something. Sooner or later, I'd make them admit it.

TWELVE

HARRIS

The next few weeks were unusual, mostly because I saw so little of John. My partners and I worked on a merger case that was impressive largely because of the amounts of paper bullshit it generated.

John was my most important client, but he wasn't my only one. At least, that's what I kept telling myself when the days continued to scrape by with no word from him. We had our ongoing Callaghan operations, but nothing out of the ordinary. Some unbelievably stupid burglars hit a house in a Callaghan neighborhood, and they were dealt with in John's usual brutal, baroque style. There were also rumors of a rat in one of the union crews...blah blah blah. I reminded myself it was normal for there to be dry spells when it came to John. Usually, it meant good news, that things were running smoothly. But I'll admit—I was counting the days until I heard from him. John was one of those people who blaze into other people's lives, and without the stress and the drama of his world, everything turned dull and ashen.

Then one morning I got a call.

It was on my burner, the one that only John's people know

the number to. John had programmed it to ring "Danny Boy," as a special nod to my "black Irish" heritage, and usually it made me laugh, but that day (a dry, unusually warm September morning), it made me jump. When I answered, I heard a high-pitched, panicky voice.

"Harris—Harris, i-is that you?"

"Hold on," I said. I dropped the phone into my suit pocket, then poked my head out of the office and told my secretary I'd be taking an early lunch. She nodded and went back to filing, and I strode out the firm's back door, up to the sunlit roof garden on the top of our building. Once I was sure I was alone, I turned back to my phone.

"Who is this?" I asked.

"It's Kevin Holt, one of Babe Molloy's boys," the voice said. "I'm in a bad way." His breathing was heavy, each word a high-pitched struggle. Strange. Babe was one of John's button men, a true professional, and his boys were all aspiring toughs. I'd never heard Kevin so worried, not even when he'd lost six teeth in a mysterious "errand" for John that I'd never learned more about.

"Tell me what you need," I said, immediately switching into competent-lawyer mode. I sat down on a rickety bench. A sparrow tilted its head at me from the edge of a marble basin.

"I—I'm fucking *bleeding* all over the place, I can't just—"

"No details, just *tell me what you need.*"

"I was setting off...a....a...present, a Molotov, uh, firework, in this deserted lot. Not to, uh—just to...uh...*remind* this guy Don—this guy D, who was starting to make a fuss in Nob Hill about not wanting to...uh, be one of our customers...and—" He swallowed, and I thought I heard a growl of pain. "The—the firework, I mean, the thing, bounced off the windshield. It bounced off the *fucking* windshield, Harris, and back onto my car. I got out, but it got me in the back when it exploded and I

—I—can't see exactly where it hit 'cause of the angle. It hurts like a motherfucker. I'm bleeding all over the fucking place and I'm not sure where to go..."

"Where are you?" I asked. I had no choice—I'd have to risk him saying the address over the phone. He mumbled one. Not far. We could get there soon. And not the scene of the crime, either, thank God.

"I'm fucked," he whispered. "Aren't I? I'm gonna get—"

"Fired?" I prompted. Last thing I needed was this idiot using the word "killed" over the phone.

"Yeah, uh...fired. The—the boss, uh, he's gonna...fire me, isn't he?"

That explained why he'd called me first. *Fuck.*

I hung up and made a few quick calls. Kevin wasn't going anywhere, and I had my priorities. At most it probably took a minute, but Kevin kept calling me the whole time, over and over. I must have declined his call five times before my business was over and I could finally take the sixth.

"Okay," I said, cutting through his cursing and whining, which was sounding increasingly like it was coming from underwater. "Wait there. The vet is on the way."

"The—the vet? Why the fuck would the *vet* come?" There was anger in his voice now. That was good. It meant he wasn't losing too much blood.

"You can't go to a fucking hospital covered in residue from a Russian firework you failed to set off correctly, now can you?" I said, rubbing my temples. "The vet's on his way. In the meantime—is everything cleaned up?"

"The only damage was the car, and I drove that to the junkyard," he said. "It's been smashed—"

"You're going to have to tell Him," I said, and Kevin started to swear, his voice thick and wet like he was holding back tears. "But not right now," I added. "Right now, just wait for us to get you."

I heard sharp inhaling at the other end of the phone, then a muffled sniff. He was crying now, barely even trying to disguise it. "I'm scared, Harris," he said.

"I know, but help is on the way. Okay?" I hung up before he had a chance to respond, cursing under my breath.

I waited there, on the roof, for about two minutes—long enough, I figured, for the necessary thing to happen. I looked at the flowers in the center of the courtyard. The thick strands of bougainvillea were starting to wilt in the noon heat. *Someone has to water that,* I thought. I made a mental note to tell my secretary.

———

I met John later that day in his "mobile office," which is what he calls his black tinted town car when he feels like working from it. "A place away from the bugs," he always said.

When I got in, he was frowning, but he didn't seem as mad as I'd feared.

"All taken care of?" I asked.

John nodded.

"And?"

"He was a stupid motherfucker."

"Was?" I asked.

John eyed me. For a minute I thought he was angry, but then a smile broke across his face. "Jesus, Harris," he said. "You're getting soft. Sit back, have a drink." He gestured to his minibar. I looked around the car. There was a stack of manila folders, and John was wearing his reading glasses (gold-rimmed, $3,000 at his favorite store in Maiden Lane), but I didn't think he'd been working. He was holding a half-finished whiskey, still frosted from his breath. I'd never have guessed he'd be this calm when Kevin had fucked up so bad.

"Did they get to him before—"

John nodded. "He was practically gone when we got there," he said. "Just needed a little push to the other side. Babe did it himself. Eased him into it, he said."

"Better than a trial and a long sentence," I said, and that time I did reach for the minibar. John's guests got top-shelf whiskey, which I didn't care for, but he kept a bottle of tequila just for me. I poured myself a generous helping, enjoying the clarity of it in the glass. I loosened my tie.

John didn't say anything, just touched my glass with his, enjoying the clink. I waited for him to drink first, an old habit. But he didn't move the glass to his lips. He looked out the window instead, at the rounded bronze cupolas of the Russian Orthodox Church we passed by. His smile faded. He finally turned back to me, his glass still raised, his eyes serious.

"To a loyal soldier," he said.

"One of the family." I raised my glass high, but at that moment the car went over a pothole, and tequila sloshed out of my glass before I could drink.

THIRTEEN
NEIL

Prepping for the audition took over most of my life over the next few weeks. But soon enough, I found myself mixing cocktails in one of my best suits. We were having Mikey Fitzgerald over for dinner. It was my idea, killing two birds with one stone. Katie always complained that we needed more of a social life—her few dreary charity work spinsters weren't cutting it, I guess, which made sense since they were about as fun as an enema—and she said she'd been *dying* to meet Mikey ever since I first brought him up. Besides, I wanted to learn more about him, observe him at close range. It was all well and good to see people like him and Brendan at The Bar, in their natural habitat, but it was another thing to see them loose in an unfamiliar environment. "Mom just gave me the number for a new chef, I've been dying to try him..." Katie crowed.

"Don't do anything too nice," I warned her. "Nothing bougie."

"Of course not," she said. "Just tasteful."

She was true to her word: within a week, we were sitting down with Mikey at our dining room table, which was tastefully but minimally decorated. Mikey had requested his steak "bloody," a nice touch that I noted to myself for later character work. We'd offered him a plus-one, but he'd come alone, with a bottle of medium-cheap red wine that Katie had insisted we drink with the steak, even though it didn't really go.

He was wearing a button-down shirt, black, with one of the buttons missing, nice but clearly well-worn. It was a little too tight against his belly, most likely from the beginnings of a beer gut, although he still had powerful arms. I could see from his forearms that he went to the gym regularly, although he didn't feel the need to wear his shirts as tight as some of the men in Hollywood. He was freshly shaved, but no aftershave. And when he shook Katie's hand, I could tell from her slight wince that he'd shook it just a trifle too hard without meaning to. I made mental notes of it all.

"So, Mikey," Katie said, tipping more wine into her glass and mine, "tell us about yourself!" She took her cardigan off, and I noticed suddenly that she was wearing a low-cut black dress, one I hadn't seen her wear for ages. And I could smell her perfume, something I'd bought her after our wedding. Did she have a thing for this guy, or was this some misguided attempt to make me jealous? Either way, I saw him glance at her tits, and felt—I'll admit it—a small rush of pride that at least in that area, she was far from deficient. "Neil says you're new to the docks."

I almost snorted. "New to the docks?" My wife, ladies and gentlemen. "Mikey, sorry, you're clearly the first working class man we've ever—"

"No, no, it's okay," Mikey said quickly. He reached out and put a hand over Katie's. She blushed furiously. "Um, no, I'm not really new to the docks. Before I was in Eureka, I worked in LA for a while, you know, down there at those shipyards. In Long Beach."

Katie nodded, and her blush started to fade. He took his hand off hers. I watched, a little confused. He couldn't like her, could he? But still, putting his hand on another man's wife...

Then he looked down at his plate. "I don't get invitations like this often," he said gruffly. "So thank you. I'm new in town, and..." He winked at me out of Katie's vision. I didn't think she'd buy any of this *aw shucks* stuff, but he sold it, and I saw her smile.

"Well, you're not alone anymore," she said promptly. "More wine?" And she poured for him without even waiting for an answer.

"You know," she said, "Neil hardly ever takes me out. But I bet you've got a girl somewhere already, don't you, Mikey? Someone special?"

"Yeah, someone from the docks?" I sneered. Katie looked down at her napkin. Her cheeks were red again, but I thought that was probably more from wine than embarrassment. I didn't know why she was getting so sloppy.

"No, no one special," Mikey said. "I—I just like being on my own, sometimes. It's peaceful."

"I get it," I said. "You should see the Callaghan dinners— it's like everyone they kicked out of Ireland rose out of a bog to attend their first civilized meal."

Katie frowned at me. "Don't say that, Neil."

"It's true!"

"Yes, but big families—Mikey, do you come from a big family? I'm just assuming because of the Fitzgerald of it all..." She grinned like this was a terrific joke.

He smiled, too. "No, I'm an only child."

"And you grew up in Eureka?"

"Jesus, Katie!" I put in. "What's with the inquisition?"

She laughed and patted her mouth with her napkin,

smudging her lipstick. "Sorry," she said. "It's been a while since we've had someone for dinner. I'm out of practice."

"No problem," Mikey said. He stabbed another piece of steak with his fork, and I made a note of how exactly he'd done it: tines facing front and with more violence than was necessary. "I'm enjoying every minute."

And you know what? He was wasted as a longshoreman, because for a minute I actually believed he was.

————

At the end of the night, I said goodbye to him at the door while Katie was doing the dishes. "Sorry about her," I said. "She's just..."

"Lonely?" he offered.

I laughed. "I was gonna say socially inept," I said, "but let's go with that."

Mikey laughed too. "No harm done," he said. "So—I'll see you at The Bar sometime, right? I—" he hesitated, "I gotta admit, I fucking love the movies. Any behind the scenes shit is good with me. So I'd love to hear as much of that shit as you have to tell. I've listened to *The Godfather* audio commentaries like ten times."

God, he was almost shy. "*The Godfather* is *such* a classic," I agreed. "The cinematography is incredible—*so* much chiaroscuro." I could tell from his shifting that he didn't know what the term meant, and I swooped in to rescue the poor bastard. "And yeah, absolutely, let's hang out more. You can count on it."

I waved goodbye and watched him drive away. He liked me. Even in spite of Katie. It felt auspicious, a good luck charm for my movie career.

————

Then it was D-Day: the audition.

Emer Productions was a beautiful set of buildings in white near the Presidio, with rolling green lawns and the kind of manufactured gardening favored by trendy tech companies. I was led right away into a holding room off the main office, where a group of actors were all corralled together. Per my agreement with John, I'd wanted Harris to sit in the waiting room with me, but he'd said he was too busy to come for any part but the actual audition.

I don't know if you've ever experienced anything like an audition—probably not if you're not an actor. Interviews and dates come close, but not quite. One of the strangest things is the waiting room, where you sit in a crowded, ill-lit box with a bunch of slightly tweaked mirror images of yourself. You can see what they're all thinking—*I'm taller than he is, he's more jacked than I am, why would* that guy *even get a seat at the table?* And you wonder what they're thinking about you. It's like one of your most disorienting nightmares, the ones where reality starts to shatter and then you end up being choked by your own doppelganger. (Which is, essentially, a pretty good description of the audition process.)

I saw the guy next to me (taller than me, but with a slightly smashed nose and bad teeth) clench his hands into fists, crumpling the script in his hands. "Not off book yet, then?" I asked. He glared at me.

The door swung open. A giant man sauntered in, dressed in a full suit with a pocket square (same as me, but his was pinstripe, which I thought was a little much). He strode right up to the receptionist, who was just leaving, and kissed her hand. "Brock Harkness," he said, his voice booming out, killing all the tepid, nervous chatter in the room. "Auditioning for the role of Aiden Trask."

"Aren't we all," I muttered.

"Please sit down," the woman said, gesturing to the chairs

and trying to detach herself from the man's hand. The creature—Brock—didn't let go.

"They're going to give me this part," he said. Now that the whole room was listening, he'd switched from bluster to dangerous whisper. "It is a question of empires."

I rolled my eyes. One of the other guys laughed, and Brock grinned with all the subtlety of a chimpanzee. He moved to the middle of the room and took a seat. Men moved away from him like ripples in a pond, leaving him alone on the lone gray couch. He looked over at me in the shadows. "Neil Bowes," he said. "The boss' son-in-law. What do you think of my John Callaghan?" He patted his pocket square. "Authentic?"

"We're auditioning for Aiden Trask," I said, drawing myself up and neatly pulling down my lapels. "Not John Callaghan."

Brock grinned. "You just keep telling yourself that," he said. "Maybe you'll get it."

I won't bore you with the details of my audition. I went in, I shook hands, I said my lines to the camera. There was a long table set up with four people: two producers (Terry Mannix from the party, of course), a shiny gold-haired man named Aaron something, the director, Bob Sweeney, and the casting director. And sure enough, there was Harris, bundled into a corner and looking sourly out at everyone. The casting director, a humorless potato of a woman, sniffed when she shook my hand. But by that line about *The world not being enough for him* (spoken by Aiden's wife Mary), I could tell I'd won them over. The woman playing opposite me in the scene was actually slack-jawed. She forgot her last line, just like Katie had.

I left with a bounce in my step, making sure to match strides with Harris and fall into conversation with him so everyone would know where I stood. Let Brock Harkness try to top that.

In fact, I was in such a good mood that I drove directly over to see Leanne, the aesthetics consultant from the party in Marin. I'd seen her just once since the party, but we'd both enjoyed ourselves, and I wanted more, even enough to tramp over to her shitty little apartment, a dirty walkup near Chinatown.

"I'm gonna be a big star," I told her when she answered my knock.

"Well, then," she said. She opened the door wide and strode off in the direction of the bedroom, shedding clothing as she went.

FOURTEEN
BRENDAN

"It's in the papers, Brendan," Jimmy said. He put his phone in front of me and leaned back in his chair. It was a few weeks after the burglary cleanup, the end of September, and we were at The Bar on a Friday night, gearing up to go play poker in the back room. Friday was drop night—the night when all our "clients" made their deposits for the week. Technically this wasn't my crew's job at all, but we liked to hang around anyway. This was the one time (besides meetings) that a huge group of John's men filtered in and out. It was our little social club. And that particular night, thinking about my promotion, I thought it was a good idea to show my face and network a little, memorizing the names and faces of the most important fucks.

"What's in the papers?" I asked, only half paying attention. Jimmy shoved his phone in my face.

There it was: local section, about a third of the way down on the main page. SEVERED LEG FOUND ON BEACH. I scanned the article: "*alleged ties to organized crime...identified as the leg of one Joshua Massey...a convicted burglar wanted for questioning in multiple ongoing cases, including a break-in in the*

Nob Hill area on September 3rd...torn off post-mortem...presumed missing, along with several associates." I'd seen it other places, too—the tabloids were going nuts trying to out-pun each other ("SEA VIEW COSTS NO ARM...BUT A LEG" was Colin's favorite).

"They didn't find the rest of his body?" I asked innocently. Jimmy grinned.

"It's just like John fucking said," Jimmy whispered. "A jogger found the leg on the beach three days after we... helped."

"They'll get the message now," I said.

"Who will?" Colin asked. He was finally over his cold, but still drinking tea, that fucking awful herbal stuff that smells like a tree took a dump in a cup. He'd even brought it with him into The Bar.

"Everyone," I said. "That was the whole fucking point, Colin. Don't you get it? Everyone knows whose leg that was, and now everyone will know why it was separated from the rest of him."

"So they won't be stealing from John Callaghan again," Jimmy put in.

"I heard the burglars gave back everything they stole," Colin said. "Once they'd realized whose neighborhood it was."

"So what?" I shrugged. "They stole from us. We can't take that lying down."

The door creaked open—the bar was packed, but I looked up when I heard that fucking voice. Sure enough, Casey had just walked in, followed by his little crew. He was wearing a navy-blue suit and yelling orders at Archie like he owned the place. I waited until they'd ordered and sat down —at least he knew better than to come talk to me—and then went over to the bar to get another beer.

One of Skinny Thompson's guys was there: Harry Rogers.

He's only a little bit older than me, maybe 25, but he's been shot four times and survived every bullet, so he thinks he fucking walks on water. He's an ugly motherfucker—was before the bullets, even, and after the bullets his jaw had to be reconstructed with a metal plate, so it makes this weird clicking sound. He was a pimp for a while, if you believe everything he says, but Skinny Thompson owns all the ass in our neighborhood (well, he owns it for John), and now Harry's just muscle. He acts like he's God's gift to women. Maybe he is—he's paid a lot of money for pussy.

"All right there, Brendan?" he said, grinning at me.

"Yeah, I'm fine," I said, dropping cash on the bar for the beer.

"I heard your guys did some construction not too long ago," he said. I rolled my eyes. Harry loved all the old-school gangster codes, especially the ones like "doing construction," "house painting," all the shit that meant murder. He saw it in some shitty movie, I guess. It was fucking exhausting.

Still, I liked the way he was looking at me: full on, with respect. And I was glad this news was getting around. I'd done it perfect, just like John wanted. If it was in the news and no Callaghan was in trouble, that was my doing. Good for everyone to know that.

"Maybe we did, maybe we didn't," I said.

"John still hasn't asked you to take anyone out of the box though, huh?"

Yet another old code for a kill. "Cut all the old dusty gangster shit," I said. "You sound fucking ridiculous."

"Watch it," Harry said, still leaning against the bar. He smiled again. "No, you still haven't been invited to the real show." He took a swig of beer and mimed pumping a shotgun. "You really shouldn't wait too long to pop that cherry, you know. You get old enough, maybe no one will take it."

"I got some of that kind of action back home," I said. I wasn't supposed to talk about Ireland, but I knew Harry knew about it. Word gets around. "And since I'm doing such a good job here, Uncle John just might…"

Casey, who'd just wandered over, looked at me. "That's your ambition, isn't it?" he said. "Button man to John Callaghan! America's next great assassin!" He spread his hands like it was on a movie poster.

Harry laughed. I rolled my eyes and started to head to the back room for the poker game. Casey stopped me, his hand on my arm. I glared.

"You might want to rethink that," I said. He grinned and slowly removed the hand, then sighed.

"Did you ever wonder why you were asked to bury a bunch of bodies near a crane next to a wall?" he asked.

"How the fuck—" I started to say, then I stopped and sighed. I was too tired for this shit.

Casey shrugged. "I saw something about the leg, heard a few rumors about the burglary, saw that they were letting down a sea wall in Sears Point."

He didn't even wait for me to fucking ask.

"It was keeping the sea out, you see," he said, "but now they're turning that whole area into wetlands. Three days after your little trip, the wall went down. That whole area's a big marsh right now. Pretty ideal place for bodies to be buried." He paused. "But you knew that, right?"

I shrugged him off and headed to the back room to play poker. Enough fucking networking for one night.

———

I tried not to let that fucker bother me. Everyone knew Casey was a shit. And he was small time. John knew it, I knew it. Plus, as much as I hated my "internship" with Harris, it was a sign that John was training me for something bigger. I turned my attention to other things. Like shooting the shit, keeping my guys happy and entertained, even while we were waiting for things to go down.

"...don't know, the whores said they liked him..." I said one Wednesday afternoon. We were in the auto shop, one of John's many fronts, waiting, as usual, for a higher-up-fuck to tell us what to do.

"*Him?* You have to be joking, that guy is one ugly fucker," Jimmy said.

The auto shop is shitty, but I have to admit, it's a good front. It actually does real business, for one thing. On our way in, we'd passed a worried-looking mom frowning over a minivan as one of the guys rotated her tires, and a group of kids were playing tag in the waiting room on the first floor. We'd gone up the stairs to where the real work was done.

It was accounting day, which meant that our guy was in the little counting room working furiously, with Katie Callaghan by his side sniffing loudly and taking notes (she was his assistant now, apparently), and the rest of us were outside waiting to get paid. I was here special, though. Uncle John had asked for me personally, said he "needed to talk to me." I didn't know whether to be scared or proud, so I settled for a little of both.

We were in the "employee lounge," a shithole with blue stained carpet and crappy coffee. But I liked waiting there, because just down the hallway was another plain black door, the main attraction: the room where they organize all the district money, to be laundered later. I'd heard that it was super classy and high tech, with a wall full of safes disguised as paintings. I'd never been inside.

"Brendan, don't you think he's ugly?" Jimmy repeated. We were sitting with Harry and a few of his guys in the lounge's ugly, itchy blue chairs. People kept passing through the hallway in front of us, on their way to "settle accounts." When they opened the plain black door, I tried to crane my neck to see inside, but all I caught was a glimpse of Harris sitting in a small beige room at a rickety desk, sighing loudly over a stack of papers. "Brendan?"

I turned back to him. "Who's ugly?"

Jimmy jerked his head just as a little old man walked by. "Rhodes."

I laughed and came back to sit down on the couch. "*Rocky Rhodes*? Yeah, he's ugly. He looks like an elephant fucked a turtle." Rhodes is our accountant, this nerdy little nothing of a guy. He's fucking terrified of all of us: I have no idea how he got into a life of crime, because everything about it seems to scare him. But he's good with the numbers.

Casey and his guy Len materialized in the doorway.

"Why does it matter if Rhodes is ugly?" Casey asked. As usual, he acted like he'd been here for the whole conversation.

"It doesn't," Jimmy said stiffly.

"One of the whores told Jimmy she thought he was sexy," Colin piped up.

"Shut up, Colin, it was clearly a fucking joke," Jimmy growled. "She just wanted to get a rise out of me."

"I think she'd probably accomplished that already," Casey said, smooth as fucking silk. Jimmy frowned for a second, and then he laughed. He fucking laughed.

"Moore?" Robins—John's bodyguard, with red hair and skin the color of medium rare pork—charged into the room. I immediately sat up straight in case my slouching pissed him off. He looked around. "Where the fuck are you?" he growled.

Casey raised his hand. Robins scowled at him. I was glad to see that not everyone knew the famous Casey Moore. "John wants to see you," Robins said.

Jimmy and Colin both looked at me. I looked down at my

fingers, playing with a thread from the chair. So what if Casey got called in first?

"Don't keep him fucking waiting," Robins grunted, and Casey brushed off his shirt and left, disappearing into the inner rooms.

"Anyone want a burrito? I'm fucking *starving*," I said. I went to the little minifridge, opened the freezer, and pulled out a burrito in orange and green wrapping. I put it in the microwave, punched the buttons.

"Why does he get to see John first?" Colin asked.

"Because he's fucking important," Len snapped. Jimmy stood up and got in his face. Len was taller, but Jimmy looks mean, and he's big. Harry got in between them.

"Don't fucking do that here," he said. He glanced down the hall, toward John and Robins.

Jimmy flipped Len off, but he came back and sat down next to me.

I felt like he was waiting for me to talk. The microwave beeped, and I got up. Harry and his guys started talking again. Len went off and sat in a corner, reading an auto parts magazine.

"Why's Casey so fucking important?" Jimmy asked, a few minutes later.

I'd just bitten into the burrito, and melted cheese hot as fucking lava gushed down my face. "*Fuck*," I whispered. I kept my eyes on my plate.

"Casey's a fucking *legend*, that's why," Len spat. "None of your phony gangster shit." I could feel Jimmy balling his fists, although I still refused to look up and dignify this little hissy fit with any of my attention. I kept my eyes on my food.

After a few seconds Len continued. "Casey got a line to the Mexican cartels when he was fucking fifteen years old. They needed white guys around here to sell—a door-to-door operation. Soccer moms and stoner kids and all that shit, they want drugs like they want a pizza delivery: fast, reliable, clean. And that's what we provide."

"Why do they have to be *white*?" Harry asked. His chest was starting to swell. He's fucking one-eighth Miwok and thinks this gives him the right to educate us all on race relations.

Len laughed. "You think soccer moms are going to answer the door if a thug's on the doormat? No, this is fucking upper-crust-y drugs, for the PTA and the debutante ballgoers."

"Big deal, hooking white people," Jimmy scoffed. "John's been doing that kind of stuff for years. Peter has the whole neighborhood."

"*Now* he does," Len said. "Because Casey agreed to join him."

I snorted. "John doesn't *ask* people to join him. They join him because the other choice is the end of a fucking rope." I raised my eyes to Len.

"Fuck off," he said dismissively, tossing his hand at me. "Like you're hot shit just because you, what—share a few fucking chromosomes with the guy?"

I stood up so quickly the paper plate fell off my lap. The burrito hit the floor with a wet *thwack*. "Don't talk to me like I'm one of you," I said. Len crossed the room again, and this time I was ready. Blood was pounding in my head—enough was *fucking* enough.

Before we could move toward each other, though, there was a blur, and then Harris was there, thick and solid between us, holding his arms out wide in either direction. "That's *enough*," he said.

"Apologize," I said, staring at Len, not moving an inch.

Len laughed.

"*Apologize*," I repeated. I felt Colin and Jimmy behind me.

Len sighed, looked around at all the faces, and seemed to

remember Casey wasn't there. "I'm sorry," he said, "that I told you to fuck off. That was rude."

I didn't like his tone, and opened my mouth to say so, but I heard a shout from down the hallway.

"Rorke!" It was Robins.

I scowled but knew better than to keep them waiting, so I headed out, past the safe room and down to the left, where the manager's office was. To keep up appearances, this was just as shitty as the rest of the place, except for a real wood desk. John was sitting behind it, his hands folded in front of him. He smiled when I came in.

"Brendan, good to see you," he said. He got up and extended his hand, and I shook it. He's got a fucking firm handshake, like "the crushing grip of an anaconda," as *Dark Was the Night* put it. I gripped his hand back, but all I could think of was Casey.

"You're probably wondering why I sent for Moore first," John said, eyeing me. It was fucking spooky, how he did that. Like a fucking mind reader. I looked away and mumbled something.

"Believe me, it wasn't because I wanted to see him first," he continued. He gestured to a chair opposite the desk and then sat down himself. "He may be a smart kid, but he's not our blood."

I raised my eyes a little. "Of course, sir."

John tapped his fingers on the desk. "I wanted to say, first of all, that I appreciate all the work your crew has been doing. That burglary...problem was a big job, and you did it flawlessly." He leaned back in his chair. "I bet you're probably getting a little bored with just cleanups, though."

"A little," I admitted.

He grinned. "I would expect nothing less from Brendan Rorke. I have a job for you, an important job. One of my guys is out this week—for a fucking ACL surgery, if you can believe it—and I need your crew."

I leaned forward. Finally. The clock on his desk ticked to the rhythm of my heartbeat.

"It's just grunt work," John said, "but important. You know we do pickups on Fridays, when everyone sends us their..." he paused to grin, "...tributes." He ran his hands through his graying black hair, which he kept slicked back like Liam's. A gold ring glinted on one of his fingers. "I need you to cover the next drop night. You and Colin and Jimmy. You'll get a piece of it, naturally." He quickly explained the mechanics. "Do you think you can do that?"

"I know I can, sir."

"Good!" Uncle John slapped the table and stood up. "Thank you, Brendan. I really appreciate it."

"Anytime, sir."

———

That Friday was the pickup. When I got to The Bar Colin and Jimmy were already sitting at our usual table. Jimmy was half drunk, his eyes glazed over, and Colin was reading a newspaper.

We set up shop in the back office, and by eight you could hear even from back there that the bar was packed, full of yelling and the smell of sweat, beer, and peanuts. Every few minutes a group of our guys would walk in, make their way down the hallway, and knock on our door. Either me, Jimmy, or Colin was there waiting for them (John had told us to alternate) and a quick handshake would turn into an even quicker delivery of a thick manila envelope, slid under the table and added to a growing pile near the safe. I took the first shift, and after an hour or so it was Colin's turn. I got up, deciding to stretch my legs.

I walked over to where Harry, his crew, and his buddy Ian were sitting. From the way they were leaning, they looked about four or five pints in.

"Hey, the man of the hour!" Harry roared. His metal jaw clicked loudly. It always clicks worse when he's drunk.

We all sat down. "I'll buy this round," Harry said, gesturing to one of the waitresses.

"Jesus, that's unusual," I said.

"*Jaysus*," one of Harry's guys imitated me. (No matter how much I try, that fucking word never comes out of my mouth right.) Harry glared at him. "This guy's done a fucking great job for John Callaghan!" he said, a little too loudly. Ian tried to shush him. The shushing worked about as well as it usually does on drunk people.

"I heard John talking about you," Harry said. "With Peter. He said you did a great job."

I raised an eyebrow. "You shouldn't be listening to John's private conversations."

Harry snorted. "What are you, the fucking hall monitor? Don't pretend you aren't pleased. I can feel your erection through the table."

I considered being annoyed, but I was in too good a mood. It was Friday, a pickup day, and my crew was in charge. We all laughed. I took a big slug of my Guinness (the pricks always bought it for me, because I'm Irish). Jimmy came out of the bathroom and sat down next to me.

"They should send you on that other mission," Harry said. He pointed at me and blinked a few times, like I was going in and out of focus. "Rat poisoning."

"What the fuck are you talking about?" I asked.

"In fact, they should send both of us," Harry said. His eyes closed, just for a second, and when he reached over to grab my arm, he knocked over my beer. I swore and yanked it back up. My sleeve was all fucking soggy.

"Seriously, Brendan," Harry said. "You could do it, man, you and me." He leaned in and added (in a whisper louder than my speaking voice), "Ditch your fucking cleanup crew and we'll go solve all of John's problems. I'm indestructible," he tapped his metal jaw, another *clink*, "and you fucking get shit done. Together we can do anything."

Jimmy rolled his eyes.

But I was still curious. "What job are you talking about?"

Harry leaned forward across the table. His breath was fucking terrible, like a vodka swamp. "There's a rat," he said, "in John's crew."

"No there isn't," Jimmy scoffed.

"There is! I heard Peter talking about it, and then they got all quiet when they knew I was listening. A fucking rat, only they don't know who and they don't know how to find out."

"Bullshit," I said, sitting back.

"It's fucking *real*," Harry insisted, leaning forward again. "It's fucking *real,* Brendan Rorke, and if you don't think I can tell the difference, then you're fucking—"

I drowned him out after that. I had to concentrate on work, the pickup, all the stuff John wanted. Harry was a coke-fueled moron. You couldn't trust a thing he said. But still—he saw something in me, and he'd been around a long time. So that night, as I watched Archie wiping down the bar, I couldn't help thinking of, as *Dark Was the Night* put it, "the glittering future."

That was probably my first mistake that night. I focused on the future, and I should've...ugh, there were so many other things I should've fucking done. But fucking Casey and fucking Harry and Colin and all those other fucks distracted me. What happened next was as much their fault as mine. But sure as shit, I was the one who ended up paying for it.

FIFTEEN
HARRIS

You don't easily forget a man killed by his own Molotov cocktail, so I thought about Kevin Holt a lot in the following days. As it turned out, though, it took a while for someone else to miss him. It wasn't until about a week later that I was back in North Beach, dealing with another unpleasant task on John's behalf. Kevin Holt's girlfriend Iris was starting to ask questions, and I had to go reassure her that while we didn't know where he was, "he'd probably turn up soon." I brought Brendan with me—another chance to learn from his little "internship."

The girlfriend—Iris—had this cramped apartment above a laundromat, and every time the wind shifted, the smell changed: sometimes it was the warm breath of clean clothes, sometimes the heavy industrial scent of bleach and chemicals. There was a dog, too, this little white scruffy thing that wouldn't stop barking as it leapt up over and over, nipping at our legs. "Poppy, no!" Iris kept saying. She took the dog by the collar, laughing nervously. "Don't worry, he's harmless," she told me. When she turned her back, Brendan took a swipe at it.

She gave us a plate of dry brown cookies that looked like they'd been made for Poppy, and then sat down and burst into tears. At first, she thought Kevin might have a mistress. I discouraged this idea, but only to a point, hoping the thought would fester in her mind, driving out all other possibilities. Then she said she'd called Kevin's mother, who lived in Arizona and hadn't heard from him. Then she'd called his cousins, then a few of his friends, and then me. She'd even tried to call John (which was why I was there, although I pretended not to know this).

She started crying again after she'd listed all the people she'd called. In her sorrow, she dropped Poppy's collar. Dizzy with freedom, he sprinted to me and gnawed on my heels. I scooped him up and held him, my hands forcibly keeping his muzzle shut. He wriggled and growled like a broken radiator. Brendan huffed in impatience.

Iris sighed. She didn't even seem to see the dog in my lap. Her face, even red and splotched with tear streaks, was delicate and sweet. She was a pretty little thing, Chinese, I guessed, with long thick hair and huge eyes. Her mouth was half open, revealing one slightly overlarge front tooth, and when she smoothed her hair back one strand stuck up like a question mark. It was hard to imagine her with Kevin Holt, who I remembered as long-nosed and rail-thin, with acne scars and a scraggly half-beard. What had she seen in him? Good money, I guessed, and that gangster swagger that most of our guys have perfected, at least when they're out of John's shadow. When she finally noticed the dog on my lap, she laughed. "I'll take him," she said, holding out her arms.

"I think he's better off being quiet," I said. He'd stopped growling. He seemed resigned to his fate. "Now Miss Chen, I assure you, we're doing everything we can to find Kevin."

"My mom says I should go to the police—"

Brendan scoffed.

I sighed and gripped Poppy's mouth a little harder. "Iris, you don't want to do that, not yet. What if—" I hesitated, with my best pitying pause, and dropped my voice so she had to lean in a little. "What if he's fallen off the wagon again? If the cops find him with drugs, he'll be arrested."

"But maybe that's better than what's happening to him now!" she said. "I mean, if you don't know where he is, maybe some other gang has him, or—"

"Maybe he went on fucking vacation," Brendan interrupted. We both glared at him.

"If another gang has him," I said, "we'd know by now. There would be a ransom." The growling started again. Poppy was mounting a second attack. I finally gave up and let him go. He barked in rage and sped around the apartment, his claws clacking on the cheap, off-white linoleum.

"No," I said, as if I'd weighed all the options, "I think we just need to be patient. He's probably out on a bender—I'm sorry, but it's true—and he'll show up again in a few weeks."

"Or he'll show up dead," she said dully. She'd stopped crying now. She grabbed the dog's collar as he lunged at me again. "This fucking dog," she snapped. "It's Kevin's. I never liked him, and he never liked me." Then she looked up at me, her eyes big. I wondered if she'd practiced this look, if she knew how effective it was. "Would you take Poppy?" she asked. "To John's or somewhere? Just until Kevin gets back?"

"Oh, I don't know—"

"Please," she said, "I can't afford a kennel. And John—Mr. Callaghan—has grandkids, right? Maybe they'd like to play with him. Maybe..."

Maybe if I do something for John, he'll look for Kevin. Maybe if I give the crime lord a dog, he'll remember his humanity. I could read it all on her face. My stomach clenched. "Uh, well," I said. The dog had stopped fighting, finally. I wondered if he was as tired as I was. "I—I don't think that's such a good idea.

He's not really a dog person. But I'll be sure and tell him you offered, since it was such a kind gesture." Her face fell. I reacted without thinking. "But I'll take the dog. I have friends who foster, and they'll find him a good home."

She smiled like it hurt. But she didn't forget her manners. "Thank you," she said, "and thank you for coming by. It means a lot."

"You know we'd do anything for our employees," I said. The words sounded even more ridiculous than usual, but she nodded, thirsty to believe them. Then she showed us out, stopping at the door to load Brendan down with dog toys and leashes and a crate marked POPPY in peeling letters.

"Thank you," she said again at the door. "I know you'll do everything you can for Kevin."

It was more of a prayer than a declaration, but I nodded anyway, and took the dog (now howling in confusion in the dark of his crate) out the door with me.

As we walked to the car, Brendan kept shaking his head. "Stop it," I said. "She'll be watching from the window." He reined it in until we were safely driving away, with Poppy in the backseat. Then he turned to me.

"Kevin's dead, right?" he said.

I nodded, a little reluctantly.

Brendan drew in his breath. "That's fucked up," he said. I raised my eyebrows.

"You want to be a button man," I said, "and *that's* fucked up?"

"There's a difference," Brendan said, crossing his arms, "between an honest kill and a lie like that. One is just a job—the other is...like—" he paused for effect, "a *sin*."

"Congratulations," I said. "That is a real Catholic sense of ethics you've got there."

I didn't talk the entire rest of the drive home. Poppy started yowling, though, just one long, low whine all the way.

———

We dropped the beast off with my friends (I hadn't lied, and they were delighted), and then I left Brendan at The Bar. I was driving back to my law offices, thinking about all the work I'd like to avoid, when I realized I was close to Emilia Salvare's strange green house. I drove there without thinking.

She opened the door wearily, and when she saw me, her eyebrows went straight up. "Mr. Harris!" she said. "My goodness." She was wearing a housecoat, a green, quilted, ugly thing that smelled like it had just escaped from a closet, and her hair was coming loose from its bun.

"I'm sorry, you weren't expecting company," I said, but she shook her head.

"No, no, come in, come in! I was just getting dressed." Her eyes brightened as she led me in and sat me down at the same place on the sofa. "I'll be just a minute," she said. "Would you like some tea?" She bustled out without waiting for a reply.

She was gone at least fifteen minutes, long enough for me to go into the kitchen and fix the tea myself as I tried not to wonder what had brought me here.

As soon as I'd set out the tea tray in the living room, she reappeared in a neat navy suit, her hair brushed and shining. Again, I got a flash of what she must have been years ago: the stylish young wife of Frank Salvare, bejeweled and glowing with the confidence only wealth can bring. She smiled at me looking at her, then shook her head at the tea set out before her. "I didn't even hear it whistle!" she said. "What a terrible hostess."

"My fault," I said. "I dropped in on you with absolutely no warning."

She waved this away and sat down across from me. She poured my tea first, then hers, and wouldn't rest until I had enough sugar and milk and she'd handed me my tiny spoon. I told her I'd already eaten, but she brought out a plate of cold cuts anyway, ("the Italian stereotype," she laughed) and I devoured them. She watched me eat, her eyes flickering with a different kind of hunger.

When I'd finished, I realized she was waiting for me to say something.

"How have you been?" I asked.

"Oh, fine, fine," she said quickly. "You know. It's been difficult, of course, but people brought so much food after the funeral that I haven't had to cook at all! It's like a little vacation for me. I didn't even buy those," she said, gesturing at the platter in front of me, which was now empty except for a few forlorn lettuce leaves.

Then she was quiet, again waiting for me to speak, but I was coming up empty. She sighed, looking around at the photos and knickknacks on the shelves.

"My parents were crazy about Frank," she said.

She looked up at me. It was as if we were continuing a conversation from earlier. Maybe we were. Or maybe I was her only option.

"Yeah, they loved him," she said. "And not just because of the money. He was really charming with them. Pulling out my mom's chair for her, taking her coat, saying she looked like my sister. My *sister*." Emilia snorted, and I smiled.

"But," she continued, looking at her hands, "he wasn't a good person all the time."

This was too true to deny, so I just waited. She fiddled with the silver bracelet on her wrist, and it caught the late-afternoon sun, blinding me.

"At first it was just little pain in the ass stuff, like he was always coming home in a fucking terrible mood. He'd slam the door and start grumbling right when he walked into the house, just this and that about how they didn't appreciate him, and he was always complaining about immigrants and vagrants and n—"

She stopped and looked at me. "I'm not prejudiced," she said quickly.

"Of course not," I responded. I said this so often it was like they put a quarter in me and out popped the little prize: a piece of paper reading BLACK GUY CONFIRMS: YOU ARE NOT RACIST.

She smiled a little, like she'd been caught out. "Sorry," she said then, a little more gently.

I rolled my eyes inwardly. No time for this, not today. "At first," I prompted, "it was just little stuff, but..."

"He used to hit me," she said. "A little at first, just slaps when I forgot to do something, or a quick pinch if I was annoying him. But once Edie was born, it got worse. I didn't get my figure back quick enough, or so he said. One night after he'd gotten back from some job for Mr. Cerullo, he insisted I make dinner instead of our chef, and he called me a 'lazy fucking pig' when I burned the meatloaf. Another time he broke a glass and told me to clean it up. Told me it was my fault he'd done it. I can still see him, standing over me, glaring, saying, 'See what you made me do?'"

Maybe she could feel my eyes on her, then—I don't know. She looked up, just for a second. Then she dropped her eyes like she'd been burned. Her mouth twitched. She twisted a ring on her finger, around and around. "He was always sorry after. He bought me this." She extended her hand and I saw the ring she'd been twisting: a silver band with a huge diamond glinting on her left middle finger. She worked it off and handed it to me. I looked at it, quickly at first, but then more closely.

"It's...beautiful," I said, when I saw her watching me. This seemed to satisfy her. She laughed.

"It's a big diamond is what it is," she said. "But it's nice."

I looked down at it again. I'd seen plenty of diamonds in my dealings with John and Deirdre, who had a new diamond for each child she bore. But I'd seen even more fakes, passed off by crooks as the real thing. Emilia's ring wasn't a diamond. It was cheap cubic zirconia, costume store jewelry.

When I looked up, she was smiling proudly, hand outstretched. I put the ring in her palm, muttering more compliments, and she slid it back onto her finger, tilting her head fondly as she examined it.

I started to wish I was gone again. I patted a pillow on the sofa—green, of course, and embroidered with the words "HOME SWEET HOME" in a child's clumsy stitches.

"I'm sorry to barge in on you like this," I said again, "I was just...in the neighborhood and I wanted to see how you were."

She blinked, but she still waited. Her eyes flicked to the breast pocket of my suit, and suddenly I understood. "Oh, I don't have money with me," I said. "I'm not delivering it anymore."

She blinked again, faster. I could tell from the puckering of her lips that she was angry. "Oh," she said. "Okay."

I frowned. Wasn't her monthly delivery enough? Or did she think telling sad stories would earn her a bonus?

"I shouldn't really even be here," I said, "in case the police connect Frank to John through me."

She laughed. "The police are bought and paid for around here, same as a bag of groceries. There's no need to lie to me."

I glanced at the ring on her finger and bit back a response. "I think they had one of Cerullo's guys delivering for you—do you need to know his name? He'll be back next month."

"He didn't come this month."

"Well, maybe the delivery's next week, then," I said. "I don't know the schedule. But it'll be this month sometime."

"I was told it would be last week," she said, "and there's nothing. Cerullo was supposed to come look in on me, my daughters were supposed to get a little nest egg from him... Nothing has happened. It's been over a month. I'd been told I had to be home at 11 a.m. sharp on the 27th, but I waited all day, and there was nothing."

I sighed. "Look, I'm sorry, but I don't know what to tell you. I—"

She stood up. "I understand," she said. "You can't help me anymore. Or you won't."

"No, that's not it—John and Cerullo—"

"I just think you should know something, though," she said, and her voice cut into mine, a knife striking a stone. "I've been offered a million dollars for Frank's life rights. Some LA asshole wants to do a movie about him, apparently, and they can't do it without me."

I stood up too, so fast it made me slightly dizzy. "Now Mrs. Salvare, you know that's not a good ide—"

"I need money. If I don't get it from your guys, I'll go elsewhere."

"John won't be pleased."

Her mouth twisted, almost a smile. "I wasn't pleased with my delivery. Or lack thereof."

In spite of myself, I was a little impressed. She was all steel.

"Threats aren't always the wisest course of action," I said.

"We'll see." She was still standing there, ramrod straight, looking out the window at the setting sun. I wondered if she'd consciously chosen that pose, with the warm red light scorching her face like fire.

I sighed. "This is an incredibly stupid thing to do."

Her face swung back to mine. "I don't have a choice."

"Yes, you do," I said. "Look—" I rubbed my head, "let me go back to John. I don't know why you think you've been abandoned, but it's probably just that something else came up. I'll find out, I'll get you your money, and you'll tell that producer or agent or whatever he is that Frank's life was far too dull for any work of fiction."

She turned back to the window, her eyebrows raised, but I'm paid to smell hesitation, and I could tell she was wavering.

"Please," I said. "I'm not doing this for my benefit. I didn't even have to come here today—in fact, there are a lot of things I probably should be doing." She deflated slightly.

"And there's something else that I'm sure occurred to you," I added, speaking a little more quietly so she'd have to move closer to hear me. "If you tell the story of Frank's life, even if you think you're leaving yourself and your children in the clear, you probably aren't. A good lawyer—and I happen to know many—can find the truth in any story, and that could mean jail."

"If I'm lucky," Emilia said. I couldn't tell if she was scared or sarcastic.

"Yes," I said, even more softly, "if you're lucky."

She shifted her legs and brought a hand up to her shoulder. "I just want my money," she said. "Frank's money. An old woman's pension." She turned her eyes to me. "Can you help me?"

"I can," I said. "If you don't do anything stupid." And I left the house before she could say anything else I'd have to report to John.

SIXTEEN
NEIL

I didn't hear back about the audition right away, but John sent a personal note of congratulations, saying he'd heard I'd done well—he signed it with real ink that smudged, a nice little knowing detail I stored away to tell the screenwriter for Aiden Trask. I was feeling optimistic as the fall leaves turned. Leanne was fucking me, the air was bright and crisp, and finally, *finally* I was getting my due.

It only bolstered my resolution to keep going with my research, and a few days later I decided to head to The Bar again to meet Mikey. I'd been a few times, actually, in the past few weeks, for research, and each time I enjoyed it more. I was there right at quarter to five, and he sauntered in, ten minutes late as usual.

"Bowes!" he said, reaching for my hand. "How's it hanging?"

"Hard and straight." He laughed and shrugged off his regulation army green jacket. He'd been in the service, he informed me, "once upon a time."

"So..." I asked. "How are things at the docks?" Since the

dinner with Katie this had become our inside joke. He laughed again.

"Pretty good," he said. "Some asshole is tightening up regulations. They held us up three extra hours on Tuesday, but you know..." he shrugged. "First round's on me." He wandered over to the bartender—Archie, I remembered—to grab us beers.

When Mikey came back, he was smiling, humming a song under his breath. "Good news?" I asked. "Something I should pass along to John?"

"I got laid," Mikey said. "Personally, I don't think John would give a shit, but..." He shrugged and reached for the wooden bowl full of peanuts. I winced inwardly. The same misshapen one had been sitting at the top of the bowl for two weeks.

I toasted "To your prowess!" and downed my beer in one. It was awful, like drinking bilge water, but I smiled anyway.

"Tell me something, Mikey," I said, turning toward him on my stool. "What would you do with a million dollars?"

"You offering?" he said, but just at that moment the door opened, and six guys streamed in, throwing a gust of wind into the stale bar. I didn't recognize them, but John had a million soldiers, so this didn't surprise me. They all yelled in Mikey's direction, pulling off coats and heading over to slap his back. They brought the smell of rain with them, and dust, and sweat, and somehow even the taste of whiskey: Blue Collar Man scent, distilled like perfume.

It took them a few moments to notice me. When they did, one of them (a grizzled half-blond mountain, with a gruff voice to match his beard) clapped his hands over his head and howled. "The Callaghan son-in-law himself! At a bar in the middle of the fucking afternoon. The career must not be going too well, eh?" He nudged someone next to him.

"I'm taking the day off," I said stiffly. "Fucking your wife really took it out of me."

A silence hung in the air, just long enough for me to wonder whether I'd stepped too far.

Then Mikey roared, and the others joined in, just a beat behind. "Fucker," he said, reaching over to ruffle my hair. "At least he's got some balls."

The others settled down, some next to Mikey and some at tables close to the bar. Archie, who'd automatically created an assembly line of beers, slid glasses down to them. One of the mugs still had soap in it. That one ended up in my hands, of course. I tried to scrub it out with my finger.

"...total bullshit, of course," the blond guy said. He was sitting next to Mikey on the other side of me, guzzling his beer. "You heard about this, Mikey?"

"I don't have enough ears for all the bullshit you guys throw around," Mikey said easily. "Which one are we talking about?"

The blond guy—Jared, I think his name was, or something else primitive and brutish—smiled. "You might want to hear this shit. I heard it from the boss himself."

Mikey shrugged. He wouldn't ask. I made another mental note for Aiden Trask: He never asks for anything. He just waits for people to give it to him. I adjusted my seat on the stool so I was stooped slightly, just like Mikey.

Jared looked around like he was scanning the room for spies. Then he leaned in, lowering his voice. An attempt to be secretive that drew attention to the secret. I shook my head. Here was one wannabe gangster who was never going to make it past the first rung of the ladder. The others ate it up, though. The hum of conversation, even at the farther tables, had slowed. I could see their hungry, bright eyes on Jared's back, even by the dim light of a few frazzled, overworked bulbs.

He waited theatrically for their attention. Then he said, "There's a rat in the union crew."

Mikey took another drink. "Your boss said that? Out loud?"

"He said 'rat,'" Jared said stubbornly. "And he said it was someone who worked for our union. A longshoreman."

The room went dead silent.

"Let the witch hunt begin!" I crowed.

Jared swiveled to look at me. "You think this is funny?"

But Mikey laughed. "How many times have there been rumors about that, Jared? Honestly." He stared Jared down.

"A few," Jared admitted. Then he sighed. "Fine, fucking ignore it," he said. "But when shit goes down, just remember that I was the one who brought it up." He pointed a finger at his chest impressively. Mikey glanced over at me and rolled his eyes. I smiled. Sometimes a little authenticity goes a long way.

———

As it turned out, I got the callback for the next audition for *The Reddened Hand*. I found out on a cloudy October evening. I was just leaving Leanne's house—she'd had me over for an "early dinner"—when my agent called with the good news. "Pop the corks," he said. "You're a shoo-in." I couldn't believe he'd say it and risk jinxing everything, but the odds were stacked in my favor.

"Thanks, Henry," I said. "Really."

"It'd be pretty silly if you lost this one," he laughed.

"Because I'm so right for the part," I said.

"Well, yeah, and, you know, obviously the—"

I heard a dull buzzing in my ear and checked my phone. "Sorry, Henry, I'm getting another call." I saw the ID and swore—Katie. And I already had three missed calls from her.

"I'd better get this," I said. "Henry, send me all the info you have—I want *everything*. I'm not leaving any of this to chance."

"Neil, you're the boss' son-in-law, I don't think you—" he started, but I hung up on him. Fucking Henry. Then I dialed Katie.

She picked up immediately. "Neil, honey, sorry to keep calling—I—I was at yoga, and I, uh—" she hiccupped loudly.

"Are you *drunk*?"

There was a pause, and another hiccup. "Yes," she said finally. "I went out with some friends after and we had a bunch of margaritas, I mean, a *bunch*, Neil, and—"

"I got the callback!" I blurted.

"What?" she muttered distractedly. "No, Tiff, I'm calling him, don't worry—*oh, Neil!*" She suddenly squealed, so loudly it hurt my ears. "That's *fantastic*, honey, I'm so *proud of you!*"

I smiled into the phone. She was sweet, and she really did want the best for me. "So," I said. "You want me to come get you?"

She sighed. "Yes, please. Thank you."

"I'm on my way."

———

By the time I got to the restaurant in Hayes Valley, her friends had disappeared and she was sitting at a table in the window seat, nursing yet another drink. I felt a pang looking at her, sitting there all alone. She lit up when she saw me and hurried over to hug me. "Thanks, sweetheart," she said, her words still slightly slurred. "Sorry I got so..." She pinched her temples. "Well, no need to talk about it now. Let's go." She hooked her arm in mine, and we left the restaurant.

"Can—can we walk a little?" she asked when we got outside. "If I get into the car right now, I might just—" But thankfully she didn't finish her sentence, and I nodded. A block or two wouldn't kill me. Anything was better than her projectile vomiting in the Lexus.

It was slow going—she was wearing heels, and a little unsteady on her feet. We probably made it about fifty feet before she had to stop. "I don't feel so good," she said. She did look pale. I moved away from her, to give her room and air. When she started to make ungodly sounds, I turned away. We were outside a diner, one of the fake old-fashioned ones popular in the trendier districts. Two men sat in the corner directly opposite me, drinking coffee. Unremarkable at first glance, but something stopped my eyes—one of them looked familiar.

I moved out of sight of the window and rushed to Katie, who was sitting forlornly on the curb. "Katie!" I hissed. "Turn around! Isn't that Mikey?"

I knocked on the window. The two men turned, and sure enough, one of them was Mikey, wearing jeans and a t-shirt. The other one had a crew cut and wore a cheap suit. They both jumped when they saw me. I waved, and Mikey waved back automatically, but the look in his eyes was strange—they wouldn't settle on me, and right when I was about to head inside to say hi, I felt Katie grip my arm.

"Oh, leave him alone, Neil, I'm too *drunk*," she said. I stayed where I was, but I didn't go in. Mikey had turned back to the other man, and they'd started talking again, but I could see even from outside how tense he was. He kept darting little glances in my direction.

"Why is he being so weird?" I asked. "It's like he doesn't even want me to—"

"Who gives a fuck," Katie said dully. She tried to pull me away again, but I still didn't move.

"Come *on*, Neil," she begged. "Can't we just go home?"

My eyes hadn't left the two men. The crew cut guy—there was something about him that just didn't feel right.

Finally, Katie tugged so hard at me that I thought my arm might fall off. "Okay, okay, I'm *coming...*" I said. We hurried back to our car.

It wasn't until we were all the way home, walking from our driveway to the front porch, that I realized what had nagged at me when I saw the crew cut guy. He had an aura, an unmistakable vibe that just screamed Law Enforcement. What the fuck was Mikey doing meeting with a cop?

———

Things happened pretty quickly after that. They had to. As soon as I started to really suspect anything, I got in contact with John, and not twenty-four hours later I was sitting down with him on a bench in his backyard, under the big linden tree that kept spitting out little leftover seeds like it was determined to irritate us. John kept picking them neatly off his jacket.

"Go over it again," he said. "Exactly what you saw."

I groaned inwardly. I'd told him three times already, but that wasn't the sort of thing anyone pointed out to John. So I told him again. John crossed his legs, looking out over the lawn towards the house. Deirdre was in there somewhere, probably humming weirdly and pretending to do housework, and I thought I'd heard Owen and Martin banging around, but here we were, just the two of us.

"All right," John said, "I'm going to tell you something, Neil. Because you've earned it." He turned his head slightly to look at me. "You've actually managed to do something extraordinary."

I blinked. "Sir?"

"You've found our rat."

I didn't know what to say, so I stayed silent.

"You've heard the rumors," he said. "They were true this time. There was a rat. And you found him. It's Mikey."

"I—"

John reached into his suit pocket and pulled out a flask. He handed it to me—it was engraved with the letters JFC. "I should be thanking you more formally," he said, with a wry grin, "but this'll have to do for now. We don't want this getting out."

I took the flask and drank deeply from it, coughing as it burned my throat. John laughed and clapped me on the back.

"Sir—John—I—I'm a little confused," I said. "How can—"

"Mikey's a cop," John said. "Undercover. You saw him meeting with his handler. Also a cop, as you guessed. They were trying to get dirt on me." That drew another smile out of him. "Thanks to you, we can make sure they won't find any."

I took another swig from the flask. It was all happening so fast. I'd seen Mikey last night with Crew Cut and now here he was, an undercover cop? Mikey? My Mikey?

"Thank you, Neil," John said again. "You've really proven your worth today." And with that, he stood and walked away, leaving me with the flask, the news, and a mind buzzing with unanswered questions.

———

"You're *kidding*!" Katie was waiting at the door for me when I got back home. We wandered into the living room. "Mikey— *Mikey* is a rat?"

"You're not supposed to say anything!" I said. "I probably shouldn't have even told you. John wouldn't want it getting out..."

Katie sank onto the couch. "He seemed so *nice*. I can't believe it..."

"Well, that is the point," I huffed. I kicked off my shoes. "He was probably trying to worm his way in, and I was a good target, being so close to John and all..."

Katie nodded, thinking. "I wonder if Daddy—"

"John wouldn't want you to wonder," I said sternly, although of course I was wondering myself. I put a hand over hers. Her knee was jumping up and down. "It's okay. I've handled it."

She looked at me and smiled. "You're right," she said. "I shouldn't worry. I just...it's a shame, really. I liked him."

The look on her face was so pitiful that I kissed her cheek. "Yeah," I said. "I did, too."

We both sat there for a while. I couldn't speak for her, but all I could think about was the future, Mikey Fitzgerald, and the kind of traps John Callaghan set for rats.

SEVENTEEN
BRENDAN

Things were quiet after we covered the drop night. For a while, anyway. But about a week and a half later I got a call from one of John's guys and within the hour I found myself fumbling with chopsticks at a restaurant John loved in Chinatown. It was one of the tourist traps, empty on a Monday afternoon, dark and grand with huge wooden panels like confessionals separating the tables and red and gold lanterns hanging from the ridiculous high ceiling. Each table was lit with a candle with a little statue head—the Buddha, I figured, or Confucius: one of those fucks.

John sat across from me, his hands on the table. He wasn't eating, although he had a plate of noodles in front of him. He'd urged me to eat, ordered for me, and laughed when they slapped a plate of fried rice down. He nodded to the waiter, an old man with a thin mustache. "Give Baby my regards," he said, and the man grinned. Baby was Baby Huang, the heir to the Huang empire, who often operated out of one or more of these places, in some shitty back room near the lobster tank.

John watched me try to pick up rice with my chopsticks for at least thirty seconds. There was no fork—I'd checked—

and I knew better than to ask for one. He'd called me in without saying why. And now here he was, in the half-dark, staring at me. Should I ask? Better not, better just to—I finally gave up, grabbed a handful of rice, and shoved it into my mouth.

"Do you know why you're here?" John asked the moment I swallowed.

I looked up at him.

"I won't play with you," John said, sighing. "I don't have the time. Your pick-up day was fucked."

That last fucking bit of rice was stuck in my throat—I coughed it down.

"Sir, I—" I tried to think back to that night. "I don't think so. I counted all the envelopes we got, just like you said, and so did Jimmy and so did Colin—"

"Did you count the money *in* the envelopes?" he asked. Somewhere in the background I heard muffled voices, his bodyguards (probably Robins) at another table.

"Of course, sir! I counted, everything was counted—"

"Did Jimmy?" he continued. "Did Colin?"

I stopped. *Fuck.* Had I seen Colin and Jimmy counting? We'd been counting all night, it seemed like, but I didn't remember bills fanned out in their hands.

John straightened in his chair. "I'll spare you the suspense, Brendan." His voice crackled like fire. "Colin didn't count. He fucked up. He fucked up, and since he's part of your crew, that means *you* fucked up."

I swallowed. *Fuck, fucking Colin, of course it would be fucking Colin.* "Sir, I—"

"Are you sorry?" John sneered. "Oh, good." He stood up suddenly, fastened his suit coat button. Robins oozed out of the dark. "I don't have time to argue with you," John said, "or hear your excuses. Colin needs to be punished. Can I assume you'll take care of it?"

He didn't wait for an answer, just slammed a few bills on the table and left. As I slunk out of the restaurant a few minutes later, I stopped by the fish tank to glare at the puffer fish and pull a fortune cookie out of the bowl.

"CHEATERS NEVER PROSPER," it read.

"That's not a fucking fortune," I growled.

———

"What the fuck, Colin?" I slammed my hand into the wall of his dull gray apartment. You could hear a baby crying next door. "Did you realize? Did you notice you hadn't fucking counted?"

He muttered some excuses, some shit about counting the number of bills but not looking at the amount. I left almost immediately—I was too fucking angry. I knew I had to punish him, but punching him in his apartment seemed too small, and I didn't want to hear him sniveling.

———

John came by The Bar the next day and made me get in his black town car, which was parked in the back alley next to the dumpsters. When I closed the door, he launched right in.

"What's Colin's punishment?"

I thought for a few seconds, watching a skinny gray cat slink around the corner of the alley. "I saw him yesterday, he—"

"Did you do anything?"

"I screamed at him for a while," I said, knowing immediately how lame that sounded.

John sighed. "Brendan," he said. "I'm losing patience with you. If you can't punish Colin, I don't know where the fuck you fit in."

"I—we could—" What, exactly? Beat him up? Was that enough? All the *Dark Was the Night* shit was flashing through my head. Nibbled by dogs? Too big. Set on fire? Ridiculous. Grounded from next job? Too small. What else? Dock his pay? But John was waiting. I had to say something to buy time.

"How much money was it, sir?"

"You should be smart enough, Brendan," he said, "to know that the amount doesn't matter. It's my money, and it was short." Then he sighed. "It was a hundred bucks." I felt a flash of irritation—a hundred lousy bucks.

I still didn't know what to say. I watched the gray cat scoot past me and curl up on the top of the dumpster lid. Guess it was warm.

"Time's up," John said finally. "You don't get to decide anymore. Tim Smith and I are coming to pick you up at The Bar—all three of you—tomorrow night. Be ready at eight."

Then he opened the car door, barely waiting for me to close it again before he sped off.

———

I didn't dare tell Colin or Jimmy what was going on. I just told them we had a job. Jimmy, who knew what had happened, looked suspicious, but Colin, the naïve fuck, bought the whole thing. He told me he'd gone to see John personally, delivered the missing money from his own bank account, practically groveled at his feet. So, he said, he was off the hook now. I grunted in agreement, trying not to give myself away.

I tried all day not to worry about it, not to even guess what might happen. But of course, all I did was fucking worry about it. The worst thought—that John was gonna kill all three of us—I'd already dismissed. No way John would come to a killing, for one thing, unless he really needed to. He liked to keep "layers," he'd told me, between him and most of that business. Not to mention that this shit was pretty small potatoes to drop actual bodies. No, this was more likely to be a lesson of some kind, like a scare. Make Colin shit his pants, remind me and Jimmy who's boss, and that'd be that. No big deal.

Closer to eight I could barely stop my hands from shaking, and I kept drumming on the table to hide it. Jimmy noticed. "Fucking knock it off," he muttered, but I saw his hands tremble as he lit his cigarette. Even Colin's nerves were failing. He was sweating next to me, breathing in and out so loudly it sounded like he was in labor.

Right at eight, the car honked, and we all raced out. Tim Smith was driving, still in his shitty little Volvo, but sure enough, John was in the back seat. Jimmy and Colin both lurched at the sight of him. He wasn't wearing his usual suit, just jeans and a sweater, but the way he sat, legs wide like a king, made him stand out even more. All three of us jumped in the back, Jimmy and Colin pulling faces at me. I hadn't told them John was coming.

We drove fast. It was a fairly clear night, but the streets were slick from an earlier rain, and the windows blurred from the water splashed up onto them. Before long we were in a neighborhood I didn't know, one of the nice ones in Golden Gate Heights. John didn't speak. Jimmy and Colin were quiet, too. With all three of us jammed in the back I could feel the vibration of Colin's knees jangling up and down. I hit his leg to get him to stop, but we'd already pulled into a spot on a neighborhood street (far away from the closest streetlight, I noticed).

"Get out," Tim grunted. Colin and Jimmy turned to look at me. I shrugged and we all slid out of the car. John was already outside, standing with his hands in his pockets. It was cold, but he wasn't wearing a coat. His eyes glittered in the dark.

"Walk," Tim said, and he pointed ahead of us, where John had already started walking. It wasn't a long walk—we stopped at the edge of the neighborhood, at a sidewalk half hidden between high hedges. Tim nudged us on, down the path. I felt an unpleasant itch somewhere near my shoulder blade. As soon as we'd set foot on the path, the hedges screened us from view.

The path didn't last long—maybe a hundred feet. It ended in a staircase that descended a steep hill. I looked down. It was at least at least two hundred feet to the concrete at the bottom. I saw a car pass way down at the end of the steps. It looked like a toy. The place was utterly deserted.

John moved forward, and with Tim behind us, so did we. The staircase was lit by an orange streetlamp that buzzed dully, flickering in and out.

"Take a closer look," John said—the first thing he'd said all night. We all approached, with me in front. I stopped at the first stair. He gestured downwards, to the steps themselves.

It was hard to see from this angle, but it looked like part of the staircase was painted orange, some hippy dippy sunset color. "Go down the first landing," John said. I looked up, but his face didn't give anything away.

Gingerly, I went down the first flight, probably thirty steps, expecting any second to feel a blow or a hand on my shoulder. Nothing came. When I reached the first landing, John said, "Turn around." I turned. Yes, all the stairs were painted, and from here I could see the full swoosh of color, yellows and oranges in some kind of sunburst pattern, like the new age-y shit you see at farmer's markets.

"Pretty, huh?" John asked. He waved his hand, gesturing me back up. I started to climb. Colin and Jimmy were shivering—I could see their breath. They framed the staircase, right and left, standing as far from the first step as they could without bumping into Tim, who was leering behind them. "Shame that as native San Franciscans we so rarely get to see all that the city has to offer," John commented.

His eyes were hard as I approached him, slightly out of breath from climbing the stairs. "Well?" he asked.

I didn't answer. John put a hand to his forehead. "Silly me," he said, "I wasn't clear enough. I've decided. This is Colin's punishment."

I opened my mouth to ask, but then the horror of it hit me. "You mean—"

"Not the whole staircase," John said. "Just the first flight."

I heard Colin's muffled shout, and John turned to see Tim grabbing a struggling Colin, whose legs and arms were flailing while he tried to yell with Tim's hand over his mouth.

"Not a sound," John said softly. "Don't wake the neighbors." Colin's eyes grew wider, and he struggled harder, but Tim had a firm grip on him. Jimmy kept looking at me and then John and back again. His face was set, but I couldn't tell in the half-light whether he was more scared or angry. His breath came out in sharp bursts of cloud.

"Sir—" I said.

"Take control of your team," John said. His eyes flicked to Jimmy, then back to me.

I looked at Colin, then, full in the face. I guess I hadn't before. His eyes were so fucking huge. I ground my teeth.

"Now," John said. I thought of *Dark was the Night*. Eddie Hoffman wouldn't have hesitated, wouldn't have even fucking thought about it for a second. What was it the book said? "A good soldier follows orders. The best soldier anticipates them." I'd already fucked up twice: first by letting Colin fuck up, and then by not coming up with a way to punish him.

And I wanted to be a good soldier—no, the best. For Christ's sake, I'd just gone down that flight of stairs. It wasn't that far. He wouldn't *die*.

All of a sudden, rage flooded me. Who the fuck was Colin, anyway, little Colin Hansen, who'd been a snot-nosed kid on the monkey bars, to put me in this position? *Fuck* him. He deserved what was coming.

Before I knew it the rage had taken over, and I was striding over to Tim. "Let me have him," I growled, and I grabbed Colin roughly by the collar and started to drag him. He was whimpering, whispering, "Brendan, no!" Still fighting, trying to plant his feet on the path and then, when that didn't work, going limp to make his body heavy. But he was weak, and I was strong. It wasn't long before I had him next to me on the staircase, and in even less time, I'd pushed him forward.

For a second, time seemed to hang in the air. Then he fell, quick and hard, down the stairs. He had the sense to land on his shoulder, but his body hit the concrete with a horrible *thwack* about halfway down, and then he slid almost all the way to the landing. He screamed on the first impact, but by the time he'd come to a stop he was just whimpering. All in all, it had probably taken less than ten seconds. I looked down. His arm was at a weird angle. He was alive, but he was a broken man. In those ten seconds, he'd realized how disposable he was. I turned back to all of them. Jimmy was looking at me, wide-eyed. Tim was already walking towards the car. But I was only focused on John.

He nodded at me, then reached out and ruffled my hair. "Good boy."

Colin was in the hospital for a week. John sent flowers and a card, or so I heard later. I didn't. I didn't visit him, either. What the fuck would that do? He'd learn his lesson and come back, and that was that. In the meantime, Jimmy and I were on our own. How fucking thrilling.

"I'm bored," Jimmy said.

It was about a week later, toward the end of October, and we were at a café for the day, staking out some guy for John. A labor firm guy named Vincent Bhat who'd been shaking people down. He was this big fat Indian guy with a walrus mustache and a stained tie, and all he'd done so far was spill coffee on himself and walk into the building where he worked.

"Not my fucking problem," I growled.

"When do we get to start killing people?" Jimmy continued.

"Keep your fucking voice down!" I hissed.

He looked around to see if anyone was listening, but this was the hipster side of town: gigantic headphones and sticker-covered laptops as far as the eye could see. Our lattes had cost seven dollars each, and when I asked for two-percent milk the doll-haired prick behind the counter looked like I'd just tracked shit in on my shoe. Apparently, it was only soy and almond milk at this fucking place.

"It's like none of our other jobs ever happened," Jimmy continued. "Like John doesn't even fucking *care* that you threw Colin down the fucking stairs..."

I rolled my eyes. Jimmy and I had never really talked about what happened—he'd grunted something after we'd all been dropped off about how even though Colin was a dumb shit, I didn't have to do all that. I'd said yes, I did have to do all that, and fuck off, because I was the leader of this fucking crew, and we'd left it at that. But there was a weird thing between us now, and I couldn't tell anymore whether he was joking or not.

I scanned the street. A car was passing by, a nice new Corvette, banana yellow. That was like the one the Yeti drove, only—

I jumped, spilling coffee down my shirt.

"What the fuck, Brendan?" Jimmy said. "What did you see?"

I pointed at the car, which was stopped at the light. "Are you—are you fucking seeing that?" I asked.

There was a hand sticking out of the trunk. A human hand. A stubby thumb and dirty fingers.

The light changed, and the car pulled away. "Is that one of our guys?" I asked, turning back to Jimmy. "Driving the car—or," I gulped, "or *in the trunk*?"

Jimmy looked down at his coffee, gripping it tightly. For a second, I thought he was furious, but then he burst out laughing.

"*What*?" I said. "If that's not us, then maybe it's another gang and it's one of our guys, or—"

He was still laughing. "Brendan," he said, "do you know what month it is?"

"Of course I know what fucking month it is, it's October. John sent us out here to do surveillance—"

"It's Halloween season."

I was still confused, and now people in the café were staring. I looked at the pumpkins on the walls. "What does that have to—"

"Those are fucking Halloween joke hands," Jimmy said. "You can buy them at a fucking party store, along with vampire teeth and fake blood." He kept laughing. "Jesus Christ, Brendan."

I looked down. My hands were shaking. I made them stop. For some reason, I thought of Casey. Embarrassed as I was, I was fucking ecstatic he wasn't there to see me. "Whatever," I said. "Fucking stupid holiday anyway."

Jimmy raised his eyebrows. "You're losing your nerve," he said.

"Fuck off," I hissed. "My balls are the size of fucking church bells." He half-smiled. But I could tell by the way he kept looking at me that I'd lost ground. And it was all fucking Colin's fault. Colin's, and Casey's. And, the thought crept into my mind, it was fucking John's fault, too.

EIGHTEEN
HARRIS

I fully intended to tell John about the widow and the issues with the life rights, but by the time I went over to his house again, something else had driven it completely out of my mind. For one thing, the house was packed with drunk Irishmen, so many that they were cascading down the porch steps and out into the front yard (until John spoke sternly to Robins and the debauchery was redirected to a more private space).

"It's Ackerman's coming out party!" a man yelled at me as I made my way to the living room. His beard was thick and black, and the smell of beer hung around him like a cloak. "He's finally saying he's gay!" The beard laughed and laughed. I nodded and shrugged him off, looking for John. I found him in a circle of men in the den off the living room, smoking a cigar and clapping a guy who I guessed was Ackerman on the back. Ackerman was small, with colorless hair and a short pug nose, and he wore a tiny black and white hat, like the ones prisoners wear in old movies about chain gangs.

"Harris!" John roared. "Come join the party!" Ackerman

turned, grinning, drunk off his ass, and blew a noisemaker feebly in my direction.

"I will, sir," I said, "if I can have a quick word with you first?"

The men around John booed, but when he saw my face, he nodded and pulled me away. We went downstairs, to the basement, where the noise was slightly muffled by the walls.

"Good news about Ackerman, huh?" John said when we'd sat down. "He was in for five years—can you believe it? Seems like just yesterday he was..."

"Committing aggravated assault?"

John laughed.

"Sir, I just heard—"

The laugh was still fading from John's face. "By the way," he said, "how are things with Brendan?"

"Sir?"

"I asked you to look after him," he said. "How the fuck is that going?"

There was an edge to his voice that I wasn't used to—not directed at me, anyway.

"Well," I said, "there's not much to tell. He's not a leader, though. A soldier at best, and only if he can control his temper. Honestly, sir, I couldn't think of a worse button man."

He nodded.

"He's feeling very neglected," I added. "Which is probably nothing but could be trouble down the road. You might want to—"

John waved this thought away. "He's pissed about the thing with Colin," he said. "He'll get over it."

"I don't think he will, sir—"

"Harris," John interrupted. "I meant to tell you. You probably heard rumors there was a rat in the crew."

"I did."

"Well, there was, and he's taken care of now. Or will be, very soon." John allowed himself a grin.

"Wow," I said. "That was...quick." I tried not to sound resentful, but I was. He usually involved me in this kind of thing.

"Don't pout," he said. "I would've told you, but by the time the word reached me, we already knew who it was." I didn't respond.

"Believe it or not," he continued, "other people are capable of handling this."

I bristled in spite of myself. "Sir—"

"Harris," he said. "You are not in charge of my union crews. You're not part of this."

He was right. I hadn't ever been involved in the unions. It was wiser—for him, for me, for everyone—if I had some level of plausible deniability. He flicked lint off his suit—he wore a black and white pocket square today, I noticed, to celebrate Ackerman getting out of the clink.

"How'd you catch him, sir?" I asked. "Through our friend in the police department?"

"Actually, no—he was *useless* this time around," John said, stretching. "No, it was—and you'll like this—it was Neil."

"Well, we—wait, *Neil? Neil* Bowes? Katie's husband?"

"The one and only." John was grinning again.

"How—*how?*"

John shrugged. "He saw the guy meeting someone, I guess, and thought it seemed suspicious. I don't know, and I don't really fucking care."

"But, sir—"

"I don't, Harris." He stared at me. "His intel was right. The guy was a rat, and now we've got him. That's all you need to know."

I tugged at my tie. Here I was, picking up rumors thirdhand. I was surprised by my own anger, but that didn't make it any less real. I watched our distorted reflections in the huge TV. John's was stocky and bloated, like a banker in a political cartoon.

"There may be something bigger going on," I said. "You want me to help with it."

"I don't," John said firmly. He held up a hand. "Harris, I'm serious. I've got it under control."

"But if something's—"

"Jesus, Harris. Who's in charge of this enterprise?"

I fell silent. A shriek came from above, probably a girl who'd just arrived to get her ass grabbed.

"Go back upstairs," John said. "I'll be there in a minute."

I didn't dare argue. I went upstairs to drink, trying to imagine a world in which Neil Bowes was savvy enough to uncover a plot.

———

I seethed about the rat and Neil and the unfairness of it all for a few days, but I didn't have much time to dwell on it. John was busy gearing up for election season, and he had me running errands that were just election-adjacent enough to be useful, but not so election-adjacent to be legally compromising. I was also busy with another case that Burgoyne had decided to drop on my lap: the will of an old dying man. The bulk of his estate consisted of ancient hideous knickknacks (that his grandchildren were keen to unload on someone else) and a sizable chunk of money (that his grandchildren were scrabbling for—unfortunately earmarked for the San Francisco Zoo to support gibbon research).

I'd been at the Continental Hotel all morning, arguing with the youngest, greediest grandchild, a girl named Laurie with thick blond dreads who worked as a salesgirl at a shop near Dolores Park that affected minimalism but sold hundred-dollar white tee shirts. After I glanced at my watch for the ninth time, Laurie finally understood she wasn't getting any money, and she left in a huff.

I wandered out of the hotel restaurant and into the tearoom, wondering if I'd see anyone I knew. Believe it or not, John and his fellow gangsters appreciate a good high tea. It's difficult to imagine a shady business deal being conducted at a sparkling table complete with fine china, starched napkins, and cucumber sandwiches sliced neatly into quarters. So difficult, in fact, that no one does imagine it. We trade on that: If you can't imagine it, you won't look for it. Mock the strategy all you want; there's nothing more dangerous than a lack of imagination.

I did see someone, but it wasn't who I'd expected. There, tucked in the left corner of the room (the same table her father frequented, although I doubt she knew this), sat Katie Callaghan, drab as usual in an ugly gray suit. And she wasn't alone: she was sitting across from a little balding man wearing the ugliest yellow tie I'd ever seen. They were deep in conversation—in fact, she was leaning towards him.

I stopped to watch. What was she doing here? She wasn't involved in the business beyond those little accounting notes, and John had always told me that was more for show than anything else, a way to make her feel useful. She struck me as someone who naturally faded into the background. At the Callaghan house, she always seemed half out of frame, doing dishes or murmuring in the white noise of family dinners, her features always plain and composed. But here she was, smiling and laughing. She was even wearing lipstick.

Then she looked up, right at me, and froze. Her cheeks immediately went from white to bright red, and she stood without seeming to know that she had. I crossed the room and went over to her, extending my hand. "Katie! What a pleasant surprise!"

"Harris," she said, taking my hand as calmly as she could manage. I felt guilt radiating off her in waves, and suddenly another possible reason for the meeting occurred to me. "How are you?"

"Fine, thanks," I said. My suspicion was growing stronger by the minute, aided by the fact that while her companion had stood up, she hadn't introduced us.

"I'm so sorry," she said suddenly. She smacked her forehead with her fist. "Where are my manners? This is Hugh Wheeler, a...friend of mine. Hugh, this is John Harris, my father's lawyer." I shook his hand. Hugh smiled tightly at me and then turned his eyes back to her.

"I—I'd better go, Kath—Kati—Miss Callaghan," he said. "Nice to meet you, Mr. Harris." He made a move to leave, realized he still had his napkin in his hands (it was stained red, from the jam sandwiches, I assumed), put it down, stood there awkwardly for a moment, shook Katie's hand, then mine, and then he left. I saw him shrugging on his coat, rushing through the front door before he even had both arms in the sleeves.

I turned back to Katie. Her blush had faded slightly, but her cheeks were still pink, and she was looking at the floor.

"Nice carpeting," I said, and she looked up, confused for a moment. Then she laughed.

"Yes, yes, I suppose it is," she said. Her voice was lower than I remembered. She still wasn't looking at me.

"Katie?"

She glanced up suddenly, clutching my arm. "Do you—do you mind if we speak somewhere else?" Without waiting for an answer, she steered me out of the tearoom, leaving her coat behind, and into an empty conference room a few doors down. The room was spotless except for the whiteboard, which read SALES OPTIMIZATION TECHNIQUES in neat blue ink.

"Really, Katie, I don't need an explanation," I said, as soon as she'd shut the door. "I don't even know why you're bothering with one. It was just lunch."

She heard the question in my voice, and she looked down again. "But...but what if it wasn't? Innocent, I mean?" She twisted a ring on her finger—her wedding ring.

"Do you know that man?" she added when I didn't say anything. She gestured in the general direction of the tearoom. "Hugh?"

"I've heard his name," I said. "Isn't he a businessman? Some...vacuum cleaners or something?"

"Commercial and Industrial Vacuum Cleaner Services," she corrected.

Then she sighed. To my embarrassment, I saw tears spring to her eyes. I tried to look away, but she grabbed my arm again.

"You won't tell my father, will you, Harris?" she said. "Or Neil?"

Neil wouldn't care. "No," I said, "of course not." She let go of my arm, clearly relieved. "But what exactly is it I'm not telling John?" I asked.

The tears were starting to spill down her cheeks. "It's—it's so stupid!" she said. She wiped at her face clumsily with one hand. "I—I met Hugh at this fundraiser thing that Daddy had once. You may remember it actually, I don't know. It was a gala? A pirate-themed gala? I wore a wooden leg?"

I couldn't fathom why she'd think I'd remember that. "Kind of," I said, to nudge her along.

"Well, anyway, Hugh had a parrot on his arm—a real parrot, can you believe that?" She laughed. "And...anyway— this was before I met Neil. We got drunk, and we...well, there was a connection, Harris. A personal connection, not anything—" She looked up at me again, her big brown eyes wide like a cow's. "I don't know if you know what I—" She shook her head. "Never mind, I'm just making excuses! But nothing happened that night, or ever. I didn't even see him again until a few days ago, when I bumped into him at the supermarket." Her voice thickened for a second, and she had to stop. I looked around the room and handed her a tissue from the box near the phone. She blew her nose. "Thank you," she said softly.

"You're welcome." I put a hand on her arm, a little reluctantly.

"Anyway," she said, "I asked him out to tea. Can you believe that?" She laughed again. "Only I guess I wasn't too clear about it—I was trying to be subtle, you know, because I'm marr—" but she couldn't manage the word *married* and instead switched to "because of Neil." I nodded. "Hugh didn't know it was a date, I guess, or only figured it out about halfway through." She laughed again. "Don't worry, Harris, this was a one-time thing. He rejected me."

I didn't know what to say. I patted her arm a little.

"I know I shouldn't have done it," she continued, looking up at me again. "It's *wrong*. But Neil—" she stopped suddenly, then went on, like she needed to get something out, "Neil isn't very loving."

I would've thought Neil's problem was that he was far too loving, to the wrong people. But I didn't say this, or anything else, for a while. I looked at her, her thick waist, her plain brown pumps that looked like my mother's orthopedic shoes, her nose now as red as her cheeks. It was hard to imagine Neil loving her. And she was right to be worried about John —if he caught her cheating, John would kill her lover (and possibly her, too, for good measure).

"Well," I said awkwardly. "You know you've done wrong, and that's all there is to it."

She blinked. "You—you're not going to tell Daddy?"

"No," I said. "As long as this was the only date."

"Trust me, it was," she said, and I heard a note of bitterness in her voice, poorly disguised. "No men ever want me."

"I'm sure that's not true."

"Oh, but it is true!" she said, a little too loudly, and tears started in her eyes again. "Harris, you have no idea—when I was a teenager, it was just *hell*. Of course, being fat in high school is no picnic, but—"

My phone vibrated in my pocket.

"Katie," I said. She stopped mid-sentence. I expected her to be angry, but it seemed she was more surprised that anyone had let her talk so long. "I'm so sorry," I said, "but I just realized I need to be somewhere. Do you think you'll be okay?" I handed her another Kleenex. "I can call you a cab, or—"

She shook her head and blew her nose again, then straightened and tugged her suit straight. "No, thank you," she said. "I'll find my own way home." She took my hand and shook it. "Thank you," she said again. "For listening."

"Of course," I said. She didn't let go of my hand.

"Nobody ever does listen, you know," she said. "Even when I'm feeling—"

"Katie, I'm so sorry," I said. "I really do have to go. If you ever want to talk, will you call my office? We can set up an appointment, coffee, tea, whatever."

I handed her my card and left the room before she could stop me again. I paid her bill with the waiter and then strode out into the bright lobby, shrugging off the cloying sadness of a plain woman in a dark room.

———

The widow—Emilia Salvare—called me, later that day. I didn't answer. I couldn't. I hadn't spoken to John yet. She left a message, then another the next day: no specifics, she knew that much from being Frank's wife, but it was clear what she wanted. "I didn't receive the package I was expecting," was a sentence she used multiple times. "I'm going through with my business venture unless I hear back from you."

It surprised me. She seemed too smart to threaten me, and threatening John was another rung up the ladder. I thought of her strange green house, the jewelry, the collection of figurines, the crooked playground: all evidence of an upper upper middle-class lifestyle. Were things really that bad?

Then the next voicemail came. It was short, pleading. I heard her breathe before she started to speak, a long, ragged breath as if she was working up her nerve. "Harris, *please*. I'm sorry I was pushy, or if I seemed greedy. *Please* call me back. Talk to J—your boss. I have debts I didn't even know about, our mortgage is upside down, and it turns out my husband didn't leave me as much..." The rest was just more breathing, quicker and shallower. I deleted it before I could hear her sob.

NINETEEN
NEIL

I knew better than to ask John for details about the whole Mikey situation, but obviously I was curious. I was delighted that Samhain, the fake Irish Halloween party John always insists on throwing, was just around the corner. Samhain is an ancient Gaelic holiday that goes from sunset on Halloween to sunset on November 1, which is All Souls' Day. It's basically a lot like Halloween: a day when "the fabric between the two worlds grows thin, and the dead can walk among us." Owen told me once that a WASP like me could never hope to understand this holiday. He's correct. But I know John wants me there, so I go.

Katie and I arrived early. Preparations were in full swing: A man in a red apron directed the delivery of food and furniture while his workers buzzed around him like wasps in a hive; a few laborer types with grizzled scruff and loose jeans added lumber to a big pile in the middle of the backyard; another burly man hauled boxes of alcohol, and Deirdre cowered in the kitchen pretending to be helpful. Her eyes lit up when she saw me. She gave me a tight squeeze— surprisingly tight, really, considering how fragile she is. She smiled vaguely at Katie, then frowned. "Oh dear," she said. "You haven't lost the weight yet."

Katie looked down at the ceramic tiles ("newly replaced!" Deirdre had just explained).

"That's all right, darling," Deirdre said, patting her on the arm. "It's cold outside now—hard to remember to exercise."

I nearly scoffed but caught myself just in time. Katie mumbled something I didn't catch. I sniffed at the air. Some kind of thick stew was bubbling on the stove like a witch's brew, and I smelled roasted carrots and potatoes.

I left the women in the kitchen and glided my way up the stairs. Owen and Martin weren't here yet, I thought with smug satisfaction. When I passed the master bedroom, I noticed the door was ajar. I'd never been inside, and I was curious. I walked in. The master bathroom door was open, too. Light spilled out, and sound: water running, the tap of steel on porcelain of a razor clattering in a sink. It seemed too intimate, somehow: I turned to withdraw. But it was too late; John had already spotted me.

"Neil!" he said. He walked out into the bedroom, wiping his hands on a towel (green, monogrammed with JC—John appreciated the joke of his initials). His face was only half shaven, and for some reason this made me squirm. Seeing him like this felt embarrassing and vaguely wrong, like seeing an elderly relative naked. Of course, John didn't seem the least bit fazed.

"How are you?" he asked, motioning for me to sit down on the bed. I waited. He sat first. The bed was impossibly soft, with a satin bedspread in gold and silver that looked like it belonged in some sultan's palace.

"Good, sir," I said. "Thank you."

He reached up to touch his face and pulled his hand away, laughing at the shaving cream he'd forgotten about. I was trying to remember when I'd seen him this relaxed, if ever.

"You know, Neil," he said, as if he'd been reading my mind, "this is a good time for our family. Don't you think?"

I nodded.

He stood up and returned to the sink. He glanced in the mirror, smoothed his hair back, tilted his head and looked at one patch of silver near his temple. He clucked at it in distaste.

"I mean," he continued, "it hasn't been exactly an easy ride lately. First the labor union stuff, then the burglaries, and the rat...." He sighed and went back to shaving. "It's enough to drive a man mad."

"But you're not a man, sir," I said.

He paused in his shaving and looked back at me. A few stray beard hairs clung to his razor. His eyes were sparkling again. "Oh? What am I then?"

"You're an empire."

His mouth twisted. For a second, I wasn't sure if he was angry or pleased—he seemed to be teetering on the edge of either. Then he smiled wryly, pleased after all: probably more pleased than he was willing to admit.

"Good boy," he said.

He went back to shaving, a few deft strokes and then done. After that came the aftershave—Primal for Men ("Embrace the animal"), which sets you back two hundred and fifty bucks a bottle and smells a bit like an oak tree mated with a bottle of brandy. He patted it neatly onto both cheeks at the same time. Then the fresh pressed shirt over his undershirt, then the cufflinks (an old set Owen had given him with a Celtic horse detail—Emer, I realized, Cuchulain's horse in Irish mythology). I drank in every detail. It was fascinating, like watching a soldier put on fatigues.

I crossed to the window, where the workers were lighting

the bonfire. The sun was just beginning to set, tinting the backyard the reddish orange of fading embers.

"Si—John?" I asked.

He looked back, pulling on his suit jacket. "Yes, Neil?"

"What happens to Mik—I mean, what happens to the rat now?"

"You mean, now that we know he's a worthless piece of gutter shit?" The tone didn't change; the eyes didn't stop sparkling.

I nodded. John came and joined me at the window.

"What do you think should happen?" he asked, his eyes following the flickering of the bonfire.

"I—I don't know."

"What would you do?" he asked. "If he was one of your crew, and he'd betrayed you?"

The obvious solution, the gangster's solution, occurred to me immediately, of course. I watched the fire until it seared its image behind my eyes. I thought he wanted me to state the obvious, but I wasn't sure, and I was even less sure that I wanted the words to escape my mouth.

But I said it anyway.

"We could—we could kill him, sir."

John stayed silent, completely still. Only his eyes moved. I followed them as they traced the paths of the now arriving guests, who were starting to fan out in the backyard. He reminded me of a lizard on a cold morning, waiting to move until he had the sun on his back.

I tried to guess what he was thinking, see what he was seeing. A navy-colored night illuminated by orange-red flame. The backyard full of people, happy shrieks of children and the low murmur of adult conversations. Beers clinking together.

Suddenly I knew what he was thinking: *I built this.* And he was right. This party, this night, this world we were all living in—it was because of him. And I understood something else, too, something I was sure John knew deep in his bones: This world, for all of its grandeur and apparent strength, was fragile, a rope bridge hanging over a chasm. And Mikey had tried to snap a cord to bring it all crashing down.

"We—we could kill him, sir," I said again. As I spoke, I was sure this was the right answer, and it didn't seem terrible anymore. Of course. We would kill him. Mikey had betrayed us. "When someone tries to destroy you, you eliminate them."

John was silent even longer this time. I heard the grandfather clock in the hall tick twenty-seven times.

Then, finally, he smiled again. "That is one way to do it," he agreed. "And it can be effective."

"Let's do it!" I said.

John laughed. "I have to admit, Neil, I'm impressed."

I flushed, from excitement and pride.

"I would've thought it'd take a little longer for a civilian like you to come on board."

His voice was hard to read again, complimentary with a hint of disdain.

"I'm not a civilian," I said, standing up straight. "I'm a soldier."

He nodded, and I knew he understood. I felt the weight of the room change. Something momentous had happened. I'd been given a key to a door I'd long wanted to enter.

"So," I said. "How do we do it?"

John laughed again and patted me on the back. "We're not going to kill him, Neil."

I blinked. "We're not?" From outside I heard a girl shriek, *"Come on, Daddy, put me DOWN!"*

John smirked. "No. Nothing that big. It's bad for business." He adjusted his collar, pulled his cuffs straight. "Let that be your first lesson, Aiden Trask. Killing is for flashy gangsters, ones who can only conquer, not rule. And Mikey is a cop, and killing cops is really bad for business."

I said nothing.

"We'll make sure he's caught with a whore and a bunch of money. His department will fire him, or we can blackmail him. Whatever's most efficient. Either way, he's ours." He turned back to me. "No need for anything else."

I'd said the wrong thing after all. But how was that even possible? We were *gangsters,* for God's sake! Killing was part of the game! I felt strangely winded, like I'd just run a race, and more than a little irritated. If he'd known we weren't going to kill him, why ask me? To put me through my paces?

Maybe he just wanted to help you get into a gangster's mindset for your audition, a voice in my head said. He had called me Aiden Trask, after all. I decided to chalk it all up to John's strange little whims, the indulgences of a leader who'd been in power for a long time.

"Understand?" John asked.

I nodded.

"You can enjoy the party now," he said.

I understood that, too. I closed the door behind me.

———

I tried to stay positive—John had consulted me, after all. After the thing with Mikey, I was clearly important to him, whether he acknowledged it openly or not. But I couldn't help it—the whole thing pissed me off. In spite of what many Callaghans clearly thought, I wasn't stupid. I knew that John had been toying with me, the way a cat taunts a mouse it's about to eat. And it wasn't appreciated. Not one bit.

TWENTY
BRENDAN

Colin came back not long before Halloween, his arm in a sling but otherwise pretty much back to normal. He came right up to me at The Bar, apologized for what he'd done, waited for me to apologize (I didn't), and then asked if we could just drop the whole thing. That I fucking agreed to—time to move on.

I was starting to get antsy. When was this promotion coming anyway? Soon? Hadn't I passed all the tests John had set for me? And yet here I was, still some fucking bullshit intern for Harris.

Then it was the end of October, and that meant another big event on the Callaghan calendar: the Samhain party. In the olden days, I guess it had to do with the harvest and bringing cows in and all that shit, but it's not like people in Dublin are going around saying fucking "Happy Samhain" to each other. No one at home even celebrates it, as far as I can remember, except for hippies and old washed-up pagans. But Uncle John, who moved to the US as a teen, insisted that it was a family tradition, and so it was. These days, it's an excuse to drink and go over to his house—two things I'll never turn down.

When we got there a few hours after sunset, the party was already in full swing. A bonfire blazed in the backyard—Uncle John pays the cops extra to ignore it—and the house was packed. All our guys were there, from Uncle Peter to the lowest of the low. Half the neighborhood was there, too, wives and husbands and their little kids all in costumes, running around tripping everyone up and howling for candy.

It was an unusually warm night, with thick clouds. I grabbed a beer from the kitchen and headed outside to the fire, where John and his sons were grouped together.

"Uncle John!" I said. They all turned, and Liam slapped me on the back. Owen and Martin just nodded. "Uncle John," I said again, coming up to him, "we sat on that Bhat labor union guy for like two weeks and we didn't see any—"

"Not here," John said, and he pulled me aside. "No business tonight." I saw Owen and Martin exchange a grin. Then he straightened. "Enjoy yourself, Brendan," he said, moving away. "You've earned it."

I was left with the three Callaghan boys. "I heard you did good, Brendan," Liam said. His eyes were looking over my shoulder, and by the distraction in them, I guessed he was looking at one of two things: alcohol or tits. Then he looked at me. "With the job from a few weeks ago, I mean. All the *legwork*." He winked, patted my shoulder, and disappeared, still looking into the distance. Tits, then.

Owen and Martin sniffed at me. "Happy Samhain," I said. The bonfire spit a few sparks on the ground. No one said anything. "Hey, do you guys think—" I started, but they were ignoring me.

"...don't know what you're doing, Martin," Owen was saying. He had his beer gripped tightly in one hand. "Stick to the dry-cleaning business and the accounts and leave the real work to me."

Martin huffed a little, sticking out his belly. "The *accounts*? With Rocky Rhodes and Katie? That's just bullshit busy work. Dad said I could start working on big picture stuff. I've earned it a million times over."

"Dad said the person with the most experience always does the best job, and I don't remember *you* busting your ass for an MBA at Stanford..."

Martin rubbed his head, making his hair stick up. "With a few tweaks to the system we could really be increasing efficiency and our cash flow wouldn't be so stagnant around the middle of the month..."

I cleared my throat, and they both seemed to suddenly remember I was there.

"What the fuck are you looking at?" Owen said. He pursed his lips at me. It made him look like a fucking lizard.

Martin was scowling too. The two of them, standing there, were ridiculous: two dad-looking guys at a disappointing barbecue. Owen's combover wasn't fooling anyone and Martin was wearing his fucking class ring. Neither of them had ever even touched a gun. This was the future of the Callaghan family?

"Did you hear us?" Martin said. "Get lost."

I bit my lip to stop from saying anything stupid and went to look for Liam and coke. One of Owen's kids (dressed as a pumpkin) screamed and grabbed my knee, nearly toppling me over, but the little brat was gone again before I could catch her. I bit my lip harder. John knew I'd done a good job —if Liam had heard, that meant he's said it loud. Maybe I was closer to that promotion than I thought.

"Ladies and gentlemen!" I turned on my way up the porch steps to see Uncle John standing with his back to the bonfire, holding a microphone. Everyone immediately shut up and looked at him. He was smiling. The gold ring on his finger glinted in the firelight. "Welcome to the annual Callaghan Samhain!"

Everyone cheered. I saw one of the neighborhood kids blow a raspberry, but his mother covered his mouth before anyone else could hear it.

"Please enjoy yourselves," he continued. "This is my gift to the neighborhood, as thanks for everything you've all shared with me over the years." He paused for another cheer, which he waved off graciously. "I first came to the United States a little over thirty years ago, a poor Irish immigrant." He grinned. "This house was the first big purchase I made, once my first business was up and running. You may remember, it's the dry cleaners on Clay." He grinned again, and I saw Martin give Owen a look.

"My wife and I—" he reached for Deirdre's hand, and I noticed for the first time that she'd been standing next to him as she smiled shyly, "were new to the neighborhood, new even to the idea of owning a house, and everyone was so kind. Mrs. Lavella," he pointed out into the crowd at a little old lady clutching her purse, "bought us the first plants we ever put in this garden, and that tree—" he pointed to the side of the yard, "is the fruit of her labor." He smiled and everyone whooped. Mrs. Lavella blushed. "We thank you all heartily: neighbors, colleagues, employees, and friends. Family. And we hope you enjoy the party." That cheer was the loudest of all.

For a second, it looked like John was finished, but then he pulled back. "Oh, and I meant to add that tonight we have a special treat for the children (and some of the adults). This man has been a friend of my family back in Ireland for thirty years, and I only just found out he'd relocated to San Francisco." He gestured behind him, and a space cleared: I saw a little old man with a long nose and a tam-o'-shanter.

"This is James Finneran," he said, "one of the best storytellers alive. He'll be telling a story tonight."

It's proof of how much the neighborhood loved John that this also got a big cheer. I can't imagine that Harry Rogers, Uncle Peter, and Casey fucking Moore (who I saw lurking in a corner with his crew) were the types to need a bedtime story, but they raised their beers anyway. I glanced around, looking for Liam. I guessed he was where the coke and the girls were —there was always a Samhain "after party," which was where the real magic happened. I knew better than to try and find him, though, if Uncle John wanted us to stay.

The little old man was at the mike now. I was trying to place him—my mother had never mentioned an old storyteller who'd been friends with the family for thirty years. And I thought I would have remembered this guy, so fucking tiny with that long, long nose and a little tweed suit out of some kids' book about talking toads.

He was clearing his throat. When he spoke, it was with a real Irish brogue. I'd missed that, strangely.

"Thank ye to John Callaghan, a true friend. When his Irish is up, he can be trouble," he grinned and looked at John, who grinned back, "but I've never met a more loyal boy in my life. And Father Allen," here he pointed into the crowd again, to a priest holding a cup of what he hoped we all figured was cider, "tells me that no one gives more to the dioceses." Another cheer. The kids, who'd all been pushed to the front and sat on the grass a few feet from him, started to fidget.

"But enough about our John," the old man said. "Tonight, I'm going to tell you the story of Teig O'Kane and the corpse." I saw two little boys exchange an excited look.

"Teig O'Kane was a fine young man, if a little spoiled. As the only son of a rich father, he'd grown up with everything his heart desired: gold, rich food and drink, horses, fine suits of clothes..."

I saw Jimmy point to the house, and we both smiled in anticipation. The storyteller went on: Teig was a womanizer, got some chick knocked up, refused to marry her, fought with his dad.

"Colin's fucking moping," Jimmy muttered, pointing over to a corner of the fence where Colin was standing half in shadow, nursing a beer.

"What else is new," I huffed.

By that point, Teig had met the fairies.

"...twenty little men, not a one of them bigger than three feet tall, and all of them gray and ancient—more wrinkled than Old Man Ronan in the village, carrying something heavy. Teig tried to see what it was, but he couldn't tell—not until they came and stood all around him. Then they threw the heavy thing on the ground, and all of a sudden, he realized: It was a dead body."

One of the little kids gasped. I saw John smile at Uncle Peter.

"Teig's blood froze in his veins. One of the little old men approached him and said, 'How lucky we ran into you, Teig O'Kane. Aren't we lucky?' Teig didn't answer. He was still frozen, cold as Death's icy breath. The man asked again, 'Aren't we lucky?' and then a third time, still with no answer. And then the little man smiled, a horrible old smile that seemed to thaw the wrinkles on his face. 'You're ours now, Teig,' he said. 'Since you haven't a word.' For that was how their magic worked. Teig swallowed. 'Now,' the little man said, clapping his hands together, 'lift that corpse.'"

From somewhere in the house, I heard a high-pitched giggle. The girls were starting to arrive for the after party. How much longer was this story? The fairies attached the corpse to Teig's back, with its arms wrapped around his neck.

"Is that supposed to be fucking scary?" I muttered. "A corpse piggyback ride?"

The shadows lengthened. I watched Harry and Ian saunter over to Colin, who shrugged at something they said. John was standing facing the storyteller, but I saw his eyes roving all over the backyard.

The fairies told Teig he had to bury the corpse, and to do it before the clock struck dawn or whatever the fuck. So he had to go to a zillion churchyards, all across Ireland, to try and bury it. At one church, the corpse spoke to him.

Jimmy nudged me, grinning. "Lucky ours don't do that, eh?"

I laughed.

Then Teig went to another church. "...There he saw a sight no mortal should see: hundreds of ghosts, men and women of all ages all pearly white and ragged, sitting or standing on the church wall, with ghostly children running around them..."

I tuned out again. The kids in the front row were fidgeting —they weren't even scared. Teig tried to bury the corpse like three more times, and always found more ghosts or spirits or whatever the fuck waiting for him. "Come on," I said to Jimmy, "let's go downstairs."

We turned and walked away, stopping only to grab Colin. "What'd you think of the story?" I asked as we made our way into the house.

Colin shrugged, a little coldly. "It's a good lesson," he said. "Corpses don't stay buried." Jimmy rolled his eyes.

Behind us, there was scattered applause. The storyteller must've finally finished.

We made it downstairs and there was Liam, sitting with lines of coke in front of him and his hand on a girl's tit. Then more and more people flocked to the basement. Owen and Martin arrived separately and shot mean looks at each other before going to opposite ends of the room with different girls. Owen took a blonde and Martin took a redhead, and for a second, I wondered if even that was on purpose.

Harry and Ian came, too, lugging a keg of Guinness that nearly took Colin's head off at the bottom of the stairs. Someone started up the music, a thick, thudding bassline. Then came fucking Casey, and Len, and a bunch of the higher-ups, Uncle Peter, Robins, Skinny Thompson. They took a few of the hottest girls and vanished into one of the other basement rooms.

That pissed me off. Between the speech about neighborliness, Colin's moping, and the endless story about a corpse backpack, this party hadn't been much fun at all. I did a line and then went off to piss. Even Uncle John's basement bathroom is swanky—the faucets are all the real chrome shit, and there are these classy black and white nudes hanging on the wall.

When I got out, I nearly tripped over someone. It was Harris. He was sitting in front of the bathroom door, his suit all twisted to one side. He looked up at me, and his eyes were sort of filmed over. I laughed. "You're fucking wasted," I commented. Fucking buttoned-up prick, always acting like he was better than the rest of us because of his law degree. And yet here he was, nearly passed out on the floor, holding a beer like a life vest.

"Yes, I am," he agreed. He patted the ground next to him. "Pull up a chair."

I hesitated. I didn't think I could take any more fucking lessons, but he was important to John, so after a few seconds, I sat.

"I'm all out of wisdom," he mumbled, as if he'd read my mind. "I don't know shit about shit."

"Mmmm," I said, craning my neck to see what was going on in the other room, where the music had started thumping even louder.

"Do you ever—" he started. Then he shook his head, thickly, like a dog getting water out of his fur. "Never mind."

I rolled my eyes. I figured he was too drunk to notice. "Do I ever what?"

"Do you ever—I mean—what if we were just...office workers?" he said. "You know, cubicles, dumb coffee mugs with slogans, the whole bit..."

I sighed. "I don't want to work in a fucking office."

"I have a law deg—degree," he hiccupped. "I could just be in corporate law. You know? At least there the moral ambiguity would be a *little* more ambiguous...I could like, go to lunch in the Financial District, and, like, buy iced coffees and shit...I don't know. I think it might make me feel slightly less..." He made this weird shrug and some of his drink dribbled onto his suit.

"Hmmm," I said again. Liam had just walked past into another room with a new blonde. Colin and Jimmy followed him.

"John doesn't appreciate you," he said suddenly. I turned to look at him. "He doesn't appreciate anybody. Here you are, his own nephew—"

"Shhh," I said quickly, even though no one was around.

"...and he treats you like shit. He treats me like shit, too, but more expensive shit." Harris laughed a little and took a swig from his red cup. Not his usual drinking style, if I had to guess. "He shouldn't have made you do that thing with Colin," Harris said finally.

I felt my stomach twitch. I stood up. "Colin needed to be punished," I said.

"Why, though? For a hundred bucks? Or because John said so?" Harris' eyes suddenly focused on me, and I felt my jaw clench.

"Yeah," Harris said, "that's what I fucking thought." And

before I could do anything else, he'd stumbled up and sauntered off.

I stood there a few seconds, closed my eyes, counted to ten, and then left again, back into the main room. It was even more crowded now, and fucking stifling. They were smoking weed, and that combined with the smell of the beer and the girls' perfume made me want to puke. The music was pounding in my ears.

I spotted Liam. "Brendan!" he shouted. "Come with me. I need more drinks and some coke and some pussy, not necessarily in that order." I shrugged and let him drag me away.

TWENTY-ONE
HARRIS

The Callaghan Samhain party came and went like it always does. I don't remember most of it. I got raging drunk—unprofessional levels of drunk, in fact. I don't like these parties on the best days, and on the worst they're nearly unbearable: a carnival of kids strung out on candy racing around a bonfire like goblins in a folktale, followed by a carnival of adults drowning themselves in liquor and other controlled substances. Because of my unprofessional drunkenness, it took me hours to sober up. I ended up having my talk with John after the party ended, when even the whores and the most stubborn drunks had staggered home.

He was in his study, nursing one last whiskey (he always drank less than he pretended to and was hardly even buzzed) and watching a movie on his laptop. He turned the screen towards me when I walked in. The movie was a black and white gangster classic, one of those with men in hats who call each other "slick" and say things like "Tommy's a stool pigeon!" John had made me watch this particular one a thousand times, enough that I'd noted the lead gangster's penchant for pocket squares. John had clearly stolen this

187

affectation from the movie, although I wasn't sure he'd realized it. Funny to think that some costume designer (most likely an aging woman working in LA in the forties) had determined John's whole gangster style.

"Harris!" He tried for his usual smile, but I could tell he was tired. Happy, though, I thought, or as close to happy as he got. He was always happiest after all the guests had gone home.

I told him about the widow's demands before I had a chance to change my mind, softening Emilia's threat as much as possible. I ended with a clear emphasis on the "mistake of her not getting paid."

The soft smile vanished. He ran a hand across his chin. "I don't have time for this shit."

"Sir?"

"You know perfectly well what she's threatening," he said, "and you know perfectly well what happened with the payment."

"Accounting error?" I offered.

He didn't laugh. "I covered the first month. It's Cerullo's problem now."

"But he's not paying."

"No," John agreed. "That's his choice. And the widow's choice is even simpler." He paused and looked out the window at the little skritch of moon. I heard a happy, drunken shriek from somewhere nearby, and sirens in the distance.

When he turned back to me, his eyes glittered. "How clumsy of me. I didn't mean to say *choice*."

I bit my lip. "I'll handle it," I said finally.

"See that you do." He got up and opened the door to his study, shutting me firmly out on the other side.

I sighed. My whole body felt leaden, but suddenly I needed desperately to get out. Out out OUT into the air and the world that was somewhere, anywhere, else, away from the stifling house with John's tasteful mahogany furniture and Deirdre's misbegotten attempts at embroidery.

I rushed to the front porch. The breeze wasn't as cool as I'd hoped, and the thick clouds made the air muggy, but still, it steadied me. I breathed in as deeply as I could, watching the neighborhood. All the trick or treaters were long gone by now. The street was empty except for a few teenage boys in skeleton costumes, taking turns howling at the orange moon.

TWENTY-TWO
NEIL

"Bowes? Neil Bowes?"

Bless my mother—in spite of her terrible taste in men, she managed to marry one with an early alphabet letter. This makes all auditions slightly less agonizing.

I rose as the woman (plump, uninteresting, something like a secretary from the fifties) eyed me. I was used to the look, that appreciative something that flits across the face of anyone who finds you attractive. It reminded me to stand tall.

It helped that Harris had driven me over for the callback —instead of bucking my confidence, he tried to interrogate me about the rat, but I knew better. I kept my mouth shut. It actually did end up bucking my confidence, though—who better to play the part of Aiden Trask than a man with real-life gangster experience?

The callback was in a little conference room in the Emer Offices, off to the side. It had been cleared of all furniture except a long table and six chairs, where the inquisitors sat. There was Terry Mannix, and the casting director, and a few other assistants or producers. A potted plant sat on the casting director's right side. I can't tell you why, but every single audition I've gone on has had a room with a potted plant. And this one was identical to the one I'd seen at my allergy commercial callback—spiky and so green it looked plastic. This comforted me. I tried to ignore the video camera perched near it. Its red light was blinking, already recording.

"You got the sides?" the woman grunted. I nodded, clenching the papers in my hand. I'd brought them with me just in case, a security blanket. Katie always said I never needed them.

"Whenever you're ready."

I sighed, and the world centered itself around me.

You may never have experienced this—probably you haven't if you're not an artist. But there's something about the flow of acting, when you pick up the mantle of a character, that's truly extraordinary. You become someone else—colors dull or sharpen as needed, your bearing shifts, even your breath changes. All I knew was that in that moment, I *was* Aiden Trask. And he was me.

They'd chosen a different scene this time. A quieter one. Aiden Trask was sitting with his eight-year-old son, who'd just been beaten up on the playground. And he was reminiscing.

"*Time was,*" I said in my new Aiden Trask voice, which had just the slightest hint of a brogue, "*I was bullied, too. Kids in Ireland back then weren't as fucking nice as they are now.*"

I paused for the child's whimpering, here delivered by a bored PA, who was chewing gum. "*Daddy, they hurt me, they knocked me down—*"

"*I don't want any excuses. You're a man. And men rule. Men fight. Men win. And if they don't win—*" I paused artfully here, to let the tears well up and define the possibility of loss and vulnerability in Aiden's soul, "*they find a way to fight until they do.*"

"*But I'm not strong enough, Daddy—*"

"*Then you get strong enough. When I was your age, my father made me eat dirt if he thought I'd looked at him funny. And I was grateful for it, because at least it meant he was paying attention. My father—my father was a monster. But he was a powerful one. He taught me everything I know, and everything you're going to know from this day forward. My father—*"

"CUT." Terry Mannix's voice rang out. I looked up.

"Thank you," the casting director said, stepping forward and reaching for the pages in my hand. "We've seen all we need to see."

I looked to her, then to Mannix and the other inquisitors. "Are you—are you sure? I could try it again."

"No need," Terry said. "That was really something, Neil." He was grinning, sharing looks with the others. The casting director was nodding—she was even *smiling*. Terry stood up and walked past the table to shake my hand. "We know genius when we see it."

On my way out the door, I winked at the potted plant.

———

I bumped into Katie as I was leaving the offices. She'd shown up to support me, which was sweet, if a little embarrassing, so I had to go out to lunch with her. She sat and babbled over a Caesar salad about how proud she was, how her charity work for the hospital was going well, the usual nonsense. I let her talk, even ordered a bottle of champagne. She'd earned it, after all, always running lines with me.

She wanted to stay at our little table for hours, holding hands and mooning over me. But after a while, I got a little bored. I went to the bathroom and checked my watch. Two thirty. I wondered if Leanne was home. I could use a good celebration fuck. I shook Katie off and headed over there.

Her apartment was on the third floor. I hummed as I

made my way up the stairs, but on the third flight a man coming down too quickly bumped into me. Slammed into me, really, hitting me hard in the shoulder, and when I yelled at him, he looked me full in the face, opening his mouth like he was about to argue. All of a sudden, I realized there was something familiar about that dumb, thick jaw.

"Wait a minute!" I said. "I know you."

"No," he said gruffly, trying to push past me again. "You fucking don't."

I grabbed at him. "Yes, I fucking *do!*" I said. "You're what's his name, the actor." I thought back to that first audition and the dumb grandstanding meathead who'd tried to quote Aiden Trask in the waiting room. "Brock Harkness."

His eyes twitched guiltily upwards, and suddenly I understood. "You're—you're here to see Leanne?" I left him and raced up the stairs. Leanne had just appeared at her doorstep, calling out, "Brock, you forgot your—"

She blushed when she saw me. "Neil," she said. "Hi. I, uh, wasn't expecting you."

"You're fucking *Brock Harkness*?" I yelled.

"Shhhh!" she hissed. "Come inside!" Behind me, I heard Brock start up the stairs. Without turning around, I said, "Take one more fucking step, I'll bash your head in." The steps stopped, then retreated. I let Leanne pull me into her apartment and shut the door.

I watched her, making her way past me and into the kitchen, turning on the coffee maker. Her hair was disheveled, her robe tied crookedly. I didn't say anything.

"It's not like we're exclusive, Neil," she said finally. "I never said—"

"No, no, it's my fault," I said. "I should've realized you were a whore."

She flushed. "There's no fucking need for—"

"Oh, there's a fucking need," I said. I balled my fists. Her apartment was dismal, so small, so fucking *tragic*. "You're a fucking whore, and you've got fucking horrible taste if you think Brock Harkness is gonna be your ticket out of mediocrity—"

She laughed. "Mediocrity? And what, you're some kind of fucking genius? I've seen you run lines, Neil. And Brock says you're shit. He went in after you at that audition, and they were still laughing about how bad you were, fucking *terrible*, laughably terribl—"

I don't really remember what happened next—or I do, but only in flashes. I remember the mug on the counter smashing, and blood pounding in my ears, and screaming and swearing, a few thuds, and then her on the floor, a bruise spreading across her left eye and her split lip bleeding. Then more shouting.

"Get out!" she shrieked. "Get the fuck out!"

I spat at the floor next to her. "Gladly," I said. "But if I ever hear you say anything about this other than 'I fell down,' you'll be at the mercy of the Callaghans."

At least, I thought as I made my way down the stairs, I'd never really paid the whore any money. We could chalk the whole thing up to a misunderstanding.

TWENTY-THREE

BRENDAN

I spent Election Day babysitting Rhodes while he cold-called all our "favored officials," and watching Katie Callaghan, back in Errand Girl mode, spill coffee all over a hotel bedspread. Casey Moore even managed to drop by and gloat about how Bhat, that Indian walrus we'd been watching, had been "taken care of" and "folded into the business."

After that, things went more or less back to normal. To my fucking great relief, I saw less and less of Casey. Sometimes he'd stop by The Bar, talking loudly to Len and his other flunkies about some stupid shit, mentioning "Chinatown" and "opium" like he was fucking Scarface, but he seemed to know to keep his distance. I wondered if word had got around about Colin. That whole thing had been fucking awful, but then again, if it earned me a reputation...

Even Jimmy noticed the change. One day we were all playing cards at The Bar—well, Colin was taking fucking forever to shuffle, and Jimmy was texting some girl he'd met at the Samhain party. Casey and Len were there, too, leaning on the bar, talking to Archie. "He doesn't bug us nearly as much as he used to," Jimmy said, jerking his head toward Casey.

"'Cause he knows who I am now," I said, cracking my knuckles.

Jimmy raised his eyebrows. "Is that so?"

"Brendan, you should be careful," Colin said. He stopped shuffling. "I heard he—Mr. Callaghan—has big plans for Casey." A month after the incident he was finally able to say John's name, although now he almost always used his full title. It annoyed me, but at least he wasn't sulking anymore.

I snorted. "Bullshit."

"That's what I heard," Colin insisted.

The door opened, but I didn't turn around or look up until I felt a hand on my arm. Neil Bowes was there, grinning at me. "Brendan!" he said. "Are you busy? Can I give you a ride anywhere?"

"We have a car," Jimmy muttered.

"Come ride with me," Neil said, ignoring him. "I have something to tell you. Something important."

"We already heard you're out of the closet," Jimmy said lazily. Neil flipped him off half-heartedly.

"I'll come," I said. "Beats the shit out of this place." I followed him out the door, blinking in the sunlight.

———

Twenty minutes later, when we pulled into the parking lot of the fucking San Francisco Zoo, I was a little less enthused. "What the fuck, Neil?" I asked, but he just smiled and gestured me out of the car. I followed, watching while he paid our tickets and flirted (pretty well, I have to say) with the blonde ticket taker. It was like an hour before closing on a Tuesday afternoon, so the place was deserted except for a few roving crowds of little kids on field trips and teenage couples with more acne than sense who'd clearly skipped school to make out near the pandas.

Neil seemed to know exactly where he was going. We walked quickly down the paths, stopping right in front of the lion enclosure. Three gold lionesses and one huge orange lion, all sunning themselves on the big fake rocks. I sighed. "Are you fucking high?" I asked him.

"Good place to meet," Neil said quickly. His eyes were bright, and he was talking so fast I assumed he *was* high, and wondered why he was holding out on me. "I like the setting—bringing the predator to his natural habitat." He gestured from me to the lions, and it took me a second to realize he was talking about me. More authenticity talk, then. I tried not to be annoyed. The predator thing was kind of cool. The lion yawned, exposing a huge jaw and knife-sharp teeth. Neil was still talking.

"...Wanted to see you and pick your brain," he said, "but I also—I just had to tell you something." He stopped. The closest lioness was licking her paw. "Brendan—I probably shouldn't even tell you, John told me not to spread it around, but—"

"Spit it out," I muttered. I'd been bored stiff back at The Bar, but now that I was out, all I wanted was to go back, shoot the shit, drink a few beers.

"Brendan," he said again. "Have you heard—no, you must've heard, you're so well-connected—the rumor that there's a rat in John's crew?"

"Yeah," I said, scratching at my stubble, "I think Harry mentioned something about it a while ago..."

"Well," Neil said, puffing himself up, "Harry was right. There *was* a rat."

"And?" I shielded my eyes—the sun was starting to set.

"And I'm the one who found him!"

I turned. "Wait, what? You found the rat?"

Neil grinned. "He'll be taken care of shortly."

"No," I said. It didn't compute. Neil? Fucking *Neil Bowes*, Mr. Hollywood, had found the double agent in John's organization?

He laughed at the look on my face. "I guess you're not the only predator," he said. "And I caught my prey."

He leaned back on the railing near the enclosure, smirking. I turned back to the lions, hoping one of them would get up, walk across the little cage, and just tear into the other one. That was what I'd come to see if I ever went to the fucking zoo. Instead, they were just fucking lying there, like my nan's cat on her favorite rug.

"I'm not saying it's a *huge* deal," Neil continued. "I'm sure someone else would've figured it out eventually." I kept my eyes on the lions, but I could still hear the smirk in his voice and was fighting the urge to wipe it off his face.

"When I told John," he added, "he said he was impressed by my work—*fucking* impressed, in fact. And he said this would mean more opportunities for me down the line."

Neil moved toward me, and I had to turn around. "Big things are coming, Brendan," he said. "And not just for me. I'll get the part in the movie, sure, but John seems to think that—" He stopped. "I don't know how much I should say, but all I'll say for now is that if I'm climbing the ladder, you're coming up with me."

I gritted my teeth. Who was he to offer me a leg up? I'd fucking done it all—the burglaries, the leg, even pushing Colin down the fucking stairs. But I had to wait for *Neil* to pull me up the fucking ladder? I wished I had claws.

"What do you say?" Neil said. He held his hand out. "Together, we're unstoppable." I wanted to tell him to fuck off. But then I thought of Harris, and all his talk about being smart. I couldn't afford to burn bridges.

I had to make him sweat a little, so I hesitated, but only for a second. Then I put my hand in his, trying to smile. Behind him, I saw the lion yawn again. If the thing had any balls, I thought, he'd be roaring.

TWENTY-FOUR
HARRIS

After election season was over (our candidates won—what are the chances?), I couldn't put it off any longer: I went to see Emilia again. I'd called her back after that last voicemail, told her I'd do what I could, but that I could only help her if she backed off the life rights thing. She'd insisted on discussing it in person. I still hoped, stupid as I was, that this meant she was wavering. I took Brendan with me and drove over to her house.

She opened the door before I was even all the way up her third step and ushered us in like royalty. "Would you like something to drink?" she asked. "Tea? Vodka?"

"Nothing, thank you," I said. "We—we can't stay long."

Her face fell. She was wearing the same green housecoat I'd seen her in before, which was starting to fray at the edges. It also seemed slightly less green, like it had been through the wash too many times. The cynical lawyer in me wondered if this was a ploy, another setup for the "poor old woman" act she was putting on. She puttered into the kitchen to make tea. I didn't know if she'd ignored my response or just wasn't listening.

"I need the money," she said, the minute we sat down. Her hand shook as she passed me my teacup. Brendan sat in the corner, scowling into his tea—he'd already burned his tongue.

"I really need it, Harris," she said. "I've got creditors breathing down my neck and my social security barely covers what I owe on the house, let alone my living expenses."

"Couldn't your daughters—?"

She stiffened at the thought, her back suddenly ramrod straight. "My daughters aren't going to pay for my life," she said. "I was a wife and mother. Frank may be gone, but I know the rules of our world. I'm owed a debt."

I didn't say anything. She sighed and crossed her legs.

"I used to love Frank's job, you know," she said. "I liked the...the *drama* of it. The simplicity. I've been around a lot of violent men—my father was no picnic, that's for sure. Most of them hide it, their temper. It only comes out at night, like some rat in a hole. But with Frank—with all of you," she jerked her head in my direction, and her eyes flicked to Brendan, "at least it's out in the open."

The clock behind her chimed twelve long, crystalline chimes. She waited for it to finish, her dark eyes anchored to mine. "Maybe you don't think I deserve the money, since I didn't earn it myself. I didn't do much for the Cerullos, that's true, or Mr. Callaghan. I didn't move any bodies or provide any muscle or close any deals." She breathed in sharply, like it hurt her. "But I raised Frank's girls, and I kept him fed. I ran his house. That ought to count for something." Her voice was rising now, and I felt the tears rising with it, even before I saw them. She put a hand on my hand. Hers was cold.

"You must know what I mean," she said. "Maybe I didn't draw blood for Mr. Callaghan, but I got more than enough bruises from Frank. And I kept him from going completely wild. He would've been a beast without me. I made him respectable. In my own way, I've earned that money, sure as any good soldier."

I couldn't look at her. She seized the opportunity. "Like you with John, I'm sure!" she said. "Look how much you do for him! And does he pay you enough? I'm sure he doesn't. But at least he pays you. That's all I'm asking for. That's all I want."

Brendan made a noise in the background. I prayed for him to be silent.

"What about the movie?" I asked. "The story of Frank's life?"

"I'll throw the offer out, tell them there's nothing to tell, whatever you want!" She was almost hysterical. Her nails were digging into my hand.

"Unless you don't get your money."

She looked out the window, at a robin perching on a branch in the front yard, lifting its beak toward the sun. "If— if I don't get my money," she said softly, "then I'll have no choice."

John's words echoed in my head. I stood up. "You *don't* have a choice."

Emilia stood up, too. She gripped my arm and pulled me back down to the couch. "That's why I need the money," she said gently.

I wanted to yank my arm away. I felt Brendan behind me, tensing. I closed my eyes, counting to ten. Just like when I was a little boy. In, out, in....out.... It took five repetitions. I counted, focusing my whole mind on only that.

Finally, I could breathe again. I opened my eyes. She was looking at me with her head tilted, just like the robin outside the window. I almost laughed. I took her hand.

"Mrs. Salvare," I said. "Emilia." She smiled at the name. "*Please,* I'm *begging* you, drop the idea of the movie. Completely. Tell the producer to back off, and put it down in writing or something, something official, that you'll never sell Frank's life rights. You could even sell them to John."

"You think he'd pay for them?" she asked, brightening.

"I can certainly ask."

"Well, then." She wiped her face, straightened her coat, and sat up a little taller. "You ask him, and you get back to me." She patted my hand, which was still holding hers. "That's a wonderful idea."

Brendan didn't even wait until we hit the porch to offer his opinion. When the door closed, he was already mid-scoff.

"No way John is giving her any money," he said as we clattered down the stairs.

I rounded on him. "What did you say?"

"John's not giving that old bat any fucking money."

I shook my head and walked quickly to the car. He followed. "Since when are you so down on John?" I asked.

"I'm not," he said. "I just know false hope when I see it."

I snorted.

"I do!" he said, sounding irked. "I'm Irish, remember? We're practically fucking raised on the stuff."

I slammed my car door shut, narrowly missing one of his fingers. At least it made him jump. That was the one bright spot of that day.

TWENTY-FIVE

NEIL

As Thanksgiving neared, I waited and listened. I shouldn't have lost my temper with Leanne—if it got out, it would reflect poorly on the family. Leanne wasn't stupid, though, or not as stupid as she looked. There was no noise, no calls, no texts. After a few days, I breathed easier. Whores were whores, after all. No one listened to them. And fucking Brock Harkness—the slut wasn't worth any more of my time. She'd probably made up that shit she said about my audition. In fact, I was certain she had.

I turned my thoughts back to the one important thing: the movie. The callback had gone well, so there would be news soon. It was a shame that Mikey was gone. I took Brendan to the zoo, but it wasn't the same. I felt myself itching again for something—some*one*—real.

———

John had been right, of course—trapping Mikey turned out to be incredibly easy. About a week after I'd told John the news, they'd made their move. Some Callaghan flunkies got

Mikey drunk, pointed him toward a woman, some cocaine, and a pile of money, and turned on the camera. It was like perfect zoological fieldwork: set up the cage and observe the beast.

For a while, they'd waited to use it. They thought they might get more dirt on him, and in the meantime, he was good to have around. Better to have him underfoot and know exactly what he's up to. Some guys from the union started tailing him. At one point I heard they wanted to turn him into a double agent. Even if he refused, he wouldn't be any trouble to us. He was fucked. Undercover cops get some leeway, but the video was still a blowtorch to his career. "Think if the media got hold of it!" John said to me with a grin. Hardworking Americans' tax dollars paying for blow, hookers, and self-indulgence?" Worse, the undercover cop was set up by gangsters. He wouldn't keep his job after that came out. At the very least, his reputation would be tarnished, his marriage reduced to tatters. For a while, John just watched and waited.

———

Mikey didn't make us wait long. One afternoon, his Callaghan observers caught him talking to his handler (in broad daylight, at a sparsely crowded taco truck venue with a makeshift patio) about this "golden egg" he was sitting on. They realized that it was only a matter of time before the police knew more than we wanted them to. And that night, the Callaghan men moved in, quick as shadows.

It was executed the same way all the best gangster plans are: rapidly, silently, efficiently. Mikey was ours within hours. The word rang out—or rather, passed quickly from burner phone to burner phone. I heard it myself from one of John's lieutenants. He called me specifically, he said, because John had wanted me to know. They were going to make Mikey a double agent after all. A happy ending.

And now time to move on to other things, I thought. But even as my mind focused on the callback and the movie and all the glory ahead, I savored the moment. It was a victory for John, of course, but for me, too. Another feather in my cap, another sure sign I was on my way to becoming Aiden Trask.

TWENTY-SIX
BRENDAN

I couldn't believe the way things were turning out. Neil, celebrated as a fucking hero, had caught the rat, and there I was, sitting in some old bitch's parlor and getting my fingers almost crushed by a PMSing Harris, no fucking closer to anything I'd been promised. Was my "internship" ever going to end? They were dangling the promotion in front of me like a fucking hamburger on a string.

Then, finally, something happened.

It didn't even take a week—five days after my trip to the zoo, Robins dropped by The Bar and told me I was coming with him to see John right now. I jumped up. "Where?"

Robins rolled his eyes. I followed him out into the street. It was gray and damp with thick fog—I could barely see five feet down the block. "Get in," he said, pointing to John's beautiful shiny black town car with tinted windows. He motioned me to the backseat.

I opened the door and slid in. Uncle John was sitting there in a fresh pressed suit with a glass of whiskey in one hand. He looked like a fucking fancy magazine ad, the kind that come with cologne samples.

"Brendan!" he said. "Welcome to my office."

"Your—your office, sir?" I said, looking around at the black leather seats. John had papers on his lap and his burner phone sitting next to him.

"An old school gangster trick," John said. He looked up front. "What are you waiting for? *Drive,* Robins!" The engine started and we pulled away from the curb. John raised the partition, so Robins couldn't hear us.

"It's a roving office," he explained, gesturing around him. "Hard for the cops to track down, and even harder to wire. I have guys check it for me every time I get in." He grinned wolfishly.

That's John fucking Callaghan for you. I leaned back, relaxing. The grin was a good sign.

"Would you like a drink?" John asked. When I nodded, he took another glass, poured whiskey into it neatly, without spilling a drop, and handed it to me. We clinked them together.

"To family!" he said.

"To family."

The car pulled up a hill. I sipped my whiskey, enjoying the smoky taste. It was good shit, top shelf. I shifted to make myself more comfortable. I even liked the squeak of the leather.

Uncle John smiled. "Nice, right? One of the many perks of our business."

I nodded. We drove in silence for a while. I couldn't tell where we were going—at first, I tried to memorize the turns, but I wasn't good at that shit and the fog was too thick to see much of anything. I was just about to ask where we were headed when Uncle John spoke again.

"You know, Brendan," he said, "I've been thinking a lot about you lately." *Finally.* I took another gulp of whiskey. "I don't want you to get too excited," John said, putting up a

THEY SHUT ME UP

hand. "I can't name you a button man now—it's a long initiation process and we don't have an opening yet. But I can give you something else—a little piece of the family pie."

I blinked. "Thank you, sir. That would be an honor."

He turned and looked out the window. I don't know what he saw, since it was still fucking foggy, but he was quiet for a long time. I gripped my glass, smudging it.

"Do you think about your mother at all?" he asked me suddenly.

No. "Uh...sometimes, sir."

"I do, too," he said thoughtfully. "Poor little Siobhan, stuck in Dublin. And how proud she'd be to see her son right now."

I grinned. "Thank you, sir."

"My mother would be proud, too, if she were still with us." He crossed himself.

I copied him. "O—Of course, sir."

"My father probably less so," he said, still looking out the window. "Of course, you never met your grandad—he was dead before you were born. But I can see him right now, sitting next to you, looking at me and shaking his head—" He adopted a perfect, if slightly exaggerated, Dublin accent, "Ah, you've got the car and the businesses, Johnny, but do you have the presidential letterhead? Do countries bleed when you decide they should? That's *real* power.'" He smiled. "Fucking bastard."

I smiled back and drummed my fingers on the seat. I was hoping he'd get back to the promotion.

John sighed, scratching his chin. He shaved every day, but his beard was so dark he was already showing stubble. "But never mind all that," he said, turning away from the window. "We're here to talk about the future. We're here to talk about you, Brendan. As you know, the Callaghans strive to have a finger in every pie," he winked, "and that usually means acquiring more businesses. We've recently acquired a convenience store on Greenwich Street. It's not much, but it's clean, tidy, and it does a good business. I'd like you to front it."

"You mean, like, run the business, sir?"

He laughed. "Brendan, a man of your talents is wasted ringing up condoms and Cheetos. No, I'd like you to *front* it. Your name will be on all the business deeds and information. For all intents and purposes, you'll be the owner."

I tried to digest this. "Wow," I said. "Thank you, sir."

"You'll get a percentage, of course," John said, "of the earnings. Both legitimate and...otherwise."

"Do you want me to do anything at the store?" I asked, confused.

John shook his head. "No, nothing like that. I just need your name."

I took another sip of whiskey. Me, owning a store. The owner of a thriving Callaghan business. Like his own sons.

Then something else occurred to me. "I'd love to, sir," I said, "but what about my name? I know it's not my real name, but if they trace me back to Ireland..."

John put a hand on my shoulder. "Do you trust me?" he said. "Do you think I'd let them send you back to a fucking Irish prison?"

"Of—of course not, sir—" *Stupid to question him, what was I thinking?*

"Let me worry about the law," he said. "You just tell me you're in."

"Oh, I'm in! I'm in!"

He laughed. "I thought so. I'll have Rhodes and Harris ready with the papers tomorrow. You can sign them at the auto dealership." He pushed the button to move the partition down and said, "Stop here, Robins." He turned to me and added, "We're right by your apartment."

I put down my glass and shook his hand. "Thank you, sir! I won't let you down."

"I know you won't," he said. "You did a great job with those burglaries, and with Colin. You're good, and you're family. That's why I picked you."

Robins came around and opened the door for me, grumbling so only I could hear. I got out. The fog was starting to burn off now, and the wind had picked up. "I'll be in touch," John said, and he waved and closed the door. I watched the car for as long as I could until it vanished into traffic.

———

Uncle John was as good as his word—within a few days the papers were drawn up and signed, and I was the official owner of Lucky Grocery. I took Jimmy and Colin there the first chance I got so we could all inspect my new business. It was an old place, with old-fashioned lettering out front: yellow edged in red, like in a fifties movie my mam made me watch once. It had a wide front window and narrow aisles, with dusty shelves crammed together. Some of the stuff on the shelves had expiration dates that went years back, and the refrigerators in the back hummed way too loudly.

It was pretty fucking ugly. But at least it was mine.

"Not much in the way of booze," Jimmy commented, looking at the alcohol. "Had any customers yet?"

I snatched a bottle of vodka away from him. "We're not officially reopened until tomorrow." I'd wanted an "UNDER NEW MANAGEMENT" banner outside, but John said that would draw too much attention.

"Do you get, like, employees and stuff?" Colin asked. "You can't run this by yourself."

"I already fucking told you, I'm *not* running it," I said. "I can slip in and out if I want, but Uncle John is taking care of everything. He just needed my name."

"Why *your* name, though?" Jimmy asked. "You're a wanted criminal."

"Brendan Rorke isn't."

"Still a risk," Jimmy said. He sat on the countertop. Great. Now his ass print would be on my counters forever.

"Well, it's a risk John's willing to take," I snapped. I handed him a rag and pointed to the counter. If he was gonna hang around, he was gonna fucking work.

———

The store was up and running a day later, with three employees including one manager, this total prick named Anthony who kept sniffing at me whenever I was in the way. I'd made him flinch one time already, though, when he got too close, so I wasn't too bothered. I liked standing back in the storeroom, watching the customers and thinking about the future. It beat sitting in The Bar again, with Jimmy in a foul mood because of a rotten tooth and Colin trying to pick up some chick.

Of course, that was the moment when Casey Moore waltzed through the back door. "They told me you were here," he said, as if we'd had a fucking meeting. "Is it wise for you to hang out like this? People might start to ask who the glowering youth is, and if they find out he's got a record…"

"Get to the fucking point, before I stab you with one," I said.

Casey bit his lip. "I came as an envoy, with a friendly warning."

I waited.

He sighed. "Brendan, I hate to spoil all your fun here," he said, gesturing around the storeroom, "all these dusty shelves and spiderwebs, but I just thought you should be asking yourself some questions."

I still waited. My knife was in my boot, but I didn't want to shed blood here if I didn't have to. Uncle John would go completely apeshit. No stains in the new store.

"Why were you named the front of this store? Why are you the lucky star chosen out of all the multitudes in the heavens?"

I crossed my arms. "Quit talking like fucking CliffsNotes and get to the fucking point."

Casey smiled. "In our line of work, do you know who usually gets named the owner of a business? The wives, the daughters, the sisters. The useless, snot-faced weaselly little uncles who do insurance out in Florida."

My fists clenched. *Deep breaths, Brendan.* "What the fuck are you—"

"They give ownership to people who are so totally irrelevant that if the cops get wind of something illegal, it can't be traced back to the big guns."

Fuck deep breaths. "I'm not fucking irrelevant—I just fucking—"

"You're right," Casey said. "In your case, it's not so much that you're irrelevant. You're a good dog, after all—you always bite the right people." He ran his finger along the dust on a shelf. "It's more just that you're disposable, a good sacrifice to the gods if things go to shit."

It was just like that night in Ireland. I didn't think or even think about thinking: I just went for my boot. But before I could do more than touch the steel, fucking Anthony walked in.

"Oh," he said, looking between the two of us. He went white. "Oh, I'm sorry, I just needed—" he grabbed at the first box on the shelf, which turned out to be baby wipes, and took off.

That left me, breathing heavily, and Casey, who'd already edged to the door. "Thanks for this," he said. He'd taken a can of peaches. "I'll see you when I get back." He ran out before the knife was halfway out of my boot.

———

You'd expect, with all I've been telling you about family, that Thanksgiving was a big deal for the Callaghans. And it is, only not in the way you might think. Owen calls Thanksgiving "a working holiday." A bunch of the big guys in our organization and a fair amount of the Hunter's Point and Chinatown and Mission bosses all go up to Tahoe, to this resort there that we "don't own" and they decide the business for the year or whatever. I don't know—it's a big fucking meeting with a continental breakfast. I've never paid much attention to those details, shit about economics and borders and all that. But they do get to go to Tahoe.

And from what I've heard there's a family part of the holiday, with turkey and cranberry sauce and all that American shit, and then there's a bosses and crew only part, which makes Liam's Saturday nights look as tame as rides on a fucking carousel.

I wanted to go, obviously, but even with Lucky Grocery and John's trust in me, I figured it'd still probably be a while before I got an invite. I'd get to go once I got my promotion to button man, and maybe my Beretta with a silencer (the Yeti's weapon of choice), but not before. This year, it was enough that Uncle John asked me to be his point man with the crews while he was gone. I was in charge of the drop that week. After what'd happened with Colin, I took this as a pretty big sign: We'd moved on. John and I were good.

Kristie, that girl I'd been fucking, invited me to her house for Thanksgiving. She'd been excited to hear about me owning Lucky Grocery, said she was "dating an entrepreneur." I guess we were fucking official now. But there was no way in hell I was going to her house in the industrial shithole of South San Francisco, to sit with mommy and papa and her little brother, who she told me was "just adorable."

No. I spent Thanksgiving the old-fashioned way: getting stoned and shitfaced in The Bar, rereading *Dark Was the Night* until the binding finally fell apart. Just as the pilgrims intended.

TWENTY-SEVEN
HARRIS

Brendan was right, of course. John wouldn't pay for Emilia's husband's life rights. I knew this. I knew it the moment I suggested it. And yet I let her believe otherwise. Why?

To this day I can't give a clear answer, other than to say that I wanted to comfort her. I think the real reason is more nebulous than that, something to do with why I got so drunk on Samhain, or the realization that much of my time that year had been spent dealing with tearful women.

The next big event on the gangster calendar came soon after that: the big Thanksgiving meeting. Someone (I think John's brother Peter) suggested this meeting be called Thanksgetting, but that name never really stuck.

In late November, I found myself in a private jet with John and a few of the others (Peter, John's other weird brother Simon, Robins, and Casey Moore) on the way to Tahoe. It had been overcast in San Francisco, but high above the clouds it was all sunlight, and we were fizzy with champagne. John was particularly cheery. He kept toasting everyone and everything in sight ("Robins! The sky! The champagne!"). I kept my gaze out the window, at the white-capped Sierras below. It would be good skiing, the flight attendant informed us. Good powder. Robins had grinned at this and tapped his nose. "Other kinds of good powder there too, eh?" he said. John threw him a pity laugh.

It was a short flight, but John still had time to speak to me. It occurred to me as he approached that he always seemed to have time for whatever he wanted to do. I'd never seen him rushed. Even when he was angry, he always moved deliberately, forcefully, a ship's prow slicing through water.

"Do you mind?" he asked, sitting next to me. I shook my head. I'd never known him to ask permission. "The Callaghans over there—" he nodded in his brothers' direction, "are being, if possible, even more obnoxious than when we were little fuckwit boys." He spoke in a stage whisper, his half-buried Irish accent emerging. I saw his brothers scowling over his shoulder at this description, but they didn't contradict him.

Then he leaned in closer, quiet enough that the others couldn't hear. "By the way," he said, "don't spend any more nights worrying about Bhat, your labor firm guy."

I looked up, surprised. "Why not?"

"We bought him out, or folded him in, or however you want to say it," John said, leaning back. "Turns out he just wanted a seat at the table. He won't be a problem anymore."

I nodded and turned back to the window. The cloud closest to the plane was long and thin and tapered to a point.

"You were right about Brendan, too," John said. "About keeping him close and happy." Another surprise—I didn't think he'd remembered my advice. "I named him the front to Lucky Grocery."

"Sir, I—"

"I know you thought it was a bad idea, Harris, because of his record, but you have no idea how *happy* it made the little fucker. He danced around like it was Christmas morning."

I couldn't help smiling a little. "But why not pick someone safer for a front? Deirdre, or Katie, or one of the other men's wives? Why take on that extra risk?"

John waved this off. "Why pay the police to ignore something when they don't have anything to ignore? That's almost *cruel*." I looked out the window again. I could see the lake already, blue with streaks of foamy white. *A ventriloquist's dummy would be much cheaper than a lawyer,* I thought, *and you could make it say anything.*

John's gaze followed mine. "Should be a good meeting," he said. "Wei's bringing dumplings." I nodded. He stood up. "Gotta piss," he said. "There's something about pissing at ten thousand feet..." He grinned and turned away. Then he turned back, as if he'd just remembered something. He leaned down, close to my ear again.

"By the way," he said, "whatever happened with that widow?"

I tensed. "She—uh, she still says she needs the money."

He considered this. I could smell his breath, the slight fruitiness of the champagne, and his aftershave, notes of hunting lodges and extensive stock portfolios. "Give her some money," he said. "Just a few grand. Keep her quiet for a while. Take it out of the widows and orphan fund."

Relief flooded in. "Thank you, sir."

He locked eyes with me. "If she says one more word about the movie, though, it's all off. You get it in writing that she won't sell his life rights to anyone else. Have her sign them to me. Understand?"

"Yes, sir."

"In fact," he said, "I don't want to hear one more word about her until I have that piece of paper in my hand."

"Of course."

"If I hear something *displeasing*," he continued, "she will suffer the consequences."

He moved away just as the landing gear whirred beneath us, clicking neatly into place.

––––––

Thanksgiving itself was for the Callaghan family. I kept out of the way. The next day was the big business lunch at one, followed by the meeting. This day had become known as Our Black Friday (a name that stuck because John had chosen it himself). We held the lunch at the Grand Mountain Resort and Spa, a Deirdre-fronted, John-owned hotel that had all the best luxuries and amenities, including but not limited to acupuncture and a series of tunnels hidden underground that connected it to several escape routes.

The lunch itself is largely too boring to discuss: a bunch of old men sitting around starched tablecloths with steaks and cigars, trying to talk about business without really talking about it while their wives show off their latest apology jewelry. The best part of the whole meal (besides the food, which really was quite good, Mediterranean-style chicken in a mint sauce and wine from the non-criminal Callaghan brother's vineyard) was the news from the production company: Neil hadn't gotten the part of Aiden Trask after all. It was "hush hush" for the moment, though—apparently John was waiting for the "right moment" to tell him. I can't tell you exactly why this made me so happy, but between my second and third glasses of wine, it really did.

The meeting was right after lunch. The bosses were driven up into the forest, to a meadow compound filled with cabins that they'd all pooled their money for years ago. It was lovely up there, sharp cold mountain air and bright autumn sunshine. I crunched up the gravel driveway to the main cabin, the one that looked rustic and homey on the outside but came equipped with the "world's most technologically advanced conference room," as John's accountant Rhodes often reminded me. Inside it was spacious and grand, a hunting lodge fit for a king, complete with antlers mounted on the walls and a long shiny redwood table underneath a gigantic white chandelier that had once belonged to Swedish royalty.

I walked in with John a few minutes early, past the sets of black-suited men we used as security. Guns and phones were checked at the door, and the room was equipped to block all WIFI signals. As we entered the room, screens descended from the walls to block out the sun that usually spilled from floor-length windows. It created an odd effect: a dim room with blinding white light on the edges.

The table was set for at least thirty people, but in place of plates and napkins each setting had a glass of John's favorite whiskey and a pencil resting on a yellow legal pad (another joke of John's—Owen had once picked up on this and started calling them "illegal pads" until John made him stop). I sat down to the right of John's gigantic leather chair and chatted with Peter about baseball as the families started to filter in. Wei Huang, true to form, brought the smallest entourage: just his bodyguard and his brother Yao. The Herreras all trouped in together, singing loudly from some opera (*La Boheme*, I thought, because of the rumor that the Herrera boss had been a famous tenor in his youth). Lawrence Cerullo came in flanked by his men, a king leading a procession, and Tom Marks slipped in last, a shadow in the doorway.

"Gentlemen," John said. "Welcome to Our Black Friday."

Laughter spread through the room. Tomcat Marks had once observed, "The consumers think they're buying electronics, but what they're really buying is us." The room had liked that quip so much I almost thought they'd make T-shirts. Casey Moore, who was on my right (a sign of his growing importance to John), laughed louder than anyone.

"It's a clever name," he said, when I looked at him.

"You're a clever man," I responded. "Working your way up here. Brendan will be furious."

"Oh, he is," Casey grinned. "Or he will be once he understands the hints I've been dropping." He reached for his glass with an aristocrat's sense of his own importance.

"Can I ask you something?" I said.

He turned to look at me, his eyes wide and polite. His ears really were enormous. I didn't know if it was this that irritated me or the whole package. He'd taken out his earbuds, but he had them around his neck still, and I'd seen him wearing them at several meetings.

"Why do you always have your earbuds in? Studied nonchalance? Or just a signature affectation?"

He smiled and put his glass down. "It's a trick I'm experimenting with," he said. "If you have them in, people assume you're listening to something."

"So they'll assume you couldn't possibly be listening to them."

"Precisely." Casey allowed himself a smirk. "You can use it if you'd like."

I smiled. "I have my own tricks, thank you."

"Like cozying up to John?" He paused and bit his lip, as if mulling this over. "It's almost a father-son relationship at this point, isn't it? Have you asked to call him Daddy yet?"

I let the question ferment for a moment. Then I tapped my pencil on the legal pad.

"It's funny," I said, "that you think that will work on me. Brendan Rorke is one thing, a lit fuse dangled over dynamite. A kindergarten teacher could press his buttons."

"But you're different."

"I like to think so."

"Everybody has buttons," Casey said airily, crossing his legs.

"Not you, though."

"No, I have them too," he said. "But I'm honest about them. More honest than the rest."

I really did laugh at that. "You'll go far in this organization," I said. "I'm just not sure that's a good thing."

Casey grinned and opened his mouth to retaliate, but John stood and called the meeting to order. The time for petty arguments was through. For the lower-level employees, at least.

"Gentlemen," John said, "we've had another banner year. Profits are up, we've expanded our territory, and there's been relatively little strife." He paused as if waiting for adulation. None came.

"There was, I'll admit, a *problem* in my crew," John continued, "but that's been dealt with and we're now back on track." I noticed his pocket square today was red and white, with a navy suit. *Subtle,* I thought.

"You've been dropping a few bodies, though, haven't you, John?" Tom "Tomcat" Marks interrupted. He was across from John, curled in his seat like his namesake, his eyes falsely bright.

John sighed. "A burglary in my neighborhood went awry. For the burglars." There was a ripple of laughter.

"And I heard one of your low-level guys can't count!"

John's smile tightened. "Yes, Tom, that was dealt with as well. Would you like a summary? I could have Harris print you one. I'll make sure he laminates it."

"I always laminate," I put in. The laughter was louder, but Tomcat's eyes were still fixed on John.

"I could've sworn," he said, "that a certain crime boss told me that dropping bodies was a sign of weakness."

John, who'd looked down at his papers, let his eyes flick upwards. "Always good of you to remember my speeches, Tom. And here I thought no one was listening."

"Oh, I was," Tom said. "Only I'm not certain *you* were."

There was a pause. Tom uncurled himself like he was about to stand. John walked over—quickly, but not rushed, like always—and put a hand on his shoulder.

"So kind of you to be concerned," John said. "I have it all in hand. I'd suggest that you watch your own side of the street—so many of your soldiers are dying. I believe the phrase is 'high on their own supply?'"

Tom stood, fists clenched. "I don't know why the fuck we're even listening to—"

But he didn't finish the sentence—John had cocked his fist. For a horrible second it seemed like he was going to punch Tom in the face, but at the last possible moment, his fist changed course and he slammed it onto the table next to Tom, breathing hard. Tom jumped—just a little, but enough to show he was rattled. Three of his men reflexively stood, but Tom held up his hand.

After another pause, John slowly removed his fist from the table. Everyone was staring. He rubbed his knuckles.

"Enough," he said. "Enough of that." And he returned to his side of the table.

"Oh, we're not done—" Tom started, but just then Domingo Herrera yawned loudly.

"Can we move on?" he asked. "I'm fucking bored."

Tom looked at him, and then around the table at all of them. The room was silent, but I felt all the work under the surface: lightning-fast calculations of old scores, new grudges, loyalties, risk/reward ratios, wagers, and debts, all precisely weighed and measured. The room was tilting. Unclear which way it would land.

"Gentlemen," John said, "my apologies. Please, let's continue." He stood again and crossed over to Tom, whose bodyguards had yet to sit down, and extended a hand. "It's been a good year," he said. Tom made him sweat, just for a second, but then he took the hand offered to him.

The room let out a collective breath, weights and measures discarded. The bodyguards melted into the background. John returned to the head of the table.

"As I was saying," John said. "Things are good. Stable. There's plenty of money," he grinned, "and it's ours for the taking."

Gangsters are in general a skeptical group, but this was difficult to argue with. Just glance at John's books (if Rhodes will let you near them) and you'll see: Other people's misery is really good business. And it was a miserable year.

"It's my understanding that the Huangs and the Herreras have reached an agreement on their property disputes," John continued, and Wei Huang nodded, "and as I have informed many of you individually, the labor firm of Vincent Bhat is no longer an issue. He has agreed to become part of our enterprise." John flashed his wolfish grin, and I felt Casey smile next to me. "I have also brought with me, as a marker of my own smaller expansions, Mr. Casey Moore, who has also been folded into our little business."

"It was a hostile takeover," Casey said, standing up. "A kidnapping, really. He got me for a song." He stayed there, smiling like he expected the other men to laugh.

I glanced at the man across from me, a bottle-nosed bruiser who worked for the Herreras. He didn't seem remotely amused. After a beat, Casey sat back down. I couldn't help feeling a little pleased.

The meeting after that was dull, as most meetings are. But I felt something behind all the dullness, something that made my eyes rove around the table while John and Rhodes were talking. John had never let his temper go that far before, and the room didn't like it.

At the end, the floor was open to anyone. Lawrence

Cerullo, who hadn't moved all meeting, finally stirred. "You heard about this Kertner, John?" he asked.

"The man without a dick?" John said. "Works in construction, I believe?"

Cerullo smiled. He always reminded me of metal: steel-gray hair, bronze skin, cold blue eyes. "He's buying up land all over Forest Knolls," he said. "And into midtown Terrace and Golden Gate Heights."

"So what?" Wei said. He had deceptively kind, twinkly eyes and white hair: the picture of a kindly teacher ready to dispense wisdom. "Leave him to deal with the toy gangsters down there. I'm tired of wiping them off my shoes."

"It's not even my area," Cerullo said, holding his hands up in mock surrender. "I'm just telling you what I heard."

"I haven't heard anything about that," Domingo Herrera said, in his deep, rich voice. He'd been an opera singer once, if the story was to be believed, and he still had the thick hair and barrel chest of his youth. "He working through subsidiaries?"

"Of course," Cerullo said, exasperated. "He doesn't use his own name. I don't even think he's behind it all. I think someone else is horning in."

John fingered his pocket square. "I'll look into it," he said, with a note of finality. "Thank you, Lawrence." He moved on to the next question.

———

I caught Lawrence Cerullo after the meeting, just as he was leaving. He had a strange walk, almost more of a shuffle, and he grunted when he moved.

Legend had it he'd been attacked on the street as a boy by at least five other kids (some accounts had it as high as ten) who pinned him down and wanted his pocket money. No one knew exactly what happened next. He vanished and reappeared hours later on his front doorstep, limping and covered in blood that he'd proudly told his mother was "mostly someone else's."

But last year at our Christmas party, he got drunk and told me he'd fallen out of a tree when he was six years old.

"Mr. Cerullo?"

We were standing just to the side of the hall door, watching people file out. Cerullo's eyes were only half fixed on me—they flitted to the door as each person left, reclaiming their phones and guns. "Harris," he grunted. "How are you?"

"I'm fine, sir," I said. "I just wanted to ask you something."

"You really should look into Kertner, you know," he said. Now he was focused on the door in front of us, presumably daydreaming about the naked mistress splayed on his hotel bed. "Something's going on there."

"Yes, sir," I said, "but—"

"John may think he runs all of San Francisco," Cerullo said, "but he's losing his grip if he isn't paying attention." He glanced at me, and I saw metal again: gears whirring behind his eyes.

"Please, sir," I said. "Do you know Emilia Salvare?"

That got his attention. His eyes snapped to mine. "Sure I do," he said smoothly. "Frank Salvare's widow. Good woman. Excellent lasagnas."

There was a hint of metal in his voice now, too. I hesitated, but only for a moment. "Sir," I said, "she's been expecting money from you—a monthly stipend, and she hasn't received it."

"Excuse me?" The metal was sharper now: a knife.

"She hasn't received her pension."

He stood quietly for a moment. "And what the fuck business is that of yours?"

"She's got a mortgage, sir, and Frank left her with debts—"

"Frank left her with a lot of things, I'd imagine," Cerullo said. "Probably chlamydia." He paused for my laugh. I didn't give it to him. We stood there for a few seconds, in the sunlight pooling from the outer door.

"Again," he said, his voice suddenly, dangerously low, "I ask, what the fuck business is it of yours?"

"It isn't, sir, but—"

"What I do with my money is my fucking decision. If John thinks—"

"This isn't coming from John," I said quickly.

"Who's it coming from, then?" he asked. "You?"

I didn't say anything. He looked at the door again, seemingly lost in thought. I waited, knowing that interrupting would only make things worse. I watched him put his gnarled, age-spotted hand up to his face, an emerald from one of his rings winking at me.

"It's almost cute," he said finally. "You're a fucking mob lawyer, and you think we honor our pensions? Have you ever known John to pay a widow before?"

"Of course I have," I said. "He does it all the time."

"A monthly payment, like on college loans?"

I considered this. "I'm not in charge of finances."

"You ever heard the expression, 'no honor among thieves?'" Cerullo said. He was grinning now, enjoying himself. "You thought that only applied to blue-collar criminals?"

I didn't answer. He laughed again. "Fuck off," he said, not unkindly. "Go get a whore or something. Wipe that frown off your face."

———

I didn't get a whore. Instead, I followed John back to the main hotel building, even though I had no intention of staying with him; I didn't feel like seeing anyone or doing anything. The thought of entering his suite, with its gold bathtub and ridiculous silk pillows, or seeing him talking to Wei or Domingo or Casey fucking Moore, was enough to make me scream with impatience. I wandered the halls of the resort instead and ended up in the art gallery next to the gift shop.

It was a small, yellow-walled room, full of the usual paintings of flowers and old-fashioned sailing ships and a few tasteful nudes. I wished I hadn't stopped drinking, but I was too lazy to go the bar (where several gangsters might now be installed, telling dirty stories and putting their unwashed hands into the pretzel bowl). I was thinking, not really paying attention to anything in particular, until I found myself standing in front of a wall with a huge painting spread in front of me.

It was abstract—different from all the others. From far away, it looked like nothing: a big block of red. But when I moved closer, I noticed it wasn't all one shade: the first third was a rusty red, the color of rich carpets, the second third was a slightly sharper orange red, like a fire engine, and the third red was darker, deeper, red wine spilled on a white tablecloth.

"You like it?" I heard behind me. The old woman who ran the gift shop smiled when I turned around. She had a butterfly clip in her white hair, carefully arranged and matching the pendant around her neck. For some reason this irritated me.

"It's called Red," she said.

"How original."

She raised her eyebrows at my sarcasm and moved away.

I wanted to leave, but I couldn't. I couldn't stop looking at that fucking painting, particularly the last third, when the orange-red bled into the wine-red. I looked and looked, searching for the seams where the artist had stopped one red and started another. When I found it, the line where the reds changed loomed in front of me. I closed my eyes, and I could still see it. I opened them, and it seemed bigger. It also seemed to be moving, vibrating, pulsing. It seemed *alive*.

And the longer I looked, the more alive it seemed, the way a word repeated becomes both nonsense and an entirely new, dominant thing. It seemed to grow in stature, until in one wild moment I leaned back, convinced the red was going to jump out of the painting and splash itself on me. I felt a whisper on the nape of my neck, like the breath of a cold wind, and something pricked behind my eyes. I got a sudden flash of memory—Emilia Salvare's fingernails, red as blood.

I turned away. "What a stupid fucking painting," I said.

TWENTY-EIGHT
NEIL

Thanksgiving was a feast, like it always is, sumptuous and bountiful, and since John and I spent most of Thanksgiving evening together holed up in the den of a Tahoe cabin near a roaring fire, it all felt like a precursor to something big. Sitting there watching the fire glint on the tumbler that held my single-malt, I felt more like Aiden Trask than ever.

The feeling only intensified as the days went on. I was surprised, when it came down to it, how quickly I forgot things. Mikey, Leanne, Brock Harkness: they all seemed to belong to the past. Maybe this was part of the Callaghan life —we move fast and always keep moving, like sharks. As I told Katie, it was all just grist for the mill (although I never mentioned Leanne). She agreed with me.

––––––

Then the call came.

It was early December, the middle of the night. The digital alarm clock read 2:14 a.m. in electric blue. "Whaddisit?" Katie asked blearily next to me.

235

"I'm outside," Robins' voice growled into the phone. "Get dressed and get here now."

He hung up before I could ask questions.

And then before I knew it, Robins and I were in a black SUV, speeding down 101.

"What the hell is—"

"John sent me. Mikey's in trouble," Robins grunted. "Now shut the fuck up, I'll explain when we get there."

He took one of the South San Francisco exits and drove onto a suburban street. It only took a few minutes, but my mind was having trouble even with the limited information he'd given me—*of course* Mikey was in trouble, we'd gotten him in trouble. What did that have to do with me?

Robins stopped the car at a curb and gestured across the street to a midsized brick house with a pleasant stepping-stone walkway studded with small black lanterns. There were boxes of gardenias underneath both front windows, and the lawn was far greener than the drought allowed. Robins turned to look at me.

"Mikey called us today, drunk, crying. He told his wife about the whores. She left him. Took the kids, too. That's his house." He gestured out the window at the brick. "He wants out of the deal he made with us. He wants to kill himself. Obviously," he sat back in the car, "we can't allow that." I recognized John's words in another person's mouth.

"So why am I—"

"I tried to talk him down, but he said he'd only talk to you. It's like some kind of fucking hostage negotiation." Robins snorted and unlocked the doors. "I'll pull around back and meet you in the alley behind the house."

"What the hell am I—"

"Just fucking keep him alive!" he snapped. "Calm him down! Make it fucking clear that his life belongs to us, and he can't get out that easy! When you're done, come out and meet me."

I didn't say anything. He shook his head and handed me a gun. The barrel was cold. It felt heavier than it should've been, somehow. I used a prop gun in a TV movie once, and I'd even practiced at a shooting range, but...

"What the fuck are you waiting for?" he asked. He half-pushed me out.

Dazed, I obeyed, tumbling out into the night air. The car took off, quietly but as fast as he could manage. It was warmer than I'd thought, and the street held the hushed silence of late night, when most people have settled into deep sleep. I looked up and down the block, trying to spot anything unusual. Then I looked down at the gun in my hand and tucked it into the back of my jeans.

I slipped up to Mikey's door, not sure if I should ring the doorbell. I bent down and looked through the mail slot, then knocked as softly as I could. "Mikey," I said. "It's me, Neil. Let me in."

There was a noise from inside, a soft crash and a whimper, and then Mikey's silhouette appeared in the hallway. He opened the door and let me inside.

The hall light was off, and he was lit from behind with a strange orange glow, but even in the half-light I could see the dazed, blank look in his eyes as they settled on me.

"You gonna kill me?" he said dully. He scrabbled for the light switch. When it switched on, I finally got a good look at him. There he was, unmistakably Mikey. Same ragged beard, same sharp blue eyes—although now they seemed different, dyed darker than I'd ever seen, and his face was haggard, with deep circles under his eyes.

His hands were full, I realized. That explained his fumbling for the switch. He had a bottle in his left hand and a gun in his right. It was bigger than mine and he was holding it far too casually, gripping it with only three fingers.

"Come on in," he said, with a little nod in my direction. His calm disturbed me more than anything. It was like we were at The Bar again, shooting the shit. He wore nicer clothes than I'd ever seen him in, a blue button down and dark jeans, but there was a dark splotch near the collar of the shirt, and the smell coming off him was thick and rancid.

"You're the one who figured it all out, huh?" he added, gulping from the bottle. Some of it dribbled down his face to join the other stain. "That I'm a fraud."

"Uh, yes," I said. I wondered how long it would take Robins to get to the alley, whether I should just keep talking. "But uh...I would assume you wouldn't consider yourself a fraud, since you were undercover and just doing your job..."

I stopped mid-sentence and looked down at the carpet, which was thick and tan-colored. From the corner of my eye, I saw a kid's drawing on the mantelpiece in the living room: a giraffe with two necks.

"I am a fraud," Mikey said, sighing. "Only I don't—" He paused, burped, then laughed. "Only I don't even really remember who I'm working for anymore. Isn't that funny?" He laughed again, then swayed a little. "Do you remember?"

"Do I? Um, well, you're working for...well, they're not the worst people, the Callaghans. I mean, all a man can really count on in this world is himself, right, Mikey? I mean, you have to make money, for—for your family..."

He was just standing there, watching me flail. Was he gripping his gun more tightly now, or was that my imagination? I thought of all the Westerns I'd seen. If he pulled, I wouldn't be able to draw fast enough... The gun in the waistband of my jeans suddenly felt like a useless brick.

"How about some coffee?" I said.

Mikey laughed again. He took another swig and then put

the bottle down, wiping his hand on his pants. "Sure," he said, "let's have some coffee." He pointed the way to the kitchen with his gun.

I moved him there, slowly but surely. He sat down at the table.

"She left me, you know," he said, gesturing upstairs. "Loretta."

I assumed this was the wife.

"I—I'm sorry," I said. "Sorry to hear that."

"I told her about the whores. Felt like I had to. It wasn't her fault that I did it—she was always such a good wife. Came to every cop party, every bar night, every fundraiser. She was always the hottest one there, too, with her long legs and her shiny black hair..." He swayed, then hiccupped. "She took the kids with her. Rebecca, and little Sammy. Said they'd grow up under a different roof, without any of my filth." Tears blossomed in his eyes.

"What—what other memories do you have?" I asked. A lame question, but it got him talking, some nonsense that I was sure was made up about a funfair and cotton candy and a trip to the movies with his brothers and their kids... I nodded, keeping my eyes on his gun. I wished I could get it away from him, but the one time I put my hands on the table, he shrieked and gripped the gun even tighter, moving it like he was about to aim.

"Okay, okay," I said gently. "You can keep it."

I heard a sound—unmistakable, the door opening and closing. Robins was back. I must've taken too long.

Mikey stood and held up the gun. Robins raced over to grab it, but I instinctively stepped between them. "It's okay, Mikey," I said. "He's with me." Mikey eyed Robins, but I gestured for Robins to back away, and when he did, Mikey lowered the gun again.

"So," I said. "Why'd you want to see me?" I was buying

time. Maybe Robins would rush Mikey and they'd tussle for the gun. Or maybe I really could talk him down.

Mikey shrugged. "I liked you, I guess. I mean, not much, not compared to some of the other guys, but you seemed the most harmless of anyone. We were thinking of developing you as a CI, only it turned out you didn't know anything."

Robins laughed—he actually let out a little chuckle and moved forward a few steps. I glared at him. But he was close now. Just a few more steps and he'd have Mikey's gun.

"But that's not giving you enough credit," Mikey said, almost gently. "What I mean is, you seemed like you were the most salvageable. The closest thing to a human in the bunch. Like me, I guess." He laughed roughly and picked up the bottle again, taking another pull.

"I don't want to live if I'm not with them," he said. He gestured upstairs again, to the bedrooms above. His voice cracked. More tears spilled out of his eyes. "They're my life. And I ruined that life when I did what I did. So I have no life anymore. I shouldn't." He put the bottle down.

We were in dangerous territory.

"You didn't ask me here to talk about them," I said, as gently as I could. "Did you?" I was using my Deirdre voice now, trying to be maternal. I kept my eye on the gun. Robins was really close now, could practically reach out and grab it, and Mikey was distracted.

"No," Mikey said simply. "I'm too tired for that. I just wanted you to see this."

He moved before anyone else could, and a shot rang out, sharp but somehow muffled in the small space. Then he staggered. The gun fell. The world went quiet. Mikey sank to his knees, coughing and sputtering. Blood blossomed on his blue shirt, pooling at first and then leaking.

"*What the fuck?*" Robins hissed. He grabbed the gun. I

looked around wildly, half-expecting to hear sirens. "*What the fuck, Mikey—*"

I didn't move. I couldn't. As I watched, Mikey put his hand on the growing stain, and brought it back smeared with red. He looked at it, head half-cocked, like a dog hearing a far-off whistle.

"I'm not dead," he whispered. Then he looked up at us, his expression hazy. "Why am I not dead?"

"Get him up," Robins grunted. He pulled Mikey roughly by the elbow and managed to yank his body up a few feet, but Mikey wasn't cooperating, and he had to let go. There was a thump as Mikey hit the floor again. He now had both hands on the stain, which was covering his entire shirt.

His eyes sharpened, and he looked right at me. "Kill me!" he yelled. I heard a dog bark.

"*Shut the fuck up!*" Robins hissed.

"Why aren't there sirens?" I asked. Robins was still trying to get Mikey up, but I couldn't move.

"The police were told to look elsewhere for trouble tonight," Robins grunted. "But even John can only stall them for so long. Now help me get him the fuck up." He hoisted him again, a little farther up this time before another slump. "*For fuck's sake, Neil, fucking help me!*"

I jumped and hurried forward.

"Kill me!" Mikey was yelling. "Kill me, kill me, KILL ME." The words became a mantra, until they bled together into one mass. "Killmekillmekillme." Robins slapped a hand over his mouth, only half-successfully muffling him.

When I moved closer, Mikey reached out and grabbed my pants with one bloodied hand, smearing my khakis. "Kill me, please, please, Neil, just kill me, I want to die, it'd be a mercy—"

"Shut the fuck up," Robins said. "You don't deserve to die."

Mikey wailed then, an actual, honest to God wail, like the ones in ancient Greece when widows rended their garments. He turned his eyes back to me, begging.

I didn't know what to do. I wanted to help Mikey, obey Robins, but suddenly the world was a strange size. Everything was impossibly big, and I was small, like the forced perspective of a fever dream. Even as I remembered the gun in my waistband, I knew I'd never use it.

"*Neil, so help me*," Robins said, and I finally snapped out of myself and went to grab Mikey.

Unfortunately, he chose that very moment to lunge away, gathering the last bit of his strength and pulling himself up by the hallway table. He moved quickly, far more quickly than I'd ever imagined he could in that state. He was down the hallway in great staggering steps before Robins or I moved. Thick droplets of blood marked his progress.

Robins swore and ran after him. It was a small house— Mikey was already out the back door. "Get a fucking towel and meet me out here," Robins muttered, and I ran to obey. By the time I was outside, Mikey had fallen over halfway to the fence. He was moaning softly. Any minute now, lights would come on.

I rushed over, and Robins and I quickly wrapped him in the towel. "The car's down the alley," Robins said. "Grab him and let's go." I saw a gate in the wall and ran to open it, then came back and helped Robins grab Mikey by the armpits. He was groaning now, far too loudly. Robins clamped a hand over his mouth again. "If they catch you, it'll be worse for your family," he muttered, and suddenly Mikey was silent. He was heavy, so heavy, like he was made of stone, and he smelled rusty and sour. Awkwardly, but more quickly than I would've guessed, we got him through the gate and into the alleyway. The car was there, unlocked. We dumped Mikey in the back, jumped inside, and sped off.

It wasn't a long drive to the nearest ER, but it felt like an eternity. I jumped at every headlight, but we made it. A cop car passed us six blocks from the house, sirens blaring, but Robins, smooth and calm, made it past him without incident. Mikey lay in his towel, bleeding and whimpering. At one point, the towel slid off him and I caught sight of his body, caked in blood, sweat, and mud from the yard. He wheezed. It took me a second to realize he was trying to talk.

"You're—not going to kill me," he said. It wasn't a question.

Robins shook his head from the front seat. "No," he said. "You want to die, and John told me specifically—'Don't give him anything he wants.'"

Mikey laughed—or rather, he wheezed even louder. "Go figure."

"We're taking you to one of our hospitals," Robins said. "Patch you up. After that, it's John's decision." Then he snorted. "Little fuck deserves to die, you ask me."

I tried to emulate him, that authentic gangster calm, but all I could feel, even after we dumped Mikey at the ER entrance, was exhaustion seeping into my bones.

Robins insisted that I shouldn't go home, and I agreed— one look in the mirror showed me a pale, bruised man I didn't recognize. I'd spook Katie, which would lead to awkward questions. Brendan's apartment was closest, so I got dumped there.

"Jesus, what the fuck happened?" he asked when I staggered inside. He sounded, I noted, a little impressed. I looked down. There were patches of rusty red all over my clothes. My last memory of that night is a fitting one: me stumbling, attempting to kick off my bloodstained khakis in Brendan's shithole disaster of an apartment.

TWENTY-NINE
BRENDAN

I bumped into Harry Rogers in North Beach about a week after Thanksgiving. Jimmy, Colin, and I had been using our baseball bats to do some old-fashioned muscle work and scare poor Ron Callamezzo, porn shop entrepreneur, into coughing up what he owed us for protection. We were just coming out of the shop via the back alley, and Harry was just going in. Instead of a bat, he was holding a crowbar.

"What the hell are you doing here?" I asked.

"John asked me to come, make sure Ron was paying his fucking rent," Harry said. He glared at Ron, who was peeping through blinds in the window. We heard a little yelp, then the blinds straightened.

"That's why he sent us!" Colin said.

"Who'd you talk to?"

"Robins. Why, who'd you talk to?"

"One of Robins' guys, Tommy, or whatever the fuck. Early this morning." Harry sighed. "But," he added, glancing at my bat, "looks like you guys already took care of it."

I nodded. "I'll walk back with you," he said. We started off.

It was the beginning of the Christmas season, so tourists were starting to flock. We separated, trying to look like we weren't together—John always told us to avoid looking like a gang. When we got to a more crowded stretch of streets, though, where everyone was taking pictures of the flying books outside City Lights and all that shit, we clumped back together. Impossible to hear us over the shrieks of the idiots.

"Has John been in touch with you?" I asked Harry.

"Why, you hoping for a Christmas card?"

"I just—he mentioned wanting to hear about how Lucky Grocery was going, and I wanted to tell him."

"He knows how it's going," Harry sniffed. "Way better than you do." We walked past an open bakery with a huge cardboard Santa out front, and I tripped and nearly fell on my ass. "And anyway," Harry said, "he's busy. They only got back from Tahoe a few days ago, and apparently, he and Moore cooked up some big idea there, and he wants to—"

"Wait, *Moore* was there?" Jimmy asked. He glanced at me. "Casey Moore?"

Harry scrunched up his face. "Yeah, can you fucking believe it? Little shit got a spot at the big boy table and everything. *I* think it's because John wants to take all his ideas and then fuck him over, but Ian says it's the real deal. John's really pushing drugs these days and Casey's the 'innovator.'"

Jimmy was still looking at me, but Harry just kept walking. He was still talking, too, some shit about how the Chinatown guys hadn't liked the place settings at one of the big dinners, and how the whores were all asking for raises, and Skinny Thompson was pissed because how was he supposed to keep up with fucking inflation? I put my head down. I didn't believe it. Uncle John didn't trust Casey—he'd as good as told me that right before he left. Harry must have been fucking misinformed.

But what had Casey said, the last time I saw him? "I'll see you when I get back."

I took a deep breath. This didn't mean that John trusted Casey. What was that saying? Keep your friends close and your enemies closer ("so close you can smell their rotten breath," *Dark Was the Night* adds). So what if John took him to a meeting? Harry could be right—Uncle John could be buttering Casey up so he could fucking eat him. He was definitely using him for something, and it wasn't because he liked the guy. No one fucking liked Casey—he didn't play by our rules. He didn't even *know* our rules.

No. Casey may have been flashy, but he'd be gone as soon as the flash faded. And I'd be there, button man for the Callaghans, long after Casey Moore was a rotting skeleton at the bottom of a marsh.

"Where're you guys headed tonight?" Harry was saying. "Some of my girls are entertaining some pretty important City Hall guys tonight at this club..."

What was with those fucking earbuds Casey had, anyway? What fucking music was he listening to? "Brendan?"

They were all looking at me now. "*What?*"

"You want to go to Harry's party?"

"Harry can come to my promotion party, when I'm named button man," I said. Jimmy shot me a look—he was right, it was probably premature to say it, but in that moment I didn't care.

Harry raised his eyebrows. A kid in overalls ran out from a restaurant and cut in front of him. He swore at the kid, earning a glare from the father, and fell behind us in the crowd.

By the time we met up again, his expression had changed. He was looking at me the way he looked at John: with respect.

"You're going to be named a button man?" he said. "When?"

I put my hands in my pockets. "Soon."

———

The next weekend, I couldn't put Kristie off any longer. I had to go meet her family. They live in this ugly gray house in South San Francisco, "so close to the BART station that you can hear the trains!" her mom chirped. That Saturday was apparently a big fucking deal for the Scott family: The second weekend of December, Christmas tree time! I had to go with them to a fucking home improvement store and stand in the Christmas tree lot outside. It was rainy and foggy so you couldn't see three feet in front of you.

Her little brother Shane was jumping around like he was on ecstasy (he reminded me a lot of Liam the last time we went clubbing, actually), running to every single tree and yelling "This one! This is it!" before he spotted a bigger one three seconds later and completely lost his shit. ("He has... developmental problems," Kristie had told me. "He's a child at heart," her mom agreed.) The rest of the family followed him around, smiling and laughing. I thought back to Ireland —we'd never gone to pick out a tree. If I'd jumped around like that my mam would've scolded me and my dad would've...well, he would've tried to be nice to me, but that's just 'cause he's a fucking pussy.

Then I heard Shane yell like he'd been stabbed in the gut, but as it turned out *that* was just the beginnings of a pout, which then lasted for about another hour. It was all because his mother had told him they couldn't get an *eight*-foot tree. They were priced out at six feet. He insisted they needed an eight-foot one or it wouldn't be Christmas anymore. Then he started crying. I had to listen to this while Kristie hemmed and hawed, her mom apologized and stroked Shane's hair, and her dad frowned and put his foot down. It was getting colder and foggier by the minute, and Shane was still whining. I stuck my hands in my pockets. I was beginning to wish I'd brought gloves, even though that didn't do much for my gangster look.

Then I realized what Uncle John would do. I beckoned Kristie over and pulled a wad of cash out of my jeans pocket. A bunch of hundreds, just like John always had. He'd just paid me my cut of the convenience store that Friday. "Buy the kid a fucking eight-foot tree."

"Are you sure?" she asked, but she was already reaching for the money, her eyes bright.

"Have your dad pay for it with a credit card," I said, "but show him the cash. We don't want to flash it around."

She nodded and skipped off to them. I saw her talking to her parents, then pointing at me. Her dad looked like he was going to refuse for a second, but then her mom touched his arm and whispered something, and he nodded. Shane's face went from angry to fucking blissful in less than a second. It was funny, actually—the whole family laughed, and then so did I. They bought the tree and loaded it onto their truck. "I insist you stay for dinner," Kristie's mom said, patting me on the arm. She didn't ask where I'd gotten the cash—I think Kristie told her I was in construction.

I tried to get out of dinner—it was getting late, and I needed to get back to The Bar in case John called. (Although I didn't say that. I just said I had to work early.) But she wouldn't take no for an answer. They drove me home, singing fucking Christmas carols in the car all the way back. Shane was the loudest, but Kristie sang, too—she had a really nice voice, I have to admit, sort of high and pure, like this girl who used to sing in my Irish classes back home.

Dinner wasn't much: some pasta, a salad, and some bread, served on this cheap plastic Christmas tablecloth with Rudolphs and snowmen. Maybe I was just fucking exhausted from all the work I'd been doing for John, though, because it felt nice.

I thought I'd get to leave after that, but just as I was edging towards the door it opened again and her uncle came in, this fat, loud guy with a mustache who tried to crush my hand when he shook it. He and Kristie's dad started arguing about football and led me into their living room, where a vomit-yellow couch sat across from a TV that was about half the size of the one in John's den. The uncle—Bob—sat down with a groan and dumped two six packs of cheap beer on the coffee table. I eyed it and thought about going home. But a few free beers before I went back wouldn't kill me.

Four beers later, two more six packs had materialized, Bob was already shitfaced, and Kristie's dad was well on the way.

"What line of work are you in, Brendan?" Bob asked, clunking his boots on the table. Before I could answer he said, "I'm in tech, myself. Repair. I mean I drive a truck and fix phones, but that counts as tech, right?" He nudged me. I wished I was further away from him on the couch.

"I'm in construction," I said.

"Oh, really?" He let out a loud breath. "Not much money in that these days, I hear. What are you, a contractor?"

"Something like that." Kristie came into the room and perched on a chair a few feet away from us, gossiping with her mom. They were out of earshot. "It's better money than you'd think," I said.

"I've got three fleets of vans now," Bob continued. "I drive one, but soon I won't even drive—I'll just be at home, fucking my secretary, sending the other suckers out on jobs!" He laughed so loudly I thought he must've misheard his own joke. I smiled tightly.

"Do you get much pussy, Brendan?" he asked, leaning forward a little and dropping his voice.

"More than you," I muttered.

"What?"

"Bob," Kristie's dad said, "he's Kristie's boyfriend."

Was I? I wondered. The beer was dulling my senses. Had I had six, or seven? If South San Francisco was starting to look good, then I was pretty smashed already.

"Still," Bob said, leaning back. "He's...well, I don't know how much contractors make."

"He bought Shane that Christmas tree outside!" Kristie's dad said proudly. "The one in the truck!"

I glared at him. Hadn't I told him not to say that? I couldn't fucking remember. "I make plenty of money," I said thickly. "Don't you fucking worry."

Bob cracked open another beer. I heard the hiss of the can like it was far away and grabbed for my own. I'd be damned if I'd be out-drunk by some IT repair fuck. "Oh, so you're *that* kind of contractor," he said. He gave a huge ridiculous wink. "I've heard the rumors."

"Don't listen to him," Kristie's dad said to me. He leaned back and turned up the TV. "He's always gossiping. Worse than a fucking woman."

"It's not gossip!" Bob insisted. He was so loud that Kristie and her mom looked up.

"Slow down, Bob," Kristie's dad said, putting a hand on Bob's arm. Bob took another huge swig from the can.

"I know what I've heard," Bob said. "A bunch of fucking criminals and thugs, doing 'construction work,' flashing money around, acting like they're real men—"

I stood up so quickly it made my head rush. "Say that again."

"Oh, Brendan, he didn't mean—" Kristie started, but Bob had already struggled to his feet. Kristie's dad jumped up to get between us, but he was too late—I'd already pushed him aside and grabbed Bob by the collar. My knife pulsed in my boot like a living thing.

"Say. That. Again." I snapped. Bob was wide-eyed now, sweat beading on his lip, dripping into that fucking walrus mustache.

"You're a thug!" he shouted. I had to admit, I was a little impressed he managed to get it out. *Fuck the knife,* I thought. I punched him. He crumpled. I punched him a few more times, not all that horribly, but I'll admit—I did hear the nose crack.

Then everyone moved at once—a swirl of screams and yells. Bob, blood from his nose gushing onto the shag carpet, just kept yelling, "I'M CALLING THE COPS, I'M CALLING THE FUCKING COPS," over and over like some demented robot. Kristie's mom meanwhile kept running in with more cloths and bandages, and Kristie was swearing at me, although I couldn't hear any specifics. Finally, I couldn't take it—I yelled, "If any of you call the cops, you're all fucked!" That shut them up. Then I just left, strode right out the door and onto the street. Finally, some fresh air.

———

Kristie pouted for a while after that. But then I gave them some money and swore them to secrecy and that seemed to be the end of that. I also stopped by her house and dropped off this purse she'd been eyeing. Cost a fucking fortune, but that smoothed shit over.

I'd been fucking stupid. I realized that now. But as the days passed and no one did anything, I got less scared of the thought of the cops knocking down my door. Her uncle was a pussy, anyway. I actually felt a little pleased with myself, thinking of leaving him in that living room, practically wetting himself with fear. Let Casey say I was a dog; at least I wasn't the man pissing on the carpet.

———

The next Monday morning, I was summoned to Uncle John's house—his exact words, in fact, were, "Just fucking get here."

It was still early when I arrived, maybe nine in the morning. Robins let me in and gestured me upstairs to John's study. On my way through the house, I saw Aunt Deirdre in the kitchen in her bathrobe, swirling her spoon in a bowl of oatmeal and staring out into space. Katie was hovering next to her near the sink, washing a dish. She half-waved at me and I hurried away.

Uncle John was sitting at his desk, already dressed in a crisp gray pinstripe suit with a pink pocket square. Not many men can pull off a pink pocket square, but my uncle is one of a kind. My stomach loosened when I saw him. I smiled. "You look dapper, sir."

Uncle John stood up. I immediately stopped smiling. His eyes were thunderous. "What the fuck were you thinking?" he said. He hadn't even waited for Robins to close the door fully.

I put my hands together, thinking furiously. "Sir, I—"

"Did you tell Harry Rogers that you were going to be named my newest button man?"

I stopped dead.

"Let me rephrase," he said, even quieter than before. I didn't dare look at him—I looked down at my feet, but I could sense him crossing his arms. "I know you did."

I didn't say anything. The rug I was standing on was Persian, I thought, patterned with deer and flowers. Aunt Deirdre had shown it to me once, bored my ass off for twenty minutes talking about Oriental design.

"And," he continued, his voice measured but thick with rage, "I hear you've also been punching out uncles in the industrial city."

Fuuuuck.

"You know what's most upsetting about that part, Brendan?" John asked. I looked up and he moved from behind his desk, came out to lean against it next to my chair. "Who I heard it from."

My thoughts raced—I hadn't told anyone, not Harry or Ian or Robins. Who could've?

"I'll spare you the suspense," John continued. "It was Colin."

I blinked. "*Colin?*"

John smiled like it hurt. "Called me out of the blue. Since his little...indiscretion...he's been exceedingly loyal."

Now I remembered: I had told Colin. I'd bragged about it to him and Jimmy later that same night. We'd all been drunk, laughing, laid out on my living room floor, doing impressions of Uncle Bob pissing himself.

John watched me.

"What are we going to do about it," he said. I still didn't move. He sighed. "You got lucky with the uncle. He won't press charges."

"Yes, sir, I made sure—"

"*I* saw to it," John said, "through back channels." His eyes held mine. "Your crew is your own affair. But I don't see how you could possibly think you're getting a promotion if Colin is stiffing me and then blabbing about all your fuckups."

He seemed calmer now; his eyes were less stormy. I, however, was boiling.

He smoothed his hair back. "I am the head of this family," he said. "I'll be the head of this family until the day I die." He moved back to the seat behind his desk and tapped the wood. "I've got enough going on right now, and I don't need another fucking—" He paused, then started again in his earlier quiet tone. "I make all the decisions—hiring, firing, promotions, demotions, when people get to eat lunch, their fucking break-times, their—" Just as his voice rose to a shout again, he stopped and held up a hand. "I'm getting ahead of myself. A flaw of mine. One that I believe you and I share."

I swallowed my pride. "Sir, I'm so sorry, I didn't mean to, I was just—"

He held up a hand again. "Let me be extremely clear. You're not being promoted."

He let the words float in the air, and for a second, I hoped I'd misheard, that I'd just be able to blink and move on. He let the clock tick a few seconds.

"Ever, sir?" I asked.

"What?"

"I'm not being promoted...ever?"

He didn't say anything, just looked at me. "Robins," he called, "we're done."

The door opened. I left. But of course, we weren't done. Not by a long shot.

THIRTY

HARRIS

When we got back after Thanksgiving, I was busy with non-Callaghan things. I went to Oakland to visit my parents, brought my mom the banana bread from Tahoe that she'd always claimed was her favorite. I saw a woman I'd been casually dating, slept with her a few times, filed briefs, and got back to normal. I didn't see much of John. He was busy, and pissed off at Brendan for something I was too exhausted to care about.

I went to see the widow again in early December. I brought her the money John had okayed. It was just enough to tide her over, but not enough (she reminded me) to cover two months' worth of her pension. She asked again if John would buy her husband's life rights from her. I told her she'd gotten as much out of John as he was willing to part with. And then I pulled out the document he'd had me draw up. I gave her every possible reason to sign that I could think of, always leaving the most important one unsaid.

After two cups of tea and a plate of now-stale chocolate cookies, she insisted tearfully that I was "fucking with her, with her whole life!" I pointed out that if she signed away

Frank's life rights, I'd go away forever, leaving her to live her whole life. "A life in tatters," she retorted. Then she crossed her arms.

"You know, Frank would always come in the back door," she said.

"What?"

"Frank would always come in the back door when he thought he'd done something wrong. Every time he came back from seeing his mistress, he slipped in the back. Or when he had to...well, I don't know exactly what he did for Cerullo, as you well know, but one night he came home covered in blood, and he wouldn't say a single word to me. And you'd better be damn sure he came in the back door that night."

I sighed. "Mrs. Salvare—"

"Do you want to leave?" she asked. "And come in through the back door? Would that make you feel better about hurting an old woman?"

I twisted my mouth. "I need you to sign this," I said. "I don't want anyone to hurt you."

"I won't sign that paper," she said, "and you can't make me. I need money, the money I'm fucking owed. What you just brought is laughable. Barely starts to cover the debt. If that producer wants Frank's story, I'll give it to him. And if you try to make me give it to you, I'll—"

"What? Go to Cerullo? Cerullo's the one who hasn't been paying you."

She scoffed. "I know that! You think I trust that fuck? I'll tell the newspapers." Her eyes got fierce again.

"You *really* don't want to do that," I said.

She raked her long red fingernails through her hair. "I don't fucking care!" she screamed.

I sighed. "If you don't take this deal now, I won't be able to do anything more for you."

"I don't believe you," she said. "I want to talk to John. Myself. Personally. John or Cerullo. Make my case. I think they'll see my point of view."

I looked at her, at her wild eyes and the fake diamond on her finger. I couldn't tell, I really couldn't tell in that moment if she was being willfully naïve or if she really thought this might work.

"I don't want an exorbitant amount," she said. "You tell them that, all right? You tell them from me—I know how much John trusts you—and tell them I want to meet. If at the end of the meeting they still won't give me what I want, I'll sign the damn papers. Okay?" She stood up and pulled me up, too, moving me to the door.

"You need to sign these now," I said, but she clamped her lips together so tightly they turned white.

"I'll sign them after they hear me out," she said, shaking her head, and she didn't stop shaking her head until she'd moved me out into the hallway and opened the door, pushing me out into another cold, unforgiving afternoon.

———

I drove around San Francisco for at least an hour after that, past a bilingual Chinese school, a few gray churches, some laundromats. The people walking outside were bundled up against the cold like it was the Arctic, in parkas and long woolen scarves. I wanted to roll down the window and tell them how ridiculous they were. It was fifty-five degrees out, hardly below fucking zero. Instead, I stared ahead at traffic and the hill in front of me, and then the hill after that.

Then I went over to the Callaghan house, which is of course where I should have gone immediately. John was in his study, Deirdre informed me. She was in the living room, doing a puzzle. Katie was helping her. Katie looked up eagerly when I walked in, as if she wanted to continue our conversation from the hotel, but I just shook my head and pointed upstairs, and she nodded.

The study door was closed. I knocked and entered. John looked up. He had a sheaf of papers in his hands, and dark circles under his eyes. He rubbed at his forehead. I sat down. To buy time I looked at all the pictures on his desk: young Owen and Martin and Liam in matching sweaters at a pumpkin patch, Katie as a little girl with two front teeth missing, him and Deirdre in their finery, outside the steps of the cathedral, newly married. All the frames were facing out, not in: a performance for whoever sat where I was sitting.

He didn't even look up. "The widow didn't take the deal."

I swallowed. "No, sir. She wants to meet with you and Cerullo before she does."

John closed his eyes and breathed in. I saw a flash of red through the window, the wings of a bird. John didn't sigh, or move, or even blink, before he spoke again. "You know what you have to do."

———

"I just knew he'd agree," the widow said. It was about a week after our last meeting, and we were in the car, a beat-up red sedan that Robins had handed off to me that morning. I was driving, and she was in the passenger seat, practically humming with energy. She'd exchanged her housecoat for a clean black trench coat with a black suit underneath. Her jewelry was polished, her fingernails newly manicured and painted her signature bright, shocking red, her hair done up in a bun and so shiny it looked lacquered.

"I knew he'd take the meeting," she repeated. "John's a reasonable man, after all, and Mr. Cerullo, too—Frank always spoke very highly of him."

"Mmhhmmm."

"I don't want much, really," she said. "You told them that, I'm sure. It's not much, and then I'll go away forever, and everything works out for everyone. I told my daughters not to worry about me anymore."

I looked out the window, at the sidewalk and the thick drizzling rain, which poured out of the sky like a leak.

"Where are we going?" she asked. Before I could answer she waved her hand. "No, forget it, don't tell me. Plausible deniability, right?" She laughed.

I forced myself to laugh, too. I turned to look at her. "You look nice today, Mrs. Salvare," I said. "Very elegant."

She laughed again. "Thank you." She put her hands in her lap. "Turns out I don't mind your bullshit, as long as it's flattering."

I took the turn to the freeway. Her hands fluttered a little. "We're not meeting in the city?"

"Just outside it," I said. The rain was worse now, blurring the windshield. I turned the wipers up higher. "It's really coming down out there, huh?"

She nodded. "My flowers will be thrilled," she said. "And my daughter Edie would be too if she were here. She loves rain. 'Great weather for ducks!' she always said."

I smiled and turned on the heat. We drove for a while in silence. The freeway was slick with rain and clouds of water shining from other cars. I was grateful for the excuse to focus on the road. But I felt her staring at me.

"What's the matter?" she said. Her eyes were on my hands. My fingers were gripping the wheel so tightly they looked ashen.

"I hate driving in the rain," I managed.

"Why are you driving me?" she asked suddenly. "Why not John's driver, or one of Cerullo's?"

"Oh, I volunteered," I said. My voice was strange even to

me, higher pitched than usual and almost squeaky.

The widow frowned. She clutched at the cross around her neck. "What's the matter with you?" she said again.

I looked at my watch. We were about fifteen minutes out. "I—I broke up with my girlfriend," I lied.

The widow blinked. "I didn't know you had a girlfriend."

"Well, she isn't my girlfriend *officially*," I said. "But..." I scrambled for a lie. "But I asked her to marry me anyway, and she said she wouldn't. Didn't think I was trustworthy."

The widow reached over and put a hand on my shoulder. I had to concentrate to keep from flinching. "I'm sorry," she said. "That's awful."

"Do you trust me?" I asked. The words came out in a strangled rush before I knew I'd said them.

She sat back in her chair, adjusted her seatbelt. I waited. I wasn't sure which answer I needed to hear. "Of course I trust you," she said finally. "Shouldn't I?"

"Of course." I saw a sign for our exit. I put my blinker on. "Won't be long now."

"The airport?" Emilia said. "Am I going on vacation?"

I tried to smile. "There's a first-class lounge we use," I said. "We park in long-term parking and head up there, and no one's the wiser."

"Strange place for a meeting," she said. Her fingers fluttered again.

My heart, already strained, started pounding so loudly I was sure she could hear it. I grabbed for my coffee and spilled it all over my lap, swearing. The car swerved.

"Whoa!" Emilia screeched, grabbing my hand on the wheel. "Careful!"

"Sorry," I muttered. "Nearly there." We'd made our way into long-term parking now, heading for the most distant garage with the byzantine entrance half-blocked by construction. We passed through that into the open-air spaces even further afield and back into the rain, which was lighter now, a soft misty drizzle.

I saw it before I even started looking. There weren't many cars out there, and only one green Camry right up against the fence separating the parking lots from the runways. Its engine was running—I could see the smoke coming out of the muffler.

I pulled up next to it. She moved to undo her seatbelt. "No, stay here a minute," I said. "The guy in the next car is called Robins. He's going to get in this car and tell you how to get to John."

Her eyes were wide. "Why can't you tell me?"

"I don't know all the details," I said.

I undid my seatbelt.

"Wait!" she said. Her fingers scrabbled at my arm. "What are you—?" I saw tears in her eyes.

I steadied myself. "Don't worry," I said. "I'll be right over there, watching." I pointed to a space a few feet from the car. "I just can't hear what he's going to say to you. John doesn't like anyone knowing all his secrets."

She hadn't let go of my arm. Something flitted behind her eyes like a bird trying to escape a cage.

I sighed. "Okay, fine. I'll stay with you, okay?" I said. "How about that? Until he finishes talking. I'll—I'll close my ears or something." I smiled, and she smiled weakly back. "I just have to get Robins." She nodded. I got out and walked over to the car. Robins was looking at me from the side mirror.

"We good?" he asked. I nodded.

"Just get in the back," I said. "She's in the passenger seat. She's a little spooked, though."

Robins glared at me. "You spook her?"

I realized my hands were shaking. I clasped them together. I didn't answer. I just turned and walked away, as fast as I could, through the drizzling rain.

THIRTY-ONE
NEIL

The Mikey situation was heavy. Very heavy. But he'd betrayed John. And not just John, I reminded myself: He'd betrayed the family, all of us Callaghans. That was how men in our line of work understood it, and that's how I should, too. So I did what they did: just went back to drinking and forgot any of it had ever happened. Mikey had ruined his own life, and it was time for me to turn back to mine.

Still, it was a strange, anxious time for me. I was jittery, finding it hard to sit still even in our house, and of course without even Leanne as a distraction my days were especially dull. I figured I just needed to stay focused. I'd hear any day now that I was officially Aiden Trask, and the next chapter of my life would truly begin.

I was still thinking about Mikey occasionally, of course. Only he wasn't actually Mikey; his real name was Dan. Detective Daniel Everett Flanagan. At least they managed to scrounge up a real Irishman.

He didn't die. Turns out he'd aimed for his heart but missed. Robins had grumbled about that, said any worthwhile suicide is a shot straight to the head. I'd assumed that after everything, John would have ended up killing Mikey—Daniel, I kept reminding myself. But that wasn't what he'd decided.

"Are you fucking stupid?" Robins said. I'd stopped by The Bar, hoping to hear more about the whole situation, and Robins was there, smoking. "You can't kill a cop," he continued. Someone dropped a glass, and I jumped. Robins laughed. "A little spooked after your adventure?"

"Of course not," I said easily, leaning back. I watched Harry Rogers pick at his nose. "I just wanted to know how it turned out."

Robins shrugged. "The official story is he confessed to the whores, his wife left with the kids, he went crazy, tried to kill himself, failed. Bang bang, early retirement."

"What about the undercover operation?"

"He used whores and tried to kill himself," Robins said. "It's a fucking police scandal waiting to happen. They won't touch any part of it."

I thought of Mikey, rolled in the towel and covered in grime. No. I wouldn't touch him, either.

———

That night, Katie told me I'd been neglecting her, so I took her to the movies to get her off my back. She settled for a rom-com with some asshole I'd gone to auditions with in LA. *Fuck me,* I thought, but it was easier to slide into those seats knowing I was soon to be named Aiden Trask. Soon that asshole would be sitting down to watch *me* on the big screen.

Katie sat down next to me with her tub of popcorn and mindlessly pulled out her phone. "Put that away!" I said. "The movie's about to start!"

She nodded but kept scrolling. I rolled my eyes and turned to the screen. Suddenly she gasped. "Neil!" she said.

"Look!" She thrust the phone in my hand. "Did you know about this?"

It was a *Variety* headline: *BROCK HARKNESS CAST AS LEAD IN REDDENED HAND.*

I read it three times in quick succession. No—no—it couldn't be, it was just—

I thrust the phone back at her. More people were filing into the theater now. The lights were starting to dim. "That's just a fucking rumor!" I said.

"I don't think so, Neil, it's—" She sucked in air again. "Terry Mannix is quoted—'It was obvious from day one that Brock had exactly what we needed...'"

I snatched the phone back and read the article all the way through. I wasn't retaining much of it, but some phrases stood out... "months-long search...star-making part..." and yes, there it was, Terry *fucking* Mannix saying that Brock "had been it from day one."

I stood up, gripping the phone. "I have to make some calls," I said. I rushed out into the lobby. No, it wasn't true, it couldn't be, why would they—

I'd call my agent. He'd been with me through the whole process. They all had—him, John, Harris, they'd all made me think... I was shaking with anger. It took me three tries to even dial. When I finally did, my agent picked up on the third ring, already apologizing.

"Neil, I'm so sorry, they only told me today but apparently they decided sometime around Thanksgiving..."

"*Thanksgiving?*" I yelled. A girl crossing the lobby with her grandmother jumped, and I groaned and left the theater to go yell on the street. "It can't have been fucking Thanksgiving, I was with John the whole time, he would've—"

"I'm really sorry, Neil," he said. "It's not the end of the world, though, right? We still haven't heard back from the—"

I screamed. A real, primal scream, too loud even for outdoors. Then I hung up. Worse than anything, worse than not getting the part, worse even than Brock *fucking* Harkness getting the part instead, was the memory of that night before the Samhain party: me and John in his room, hatching plans for the empire and looking down at our subjects below. He'd probably known then that I wouldn't get the part. Even then, even that night with all his fake interest in my advice on how to deal with Mikey. He'd been fucking with me for weeks. As I ran out into the night, my mind clouded over with rage.

———

Katie took it even harder than I did. She just wouldn't let it go. She kept saying, "Why would Daddy do such a thing?" and shaking her head over and over.

We were in our kitchen, and she was attempting to cook. Chicken and some pasta with red sauce. She was wearing an apron that must have been a gift from her mother, because it was pink and frilly and too small. The ties wouldn't close in the back. One just hung down dejectedly.

The pasta started to boil over, and she panicked and hurried to it. When she'd switched off the stove and mopped up the mess, she turned back to me, her face pink and her hair wild from the heat.

"He shouldn't have done that, Neil," she said.

"No shit," I muttered.

He'd called me, said he was hands off with the production company and there was nothing he could do. Bullshit, of course, but when he added that he "trusted I would understand" and that he'd "make it up to me down the road if I didn't make a fuss now," I caught the whiff of a threat. I knew better than to push it further, at least for now.

She shook the pasta out into the colander, causing a rush

of steam. I listened to her banging as she washed one pot and added the sauce to the other.

"Daddy shouldn't have done that," she said again, once the sauce was mixed.

I sighed. "It's the business, I guess." I had no idea why I said it, when her own anger so closely matched my own.

She put her hands on her hips. "That's ridiculous, Neil," she said, in the loudest, sharpest tone I'd ever heard from her. "Daddy runs Emer Productions. He made this decision. Don't let anyone tell you otherwise."

"What do you know?" I scoffed. I sat down at the kitchen table, fingering the place setting. Another gift from Deirdre— red and green "for the season," with pictures of big-eyed snowmen ice skating.

Katie sat down across from me and put her fingers up to her temples. "He owed you that part, Neil. You were perfect for it. You're a Callaghan, and you weren't even born into our family."

"I know," I muttered. "Your father never lets me forget it."

"No," she said. "What I mean is, my dad built this world," she gestured all around her, "but most of the rest of us were just born into it. We didn't work for it. We didn't earn it. You did."

Was she implying that she knew I'd married her for her father? I suppose she knew, of course, but we never discussed such things. I felt a sharp twinge of pity, and I reached out and covered her hand with mine.

She put her other hand on top. It was slightly damp from cooking. "You should be furious, Neil," she said. "Especially after everything you've done, with Mikey and all that. It's absurd."

The pity I felt for her merged into something else: a rush of emotion that I suddenly recognized as pride. She was far more observant than I'd ever given her credit for. Her eyes were gleaming with love and a strange ferocity. And she was right, of course. The whole thing was absurd.

———

Even Harris agreed. I cornered him at a benefit a few days later.

"Harris," I said, snatching a shrimp off a tray nearby, "I suppose you've heard the news."

He stared at me blankly. He looked ill, I noticed. His face was gaunt, and his eyes were red. "About Mrs.—how would you have—" he started, but then he stopped.

"I thought you would've heard by now," I said, "that I didn't get the part."

He was quiet for a few seconds. I could tell he wasn't listening.

"Hello?" I said. "Harris? I didn't get the part. Aiden Trask in *The Reddened Hand*. After all that *fucking* work, hours of prep and line reading and research with Brendan and all that time on auditions and...Jesus, Harris, I don't know about you but I'm starting to think John is slipping..."

"Mmmhmmm," he said. His eyes were still far away.

"...don't mean to speak ill of anyone, especially a member of my family," I continued, "but I don't think that John really appreciates all the men he has here."

He looked up. Now he was listening. "You're right," he said. He looked down at the beer in his hand and took a long drink.

"He really doesn't have an eye for the *real* talent," I continued, "yourself excepted, of course. I should be the face of the Callaghans, don't you think? I thought I would be *ideal* casting for Aiden Trask, what with my theatrical background and my knowledge of the family."

I was still keeping it light, but I felt my anger, a small

crack on a field of ice. And I knew suddenly that I'd regret staying any longer. Better to get away before the ground broke underneath me.

But before I could make my excuses, he was speaking again. "You're exactly right, Neil," he said. "I have to go now, but..." He looked at me. "You've given me a lot to think about."

And he left. For a few seconds I just stood there. Was he messing with me? It was always hard to read Harris. But when I thought back to our conversation, I was certain that he'd been serious. I'd never seen him look so withdrawn, or so serious. We'd had a moment. A small moment, maybe, but a decisive one. It got me thinking. If even *Harris* thinks John is wrong...

THIRTY-TWO

BRENDAN

After that meeting with Uncle John, I was fucking pissed. He'd never talked to me like that before. And after all that I'd been through, no promotion? For the next few days, I kept my head down, stopping in at Lucky Grocery, doing all the cleanup stuff we were assigned (just a few dustups and some knuckle-cracking), and I tried to think.

I half expected Uncle John to call me back again, tell me he was sorry for getting so mad. I knew I'd fucked up, but of all the fuckups in that family... Jesus. Martin and Owen were still feuding over who should get the bigger portion of the dry-cleaning money, and Liam was out chasing pussy, never having worked a goddamn day in his life. Harry Rogers was a fucking snitch, Robins was practically braindead, and Skinny Thompson could barely count to ten. Not to mention fucking Colin—he'd stolen John's money and sneezed on that fucking leg, and *I* was the one in the doghouse? But John never fucking called.

Probably a week after that, we caught another body. Tim Smith showed up at The Bar one afternoon, just as the sun was starting to set, and told us to get our bag. We had it ready, actually—Colin had just been cleaning it, because he'd lost a bet about how many bar peanuts he could fit in his mouth.

We were on the road in minutes.

I guess I should've been relieved, and I was a little. A body was a big job: a good sign that John had forgiven me, and things were starting to blow over. I tried to ignore my anger: I still didn't think I'd done anything all that bad, but better to keep quiet and keep John on my side. Maybe this meant good things for the future, too, maybe even a promotion sometime down the road.

I don't know where I'd thought we'd be going, but when Tim got on the freeway, I was surprised. I was even more surprised when he took the exit for SFO. "Are we flying somewhere?" I asked. Tim glared in the rearview mirror. A trip was too much, but I was just starting to hope we were meeting someone important in some fancy first-class lounge when we turned off into long-term parking.

Tim kept driving and driving, past probably hundreds of cars to the most distant lot, which was almost completely empty.

It had just rained, and there were puddles everywhere. We pulled up two spaces away from a dusty red sedan, which was parked right at the fence that separated the lot from the runway. It was loud as fuck—all the rush of the wind and engines and planes taking off. I glanced around. There was no one in sight. "What the f—?" I started to say, but Tim pointed to the red sedan. First, I noticed the blood on the dashboard, then the body slumped in the passenger seat.

"That's your fucking cue," Tim grumbled. I looked at Jimmy and Colin. Colin got out first, to get the bag out of the trunk.

"We'll bury her in the marsh," Tim said. "It's closer to here anyway."

"Her?" I said. Tim ignored me. Jimmy opened the door to the sedan, which was unlocked. It squeaked. I was still standing several feet away, but I could see that it was a woman, a little old woman in a black trench coat, shot in the back of the head. A neat shot, too, in and out. Not much blood, considering. Like a Yeti kill shot—really professional. Her face was hidden, her body slumped forward.

Colin looked at me. "Why would they kill an old woman?"

Something was bugging me—something about the old woman. She felt...familiar. "Don't fucking ask questions," I said. "Let's—let's just get her—it—out of here."

"You first," Jimmy said. He was standing in a puddle, his arms crossed. It started to drizzle. I looked up at the thick angry black clouds.

"Give me the bag," I said. He handed it over. I put on my gloves and made the first move. Once I'd touched her hair, I pulled her upright. Then I jumped. Of course she looked familiar. It was Harris' widow, the old woman with the green house.

"What?" Colin asked. "What's the matter?"

I didn't answer.

Her fingernails were bright red, her hands white, but the veins stood out bluer than I'd ever seen. I tried not to look at the mess behind her head. I concentrated instead on her face, which was almost calm, just the one mark between her eyes where the bullet had exited. It looked like one of those dots Indian women wear. Her eyes were wide open, and she was already stiff as a board, but she couldn't have been dead long. Her coat was still wet.

"Why would they kill her?" Colin asked again. He was hovering next to the car. I realized I was kneeling in something sticky. I pulled back, groaning in disgust, but it wasn't blood. It was coffee. Someone had spilled coffee in the front seat and on the gear shift. Jimmy still wasn't fucking moving.

"Are you having the fucking vapors?" I hissed. Here I was, stretched out in the front seat with my ass next to my elbows, and he was just standing there. "Fucking help me."

Jimmy hesitated, but when I glared, he went to the other side of the car and opened the door. With his help, we managed to haul her out of the car and onto the asphalt, where Colin had spread the tarp. I looked over at Tim Smith, who was smoking and reading the paper in the other car, one eye on the rearview mirror.

"Seriously, though, Brendan," Jimmy said in a low tone while we wrapped her up, "why kill this old lady? Isn't she the one whose husband—"

He did remember after all. And he hadn't even tracked mud into her house or broken one of her figurines. "Calm down, pussy," I snapped. "She's not your fucking grandma."

"I know, but—" he glanced at Tim, "what could she possibly have done? Why would John want to—?"

"Just shut the fuck up, okay?" I said. I grabbed his arm. "Look." I pointed down at the body, wrapped neatly in the tarp. "Just don't think about what's in there. It could be anything, right? A rug, a thing of steel poles wrapped together."

Jimmy just looked at me. I glowered at him. It was still fucking raining, and my jacket was starting to stick to my skin. "Time to finish this," I said.

"Fine," he said finally.

"Colin?" I asked. "You done with the car?"

"All clean," I heard him say, with a muffled something in his breath. We got back up—he'd scrubbed all the blood off the dashboard and held a gun in one gloved hand. "This was in the back," he said. "I'm guessing it's the murder weapon."

"Thank you, CSI," I growled. "Bag it." We headed back over to Tim.

"You done yet?" he said. I opened my mouth to let Tim have it, but right at that moment, a jet took off over our heads, and my response was drowned out. "Good," he said. "One of you drives the car back to the junkyard, have it crushed. The other two come with me, to the marshes."

"I'll take the car," I said. "I'm fucking sick of you people." And I got in before anyone could say anything else. The keys were in the glove compartment. I was gone in seconds.

———

I expected a call from John after that, some kind of good job shit. But I got nothing. I kept thinking about that old woman. Jimmy had asked why she'd been killed. I thought I knew. I remembered what I'd told Harris the last time we left her house, that he was giving the widow false hope about some money she'd wanted from John. Obviously, she hadn't gotten it, she'd threatened John, and that had ended for her about as well as those things usually end. I didn't know why I kept thinking about it. I'd hated the old bitch. But the thought kept knocking. I kept seeing her red fingernails and that face, with those eyes wide open.

———

And life went on, just as fucking usual. Then it was time for another sacred event: the Callaghan Christmas party. I was invited, another good sign that I was back in with John.

That Saturday night, I put on my best suit (this green one that's tight over the biceps) and Colin, Jimmy, and I headed over to the Callaghans'. Our girls were meeting us there. I was carrying a bottle of wine from Lucky Grocery, the best we had. It wasn't very good, a dusty bottle of red worth about thirty bucks, but I'd brushed most of the dust off at least.

We got there right on time, which was unusual for us, but nearly everyone was already there. Uncle John has a habit of starting parties earlier than he says he would, for the element of surprise, I guess. It's a strategy the Yeti used in *Dark Was the Night*— "Arrive before people are expecting you, like a plague or a foul wind."

The house was packed, just like for Samhain, but in a very different way. For one thing, everyone was in "formal attire," which meant a bunch of old wives in weird velvet dresses and diamonds and a few whores and low-level gangster groupies lurking in the background in oranges and reds, trying to look classy.

People nodded at us as we walked in. I liked that. My mood started to lift. I saw Harry Rogers out of the corner of my eye. I winced. Seeing Harry Rogers in a suit is like watching a chimp put on makeup. He waved to me like we were fucking buds, but I just gave him a look and moved on. Uncle John might be over my fuckup, but I was still pissed about the whole thing. I saw Casey in a little huddle, giggling with his guys about something, and Skinny Thompson, Tomato Mulligan, Harris, and Robins all gathered near the roaring fireplace. They were holding tongs, and it took me a second to realize they were actually roasting chestnuts—Uncle John was a stickler for Christmas traditions. They all looked fucking miserable, especially Robins, crammed into a too-tight suit like a bad sausage casing.

Waiters dressed in red and green plaid with bow ties floated around, offering people shrimp. I grinned just looking at them. Only Uncle John could make a classy San Francisco catering company enforce that kind of dress code, and I was sure he'd gotten a fucking discount, too.

We made our way into the center of the living room, where Uncle Peter and the Callaghan boys were. I saw Neil and Katie out of the corner of my eye and tried to duck out of Neil's eyeline. I'd heard he'd thrown a hissy fit after he hadn't gotten the part in that movie, and I was desperate to avoid hearing his side of the story. I only had so many years left to live.

Then I bumped right into Uncle John.

"Oh, Christ, sorry, sir, I—" I muttered, but he just laughed. That gave me the courage to look up. He was wearing a black suit with the skinny tie slightly loose, and he held a glass tumbler in his hand.

"It's okay, Brendan," he said. He put a hand on my back. "I forgive you."

I took a breath. "Thank you, sir," I said. Then Jimmy nudged me, and I remembered the bottle in my hand. "Oh, sir, this is for you." I handed it to him.

He took it, read the label and smiled. "Deirdre!" he said. Aunt Deirdre appeared next to him, wearing this weird poofy blue dress that made her look like an old mermaid. "Look at this, our nephew brought a bottle of wine."

"How sweet," she cooed. She took it and looked at the label. She stared at it for way too long. Did she have fucking tears in her eyes?

"Well, we'll let you get back to the party," John said. I could tell he'd seen the tears too, and he was just as uncomfortable as I was. "Enjoy yourselves tonight, boys. You've earned it."

He moved away, one hand gripping her shoulder.

"That wasn't so bad!" Colin said. He was still a little shaky around John but had decided to channel his fear into full-on kiss-assery. "He said he forgives you."

"That could be just for nearly fucking knocking him over," Jimmy grumbled.

"Keep me the fuck away from Harry," I said. "And Casey." I looked around the room. Kristie had just walked in, carrying the purse I'd bought her, and she was already clumped in a group with Owen's wife Anna and Jimmy and Colin's dates. She waved and made a sign for me to go rescue her.

I don't really remember much from that part of the party. Kristie and I followed the caterers around the room, snatching up all the best appetizers before anyone else could get them. It seemed funny at the time. Then I hit the eggnog pretty hard, and as we got closer to main courses I switched to whiskey. There was mistletoe everywhere—Kristie wanted to stop at every single one, which was fine by me until she pushed me away, saying my breath smelled like her dog's. Then I got pissed and left her to fend for herself. I think she went up to play with the kids at one point—they were all upstairs, supposedly "in bed" during the grownups' party.

Harris was moping in a corner. I walked over and tried to talk to him, but he just stared at me without blinking. I got a prickly, itchy feeling that he was thinking about the widow. I was sure he knew she was dead, and after a few minutes of his staring, I was almost equally sure that he knew I'd been the one to clean up after. The staring was fucking unnerving. He loomed in that corner, tall and somehow clouded over, glaring at everyone. I'd never noticed quite how tall he was before, or how broad in the chest. That night, he looked as big as John. Worse, he looked like he could give John a run for his money. I moved away as quickly as I could.

Somehow, I ended up in the room off the living room, with Colin and Jimmy and Ian and a bunch of other fucks. There were a million people in there, mostly guys like us, mid-range and drunk and milling around hoping for praise or drugs or more alcohol. It must've been late. With the fire roaring, the heat blasting, and all the bodies, it was fucking boiling. The caterers had gone home by then, I guess—I don't remember them being there. And the girls and wives were gone, too, or at least, they weren't in the room. It was all Callaghan crew, just standing around, shooting the shit.

My head was pounding, so I nursed my glass of whiskey. I was hoping the party would be over soon, but I'd already decided I wouldn't leave until Uncle John gave me a personal goodbye. I thought he was nearby, somewhere past the arch in the living room, but I didn't see him. Some of the older guys were drifting off to John's den to smoke cigars.

"...love you, man," one of Harry's guys was saying to him. He was fucking hammered, could barely stand up. Everyone sniggered at him, stumbling around the room like a baby giraffe trying to walk. "This guy fucking saved my life," he said, pointing to Harry, who he was now holding on to like a life raft. "Fucking saved me from drowning when I fell in the water that time, remember that, Harry? We were supposed to sink that fucking drug boat because the feds were on to us, and what—what was the name of that boat again? Pita, Rita, something like that..."

"*The Lupita*," Harry said through clenched teeth.

"Lupita, that's right!" the guy said. "This guy fucking saved my life on the—what was it again? The Lup—lupita..."

"Sounds like a fucking delightful romance," I said. Everyone laughed. Harry blushed, but before he could say anything a voice cut in.

"*The thing about Eddie was that he was charming. Charming and deadly, like a beautiful viper, or a dangerous dame in an old movie. The Yeti was smooth and polite—he always opened doors for women, he carried old ladies' groceries, he served on his kids' school's PTA. But Eddie was a man of two sides, killer and father, hunter and husband...*"

Everyone else turned around, but I didn't. I knew who was reading, and why he was reading it. Sure enough, Casey sidled up to me and cleared his throat. He was holding a copy of *Dark Was the Night*, the copy I'd read when I first came from Ireland.

I gripped my glass but didn't drink. Casey *fucking* Moore. "You went all the way down to the basement to find that book?" I said. "At this fucking party?"

"It's a good one," Casey said. He closed the book. Everyone was watching. I turned to face him. He was wearing a suit that was way too fucking big for him.

"I like all the contrast in the writing," Casey continued. "*Killer and father, hunter and husband.* Do you think he'll ever mention light and dark, bring the whole thing full circle?" He opened the book again. "Ah, yes, there it is. The end of that very sentence."

"Fuck off, professor," I said. Someone laughed. I turned away from him again.

He put his hand on my shoulder. I shrugged it off and fought to keep my voice calm. "Don't fucking touch me."

"Why?" he said. He looked to his crew. They were grinning. "What're you going to do, kill me?"

"I might."

Casey's guys laughed.

"This is fucking bullshit," Jimmy said. "Come on, Brendan, let's go."

I didn't budge. My heart sped up. "If you don't think I can kill you, you're fucking stupider than you look," I said. I wheeled around and jabbed my finger in Casey's face.

"Oh, I don't doubt that you could kill me," he said. "I just doubt that your Uncle John would let you."

"No one fucking *lets me* do anything, I do whatever I—"

"Oh, don't insult my intelligence, Brendan," Casey said.

"You know you're a dog on a leash. A Doberman, maybe, but that doesn't make the leash any less relevant."

"Stop talking shit," Jimmy said. "Brendan, come on—"

I drained my whiskey and slammed the glass onto a table. I felt a pulsing in my fingertips now, strange little heartbeats.

"Casey Moore," I said. "I'm fucking warning you, I've heard all your shit and I've ignored it up till now, because I know it's just hot air, but if you push me—"

"Brendan?" Oh great, fucking Kristie was here now, her eyebrows scrunched together in confusion. "Why are you yelling, you're just—"

"Shut up, Kristie." I turned back to Casey. "If you push me, I'll—"

"Oh, Brendan." Casey shook his head. "No more empty threats, okay? They just don't work when we all know you're never going to be promoted—"

My knife was out of my boot and in my hands before I knew it, and then it thrust forward towards his heart. He jumped away. I lunged again. Somewhere outside of me I knew people were yelling, but all the sound in the room had vanished, like someone turned off a switch. I could hear my breath, feel the knife handle as I thrust it forward, but nothing else. Time slowed.

I roared then, I think. Casey was getting cocky. I had him this time. I thrust again and my knife hit flesh, somewhere on his left side. But the fucker twisted away, and then I felt hands on me.

I was yanked backwards. Sound came rushing back. Kristie was crying, people were yelling, Casey's guys were screaming at Colin and Jimmy, but we were all being held back. I twisted to look behind me and got clobbered in the back of the head. Robins' voice roared, *What the fuck are you doing?* in my ear. I looked up—Tim Smith had Casey's hands behind his back. Unlike his men, Casey wasn't struggling. He just stood there, smiling at me. I struggled even harder than before, screaming at Casey across the room.

Then everyone fell silent. For a second, I thought I'd gone crazy again, but then Robins shook me, and I looked up. Uncle John was standing there, right in the middle of the room between me and Casey. He'd brought others, too; I saw Uncle Peter off to the side with Harris, Owen, Martin, and Liam, even fucking Katie and Neil.

I took a breath. "I—I'm sorry, Uncle John, but Casey was talking shit about me, about our family, and I had no choice, I had to hurt him, so I—" I looked for my knife. One of Robins' guys was holding it. It was tinged red, but only slightly. Uncle John held up a hand, and I stopped talking. He turned to look at Casey.

Casey grinned. "Don't worry, sir, it was a shallow wound," he said. He twisted a little, to show the hole in his shirt. I swore—he was right, it was just a fucking scratch, hardly even bleeding.

Then Casey looked back at me. "You know, Brendan," he said. "I should be thanking you. I'm lucky. Your knife is just like your dick—four inches of pointless thrusting."

I tried to lunge at him and opened my mouth to scream. But before I could, my mind caught up with my body and I realized what I was hearing: a chuckle here, a chuckle there. Harry laughed, and so did Ian. But I only really heard one laugh: a low, gravelly one.

Uncle John laughed. Uncle John fucking laughed.

He signaled for Robins to let me go. The heat came on me again, that black heat of anger. This time it was even worse— it fucking swallowed me. I would have killed someone, I'm fucking sure of it, but of course I didn't have my fucking knife anymore. The rage filled me, spilling into every part of my body. I was a berserker—I was the rage. It was like I wasn't even really *there* for what happened next.

THIRTY-THREE
HARRIS

I don't honestly remember much of the week after I left Emilia at the airport. I didn't binge drink, or do coke, or go wild with strippers and remorse. That's not really my style. I worked. A lot. I kept my ear to the ground, I reported to John, and I listened.

Brendan was in trouble. He'd told everyone he was getting a promotion. My plate was pretty full, but I still had time to wonder at this. It never fails to amaze me how consistently some people act against their own interests.

Things were quiet after Emilia: more quiet than usual. John should've been pleased, but I don't think he was. I only caught glimpses of him moving here and there, an ashen-faced blur. He loved to do charity work during the holidays, organized a toy drive at the local cathedral and spoke on behalf of poor children at a city council meeting. I was there for that one, and all I remember was the hot room, the acrid smell of too many people and an overworked radiator, and John's face, little half-moons of purple underneath his eyes.

After the council meeting, there was a reception for some children's charity. Tomato Mulligan, one of John's guys, was there for some reason, and John steered him over to me. He was already drunk and as red in the face as his namesake.

John slapped a hand on my shoulder. "Harris here needs a little cheering up," he said. Tomato Mulligan, who'd straightened the minute he heard John coming, smiled his big, ridiculous smile.

"Ah yes," he said, "I heard about your sweetheart."

I frowned, confused. Had my lie about a breakup made its way through the rumor mill?

"The widow Salvare," Tomato said in a stage-whisper.

My throat tightened, but before I could do anything, John had grabbed Tomato by the tie—smoothly, quietly, but he still had him by the neck. "Let me help you," he said softly, drawing Tomato closer. "You've got a stain on your shirt."

"Sir, I—I'm sorry, I didn't mean anyth—"

"Discretion, Mr. Mulligan, discretion," John said. He let go, and Tomato heaved a sigh. He'd taken a step back and almost collided with the table behind him.

"I—I'm sorry, sir," he said. John tilted his head in my direction.

"I—I'm sorry, Harris," Tomato said.

"I accept your apology," I said stiffly.

"There!" John said, and he dusted off Tomato's shirt. "No harm done. Enjoy the party." He swept away, tossing one apologetic glance in my direction like some kind of party favor.

And then: the Callaghan Christmas party. Largely memorable for one moment: when Brendan stabbed Casey. And then Casey, true to his nature, turned that into an opportunity to mock Brendan's penis size. A clumsy joke, I thought, but John laughed. And Brendan, cornered and totally friendless, screwed up his face and balled his fists, all the pain and anger building inside him until it was almost visible. And then he burst into tears.

———

"To his credit, though, they were *manly* tears," Casey said just a few minutes later. Brendan had just been escorted out the back gate, his face still wet as he swore at the top of his lungs. I figured John or one of his guys would quiet and threaten him before Tim Smith dumped him at his apartment.

Casey stood next to me, watching the scene play out and avoiding Colin and Jimmy, who were glaring at him from across the room where Robins was babysitting them. I predicted they'd be escorted home, too, as soon as rides could be arranged. I didn't think John needed to worry about them avenging Brendan, though—as angry as they were at Casey, they both seemed more than a little bewildered by Brendan's behavior, and I'd seen Jimmy shake his head in shame as Brendan was led out.

Casey tapped my shoulder, to see if I was paying attention. I raised an eyebrow at the gesture. "They *were* manly tears," he said again. "Not a sob, or a whimper—more like an enormous dam bursting on his face." One of his guys —Len, I think—laughed.

"You should be careful John doesn't hear you talking like that," I said. The party was breaking up, but a few groups still lingered, gossiping about Brendan's outburst and staring admiringly in Casey's direction. "Some people might say you brought this on yourself."

Casey's grin widened. "Who, me?"

I drained my glass. What was I still doing here? Waiting for John's permission to leave? Casey was the last person I wanted to talk to. But I still lingered—after all, I'd just be trooping back to my apartment's cold blue walls.

John approached, and Casey snapped to attention, even giving a little mock salute, which John acknowledged with a slight smirk. "Casey," he said in a disarmingly calm voice. "What the fuck was that?"

"Some people just can't handle their liquor, sir," Casey said airily, stretching so his cut was exposed. "I won't hold it against him."

John pinched the bridge of his nose with his fingers. He laughed, a weak chuckle. "Moore," he said, "you're too much." Then he turned to me. "I know you'll be wanting to get home, Harris," he said, "but I need to speak with you. Will you meet me on Wednesday at the Trenton Hotel, main lobby? Nine o'clock?"

I knew what he was doing. Asking me for a meeting in front of Casey and the others, giving me the chance to say no. Demonstrating my power and importance, humbling himself before me. This was the closest John ever got to an apology.

"Of course, sir," I said. "I'll see you then."

THIRTY-FOUR
NEIL

The Christmas party was a wash—the usual dullness, a feeble knife fight, blah blah blah. Finally, after everyone else had gone home, Katie decided she was ready to leave. I went upstairs to grab our coats from her old bedroom.

I'd just reached the landing when John's office door opened, and he appeared in the hallway. He was still formally dressed for the evening, in a black suit and a skinny tie only slightly askew. I usually appreciated his sartorial choices, but seeing him there, his black hair slicked back in a futile attempt to hide the grays, his suit far too tight for a middle-aged man, suddenly made me furious. *This* was the man who decided I wasn't right to play Aiden Trask?

Still, I knew better than to express my anger. I wasn't a low-level ape, a bundle of adolescent hormones crammed into a suit. I knew how to play it. (*I knew how to play it*—why, oh why didn't John see that?)

"Merry Christmas, John," I said.

He blinked at me. "Merry Christmas, Neil." He put his hand on his bedroom doorknob.

"Could I speak with you for a moment? In there?" I pointed to his office.

"I don't have time right now." He said it calmly, but his eyes flashed. He turned to yell down the hall, "Katie! Don't forget the garbage before you leave—"

He stopped when he saw I was still standing there.

"I think you need to make time." The words were out before I even knew I'd thought them. I resisted the urge to clap my hands over my mouth.

He moved closer. I could smell his cologne, see the watch tan on his wrist. His eyes were shadowed, his skin a shade too pale and drawn tight across his face. "When I say I don't have time for something, Neil," he said, still advancing, "that's my way of being polite. What I really mean is *I don't care about this.* Do you understand that?"

In my confusion, I nodded, but I felt resentment building in my stomach. He was acting like he was humoring me.

"Good." He left, passing me on the way down the stairs. At that moment, the front door opened, and Owen banged in, complaining loudly that his kids were "driving him fucking crazy."

I should've gone straight home, but I stopped at a bar on the way back instead—or several, possibly. It's all a little hazy.

Somehow, I got home, and as I was violently ill into the flower bushes outside, I realized that I actually had a fever, not at all aided by my drinking. I spent the rest of the night sweating and tossing around in my bed, replaying my conversation with John over and over like a skipping film strip, but always from slightly uncanny angles. At one point I distinctly remember seeing John leaning over me. Something was blurring and rippling his face, like I was looking at him from the bottom of a well. After that I gave up on sleep and waited for the sun, which rose pale and wan in a gray sky.

THIRTY-FIVE
BRENDAN

My memory of the morning after the Christmas party is a little murky, but I remember waking up in my cold bed with the worst, spikiest hangover of my life. The apartment was fucking freezing—guess I was too drunk to turn the heat on. I got out of bed, walked into the kitchen, poured myself a glass of water. The linoleum was ice-cold, and my head ached like someone had blown it up with dynamite. I tried to turn off the faucet. It was fucking leaking, a steady little *drip drip drip*. I stood there, listening.

I tried to keep my mind empty. The party had been rough, but at least I'd finally hurt Casey, shown him who I was. I watched the little bead forming on the faucet, then building, getting heavier and heavier, then falling. *Drip... drip...drip.*

The knife hadn't worked though, had it? Casey had still disrespected me, disrespected me in front of the entire fucking Callaghan family.

And when Casey disrespected me, Uncle John laughed.

Uncle. John. Laughed.

———

After that, things just went along. I had a busy December, and by the time the New Year rolled around, you could say I was a new man. Of a sort.

I'm sorry to be so fucking vague, but I have my reasons.

And that brings us right up to date—to today, January 8. I'm on my way somewhere—a car's waiting for me outside. Excuse me, won't you? That's the kind of shit Uncle John would say, isn't it? The shit you hear in old movies?

I'd like to stay, but I have an appointment. I really can't be late.

THIRTY-SIX

HARRIS

The Trenton Hotel is one of the "shining jewels of San Francisco's crown," if overinflated brochures are to be believed. Even I have to admit it's pretty glorious at Christmas. On the outside, it looks like any other nice hotel: huge and gray and imposing, with colorful flags flapping in the round driveway where people pull up in their Bentleys and Mercedes. A thick red carpet leads up to golden revolving doors, which usher you into a foyer, then onto an escalator up to the main floor.

The lobby is enormous, at least half the size of a football field and a dizzying five hundred feet high. The hotel floors ring the building, arranged in circles stacked on top of each other like the layers of a cake, leaving the central space cavernous and huge, like a cathedral dome. On the left, brightly colored red and green glass elevators take guests up to their rooms.

The lobby floor is laid out with chairs and couches and two cocktail bars encircling a grand fountain in the middle, where glasslike sheets of water empty into a gray basin. At Christmastime, a miniature winter village sits on top of the fountain, complete with a zoo, Victorian neighborhoods, an ice-skating rink, and a train that circles the scene, whistling cheerily and spouting steam.

But all this is nothing compared to the real show. Beads of white light appear suspended in midair from the far-away ceiling to the lobby floor, draping the upper levels and all the galleries above in a warm, sparkling glow. Look up and you're dizzy, caught in a flurry of artificial snowflakes. When I was a boy, I used to stand here with my mom, looking up until my neck ached, spinning around and around until the lights were a night sky full of stars. When I asked my mother how the lights stayed up like that, she told me it was Christmas magic. Even then I knew it was lines of wire, so thin as to be nearly invisible. I remember resenting her for not telling me the truth; it made me feel babyish.

I couldn't remember sharing this particular memory with John, but I wouldn't be surprised if I had. Why else would he have arranged to meet there?

That night the bars were relatively full, but the space was so big that there were large gaps between groups. John was there before me, of course, sitting on a black leather chair with his legs crossed, sipping a whiskey. Robins was lurking off to the side, drinking at a small table.

John had ordered for me, a Moscow mule. It was my favorite drink, a drink he'd insisted I give up years before, since it wasn't a manly enough order for his second-in-command. I guessed that the drink was supposed to be another gift for me, a treat for a surly toddler. He pushed it to me.

"You can keep the mug, apparently," he said, "if you get the most expensive kind."

"Wonderful. It can go on the shelf with all my other mugs."

He laughed. I sat down. I wanted to look up at the lights, but I wouldn't let myself.

He let me settle in, waiting while I fidgeted with my coat and scarf and straightened my suit. I'd been at my office all day, through several long depositions, and I hadn't bothered to shower or change. I hoped he noticed how rumpled my clothes were. I didn't say anything, just watched as a mother and a little boy got on the elevator, the little boy jumping up and down in excitement.

"Harris," John said. I didn't move. I watched the boy and his mother go up the elevator, their faces illuminated by the white lights.

"Harris," John said again. He didn't like to repeat himself. I looked at him.

He was smiling but pale. His under-eye circles were dark, and his stubble was thicker than usual. "Have you been sleeping, sir?" I asked. My tone was strange, even to me, a mixture of concern and defiance.

John raised an eyebrow. "That isn't something for you to worry about."

I took a sip of my drink. He didn't say anything, not even after the waitress had come and gone, bringing him another whiskey.

"Sir—" I began finally.

"It had to be done, Harris," he said. He fixed his eyes on me then, with that famous John Callaghan intensity that made you feel like the only person in the room.

"What did, sir?"

John's eyes twitched. He wouldn't answer.

I leaned back in my chair, looking up at the lights. I got a flash, suddenly, of the widow's house: the cabinet filled to bursting with knickknacks, the ugly, uncomfortable couch, the sickly green wallpaper. (What was it with that green? I'd never asked her. Was it her favorite color? Or Frank's? It must've been Frank's.)

I saw the living room, with its heavy, expensive, ridiculous clock. Was it ticking, even now, louder in that empty room than I'd ever heard it? I saw a mouse skittering in the kitchen, nipping at the biscotti container, and dust particles gathering on the white porcelain Cupids. That crooked playground would be rusty by now, with all this rain. Her flowerbeds might already be sprouting weeds. In the months to come, would her daughters enter the house, their feet creaking on the floorboards as they placed white plastic sheets over the furniture?

John looked at me again, and I knew he knew what I was thinking about, although of course he couldn't picture it the way I could. He'd never been inside that house. I was seized, suddenly, with white-hot rage. I gripped my mug, willing the coolness to calm me down.

"Are you all right?" John asked.

I reached for something, anything I could say. "The widow's daughters..." I said. They wouldn't find her body, but she was officially missing. I'd seen it in a paper I'd tried to avoid looking at the other day, in the local section, next to a story about the newest panda at the zoo.

"They won't do anything," John says. "As soon as they decide to stop looking for her, they'll sign the life rights contract to us. Maybe they'll even do it ahead of time."

"You don't think they'll go to the police?"

John snorted. "Not after they talk to Cerullo. Besides, what evidence do they have? An old woman disappeared. It happens."

"They'll be suspicious."

"Let them be. It'll keep them scared."

I thumbed the rim of my mug.

"Besides," John said, "they don't know enough to put together a coherent story, even if they don't sign."

"What if she had papers, a book—?"

John pursed his lips. "You really think we'd go to all this trouble and leave something like that behind?"

I didn't. He was nothing if not thorough.

"You're not really worried about being caught," he said, leaning back in his chair with a sigh. Light shone on a streak of silver in his hair. Two girls in tight, shiny golden dresses passed by us, giggling and holding flutes of champagne. His eyes followed them with his usual sense of bored entitlement. Then his attention flicked back to me.

"No," he said, "you're worried about your immortal soul."

I forced myself to look back at him. "My immortal soul expired years before today."

John's mouth twitched. "I hoped you'd say that," he said.

I waited, again. My rage subsided. I took another drink. A Moscow mule was too cold for winter, really. The bartender had probably laughed when John ordered it, unless he knew who John was.

John seemed to sense what I was waiting for. He stiffened.

"Harris," he said, "it had to be done. I needed it to be over. I'm starting to think—" He stopped himself, put his arms on the arms of his chair, took a deep breath. "Never mind," he said smoothly. "No need to trouble you with that."

"You're tired," I said, again with that strange mixture of concern and anger.

His eyes flashed, but he kept calm. "Tonight, I am tired," he admitted. Then he sat up again, rolled his shoulders. "I won't be tomorrow."

I sighed and looked down at my hands. No, he wouldn't be tired tomorrow. I would be, though. I didn't know how many more of these I could go through. She was my first widow, true. But I suddenly realized she was far from the last.

When all was said and done, I'd done the job John asked, and I'd done it well. This would keep happening. I'd keep getting summoned to paper over our sins and dispose of all the excess souls we left in our wake.

I finally looked up. Our eyes met. And in that instant, something broke inside me.

———

That brings me to today. I won't give you the date, although you know by now that it's a new year. A new world, really. A frozen sea is breaking up.

I've been busy. I'm on my way now, in fact. Where? I decline to comment on the grounds that it may incriminate me.

THIRTY-SEVEN
NEIL

I've been angry before, of course. And I can access that emotion readily for my art. But this anger was different. It was a wall, and every moment I'd spent with John in the past six months was a brick in that wall. When I stayed at home (I had ample time, now that my movie career was dead), I saw the bricks piling on top of each other. John toying with me in his room, arguing about Mikey's future: brick. The callback, with Terry's remark about "knowing genius when he saw it": brick. Robins yelling at me to help him lift Mikey's bleeding body: brick. John's face after the Christmas party, his dismissive "*I don't care about this*": brick.

Maybe you'd have thought that I'd be most angry with Terry Mannix and the other producers. After all, John had said he didn't care about these things. But Katie was right; John was in charge of everything. If he'd said, "Neil Bowes is Aiden Trask," there's no way anyone would've objected.

And he hadn't. Worse, he'd put me through two rounds of auditions, not to mention making me wait weeks even after they'd already made the decision. Worse still, he hadn't even told me like a man. I had to find out like the rest of the moviegoing public, on the fucking Internet.

And Mikey—what about Mikey? I mean, he was an idiot, and a snake. I wasn't sorry for what had happened to him. But John was responsible for that, too. John had ruined his life without thinking twice. And he'd laughed at Brendan, his own nephew, in front of everyone at the party.

I talked it over with Katie, and you know what she said? "Daddy never knows what he has." She meant it a little bit in reference to herself, I think—the whole plain neglected daughter thing—but she also applied it to me. And she was right. John, for all his supposed wisdom and swagger, never appreciated anything I did for him. If he had, he wouldn't have chosen Brock Harkness, that fucking clown, over a true artist like me.

And what about the future? John could wake up one morning and think, *I'm not sure about Neil.* And then where the fuck would I be? I'd end up like Mikey in the mud of his backyard, wailing and begging for a death that John wouldn't grant. John thought he *was* Death. And Life. And God.

That was the final brick.

———

I built the wall, and then it was up to the universe to show me what was on the other side of it. Luckily, as I've found on many occasions, the universe finds a way.

And I've found mine. Excuse me, won't you? I promise, I'll tell you when I'm done. You'll probably applaud me.

THIRTY-EIGHT
JANUARY 14

The kindling is lit. The fire is starting.

This is what I repeat to myself, over and over. I alter my steps to its rhythm.

I left the house a little early this morning. I arrive at the hotel early, just as planned. It's a surprisingly bright, warm day. I booked the room under "Reagan"—a nice touch, I thought.

When I get to the shabby room on the second floor, I close the blinds and draw the curtains. It smells of cigarettes and stale air fresheners, and everything is a grimy beige: curtains, carpets, a dull quilted bedspread. On the wall is a watercolor of a cat in weak pastels. To my left there's a small kitchenette with a minifridge that hums loudly and a cheap plywood kitchen table with flower placemats.

John will wonder why I brought him here. He's very curious, but not imaginative: a problematic combination for a leader.

He's been told to come alone. He won't. But his bodyguards won't stay with him. I've paid them well not to. And they're already looking forward to a brighter future.

My gun is in my holster. The two glasses are on the table. I pour carefully, one water, one not.

I turn on the fluorescent light in the bathroom. I lean over the cheap porcelain sink and look in the mirror.

There it is: the face that always disappointed, particularly in my teenage years: wide, with dark brown eyes, a broad nose, flabby cheeks. My dark hair is in a bun. I can hear Deirdre's voice: "Oh well, dear, beauty isn't everything." My neck is thick, my body sturdy. I don't look like the daughter of John and Deirdre, the wife of Neil, the sister of the beautiful Liam Callaghan. I, Katie Bowes, nee Callaghan, am outwardly unremarkable.

But my eyes. They're alight with something. A thrill runs up and down my spine, like someone's fingers tracing up and down a piano.

"I'm ready," I say. I usually speak in a borrowed voice, but this is stronger, deeper: the one that belongs to me.

There's a knock on the door, three quick raps.

I hide my holster in the potted plant. I open the door.

My father's there, with Robins and Tim Smith.

He checks his watch ostentatiously. "I don't have much time, Katie, I have a meeting across town—"

"I have to talk to you, Daddy," I say in my borrowed voice. "Alone."

My father sighs. "It's okay," he says to his bodyguards. He follows me inside. I gesture him to the table and as he strides toward it, I grab the gun and lock the door in one fluid motion.

By the time he's turned back, he sees me.

"What the fuck are you—ROBINS!"

"Oh, they won't stay," I say. "They've already made their choice." I knock with my left hand on the hotel door, shout "Robins!" just as loudly. I let the silence sink in.

My father's eyes widen. He takes in the gun, the two

glasses set out on the table. "What is this?" he says. I can see the panic rising in him.

"This is your death," I say. I aim the pistol at his heart.

He races to the door, tugs at the lock. It's dead bolted, of course. He doesn't have a gun, didn't carry one to the meeting he thought he was attending, but his hand strays to where it would've been, and closes on air. After a few moments, I see from the flicker in his eyes that he realizes he's trapped.

I enjoy a coy smile.

"If you're willing to bet I won't shoot, feel free to come take this." I wave the gun at him.

I can see his mind racing. He's thinking of rushing me, but I know he'll decide against it. He knows I'll shoot. I know he knows. I've imagined this part already, and he does exactly what I suspected: He slows, smooths his hair back, gestures at the table.

"Are we going to have a drink, then?" he says. Sweat forms on his upper lip. His eyes never leave the gun.

I nod. He sits, reaches for his glass, rubs it with his thumb. "Poison?"

"Naturally."

"Why not just shoot me?"

"I want you to have time to adjust to your new reality."

"I won't have much."

"You'll have more than you would otherwise."

He stares deeply into my eyes for the first time I can remember. The world slows.

He's the first to break the spell. He walks over to the table and picks up the glass. He drains it, wincing a little. "Fucking awful," he says. "And it's making my tongue numb."

"That's the idea." My hands are shaking. After all this time, all this planning, he's sitting across from me, dying.

"You were hoping I'd hesitate, right?" he says with a small

smile. "So you could triumph over me as I slowly... transition?"

I shrug. "I knew you'd down it. You pride yourself on being all or nothing. The 'transition' will be slow either way."

He laughs, and his leg twitches. I see from the flash of horror in his eyes that the paralysis is starting. He puts his hand on his knee to steady it.

"So you're killing me," he says. "What's my crime, precisely?"

I laugh. "You have *some* time, but not enough for the full list."

A flicker of a smile. "You don't strike me as the do-gooder type," he says, mostly to himself. I see his arm move furtively. He's trying to scratch his chin to assert calm thoughtfulness —a trick I've seen him use over and over, year after year. His arm isn't paralyzed yet—it shouldn't be, according to my research—but he's in too much pain to bring it all the way up. "Is this a neglectful father thing?" he says.

Now I smile. "My motivations are my own."

He looks up at the pockmarked ceiling. When he turns back to me, his eyes are fierce. "I'll meet death bravely when it comes."

"You'll act as if that's true," I say, "as long as I'm here. But that's not the same thing. Your bravery needs an audience. Show your bravado in an empty room, and then I'll believe."

He laughs again, then grows thoughtful. His thigh twitches. I hear a truck pass outside.

"You're quiet," he says.

"Well spotted."

"I underestimated you."

I shrug again.

"Is this a girl power thing?"

I laugh, this time genuinely. I switch the pistol to my other hand. "In some sense, I suppose."

We both wait. His body is tensing. The underarms of his suit are dark.

"You don't want to explain?" he asks. He speaks almost courteously, as if he's letting an old woman ahead of him in line (something I've seen him do countless times at the corner market). I feel a rush of something for him—if not affection, then admiration.

"I do," I say, "but I'm waiting for questions."

"Very well. How'd you do it?"

"Do what?"

"If you want me dead, and it's not personal—"

"Who said it wasn't personal?"

He smiles and continues, "And it's not *entirely* personal, then I can only assume you want my empire."

"The family business," I say. "Yes." I sit down in a chair. I'm almost calm.

"Kertner's been buying up land all over the city," my father says. His eyes flick to me. "You?"

I nod.

"And the labor union man—Bhat. The one we folded in."

I nod again.

"You made a problem for me, knowing I'd try to bring him inside instead of dealing with another enemy," he says. "With him inside, you'd have access to a lot of information. Not to mention with all your accounting work..."

I shrug.

"But you wouldn't end me today unless you had more."

"I do," I acknowledge. "Three pillars of your administration."

He frowns. I can tell by the way he twists at the waist that his legs are now completely numb. I watch him thinking. How many thoughts does he have left? It's strange to think I control all this.

Then he realizes. "Harris," he breathes. He's genuinely shocked. "He's been furious with me ever since the widow..."

"Yes."

"But the other two...I'd know if you had Peter, and your brothers couldn't keep a secret like this..."

I laugh. "You lack imagination. That's probably your biggest flaw." I pity the frown on his face. "Brendan Rorke and Neil Bowes," I say.

He snorts. "Pillars of my administration? Hardly." He coughs. Something ugly comes up.

"Edges of a carpet fray first. If you tie them off, you can keep the whole thing from unraveling."

"What a lovely metaphor." For the first time, he sounds angry. "They've been in on this the whole time? All three of them? Harris has been helping you—?"

I laugh. "You think I'd trust them with this? No. They...let's say, *joined my team* a few weeks ago. I recruited them. You did my work for me, really. I needed a few malcontents, and I just sat back and waited. You handled Brendan poorly first, which isn't surprising. You don't value him. You value Neil even less. It's not difficult to understand why," I add wryly. "I live with him."

His mouth twists. He's thinking hard, tracing all the paths back to the center of the labyrinth.

"Casey?" he says. "Casey Moore?"

I smile. "You're bending over backwards to avoid giving me credit."

"He's got to be helping you."

"He is," I say, "although inadvertently. He wasn't in on it, if that's what you mean. But he's an opportunist. When I saw him hone in on Brendan, I realized he was helping me even if he didn't know it, working a parallel track. But I only brought him up to speed a few hours ago." I pause. "I don't think he'll mourn you."

My father's nostrils flare.

"I was surprised how you handled Harris," I continue. "He's the closest thing you have to a soulmate. And you broke him."

He's even angrier now. I can practically feel heat coming off him.

"Peter has always hated me," he says. "I'll give you him." He glances at me. "The others in SF, Tomcat and Herrera and everyone...they know already?"

"They'll be informed shortly."

"They won't fucking care," he says bitterly. I'm quiet; I let the thought fester. "But your brothers—your brothers will never allow this—"

"My brothers are easily led," I say. "Owen and Martin will follow anyone who promises promotions and affirmations of their masculinity. Neither wants the responsibilities of being in charge."

"They'll be angry."

"They will," I sigh, "but revenge is too much work. And they're the children of inertia."

He smiles again, ever so slightly.

He tries another defense, this time casually, as if offering a suggestion at a staff meeting: "And Liam?"

"Point him at the nearest bottle. Or blonde."

"Neat," my father acknowledges. He's still smiling. Do I imagine it, or is there a note of pride in his voice? I hear envy, too, the envy of one artist admiring another, a certain begrudging *Why didn't I think of that?*

"They don't love you," I say.

The smile fades. He slides down in his chair and grips the table edge to keep from slipping farther. His knuckles are white, and hairier than I remember.

"Were you behind the rat? What's his name?" he asks. I feel another flash of pity; he's pretending he doesn't remember the name, as if all his failures aren't etched in stone in a dark corner of his mind. "Mikey?" he says finally.

I roll my eyes. "Of course not. But I couldn't help figuring it out: a crewmember hired right around election season, when DAs are trying to prove they're tough on crime? And he was too real, like some writer's idea of a working-class man. Honestly, I was shocked no one else noticed. It was like pulling teeth to get Neil to figure the damn thing out."

Another half laugh. "He was with you when he saw Mikey at the diner."

"I had to walk him right past the damn place, and even then, he didn't get it. I had to stop dead, right in front of the fucking window, and pretend to be sick."

"Neil is a lot of work," he agrees.

A feeling wells up in me, and it takes me a moment to recognize it: joy. I don't get to talk like this with anyone, least of all my father.

I hear footsteps in the corridor, and I stand up and look at John, to see if he'll cry out. He doesn't seem to be listening—his eyes are glazing over. He's fading fast. I listen until the footsteps fade, too.

I stand up and pull him straighter in his chair. His eyes widen slightly when I draw nearer. He slides down again, but not as far. He's afraid, but not of death—of me. Of what I represent. A loss of his control. His legacy warped and corrupted. For what is a story but its ending? And this is his: immobilized at a crappy motel by his little girl.

"Harris almost caught me once," I say. I don't know why I tell him this. "Before I'd decided he'd be on my side. Back when he was angry with you. But not as angry as he would be later, standing over the widow's body."

"Don't exaggerate," my father mutters. "He never stood over the widow's body—he's always long gone when a crime takes place." He won't look at me; he tilts his eyes away.

"You're right," I say. "That was embellishment." I smile and take my seat, still holding the gun. A seagull cries somewhere outside. I picture it wheeling in circles around a white sun.

"I was meeting Hugh," I say. "Hugh Wheeler, my go-between with Kertner and Bhat. At the Continental. It was stupid of me—that hotel is too well known in our circles. But I wanted to have my meeting where you had your meetings." I shake my head at this.

The paralysis has spread to his chest now, judging from the gasps. His fear is growing. The longer Death lingers, the more frightening it becomes. I feel some kind of leap in my chest at this thought, but I don't think it's joy. Hard to tell.

"I had to tell him I was on a date."

I see the confusion in my father's eyes, passing over the panic.

"Harris, I mean," I say. "When he saw me with Hugh. I pretended I was attempting to have an affair." I laugh.

I'm killing my father. The reality is starker now, looking at him. But there's no remorse. He finally crashes onto the floor, and the sight of it fills me with a rage so potent I can taste the bitterness in my mouth. I stand up and tower over him. We're nearing the end.

"I said some things to Neil I shouldn't have," I continue. I don't need to tell him this, but I can't stop talking. Suddenly he's dying too fast.

He wheezes, and it takes me a moment to realize he's laughing. Not completely gone, then. He moves his head, and I think of how awful the thick carpet must smell.

"Neil wouldn't have noticed," he croaks.

"No," I agree, and we share a smile. My rage laps at my feet like waves against the shore, but it's ebbing. "Still, though, if he'd been paying attention..."

My father laughs louder now. "Paying attention," he says.

I see a strange wistfulness in his eyes, and it makes tears prick in mine: hot, angry tears.

"Why couldn't you see me?" I whisper it first, then say it louder because I'm not sure he heard. "Why couldn't you see me?"

"That's what you want to know, in my last breaths?" he manages.

I nod. I'm not sure he can see anything—his eyes are glassy. A vein is standing out in his forehead.

"I don't know," he says. "I don't know why I didn't see you." He's quiet for a moment. "It's a shame, really."

The way he says this, the forced nonchalance, makes my anger roar back. I feel it in my chest, leaping to get out.

It makes what I do next—what I planned to do all along —that much easier.

I raise the gun and aim it squarely at his forehead.

The terror floods into his face again, contorts it. This is not the father I grew up with, the king whose authority hung over everything. This is the real man underneath all the shadows.

In that moment, I know one thing: John Callaghan will die. And I will become our name.

"Wait," he says, and the panic makes his voice higher and stranger than I've ever heard it. "Katie—"

"Kathleen." My voice has a hard edge. "Don't tell me— you'd prefer the slow way out?"

I underestimated his fear. He's twisting, scrabbling, flailing to escape death, even as he feels it closing in.

"You—you said you were going to poison me," he says.

I cock my pistol.

"I lied."

ACKNOWLEDGMENTS

You may read a book alone, but writing one is impossible without the support of a community. My thanks to:

Michael Dolan, my editor, for believing in me and shepherding a debut author through the publishing process.

Debra Lattanzi Shutika, for suggesting I enter the PitMad Twitter pitch event, which was the beginning of this book's road to publication.

My parents Tim and Priscilla Myers, for editorial and emotional support during a long process (and for getting HBO in the house when I was a crime-movie-obsessed teenager).

Pamela Chen, for the terrific author photo, and Jessica Wei, for making me laugh during the photoshoot. Thank you for your support and friendship.

My friends, who supported, encouraged, and inspired me in equal measure.

And to you, if you've read this far. A writer is nothing without readers.

The title of this book comes from a poem by Emily Dickinson that begins "They shut me up in Prose." It was constantly in my mind while I was writing. I thought of it as Katie Callaghan's inner monologue.

ABOUT THE AUTHOR

Cassandra Myers has rewatched *Boardwalk Empire* and *Seinfeld* far too often. Her work has been published in *Mystery Tribune* and *Failbetter* and her short story "Two Notes" won Honorable Mention in the Kalanithi Writing Award contest. Her journalistic writing has been published in *The San Francisco Chronicle*, *The Los Angeles Daily News*, *The Bakersfield Californian*, *The Santa Cruz Sentinel*, and others. She graduated from UC Berkeley with a B.A. in comparative literature and has worked as a bookstore clerk, an administrative associate, and a university science writer. *They Shut Me Up* is her debut novel.